Medlock

By the same author

AS B.P. WALTER:

A Version of the Truth
Hold Your Breath
The Dinner Guest
The Woman on the Pier
The Locked Attic
Notes on a Murder
The Garden Party
The Treehouse
The Winter Visitor

AS BARNABY WALTER:

Scuttle

S. G. HARTNELL

Medlock

SPHERE

SPHERE

First published in Great Britain in 2025 by Sphere

1 3 5 7 9 10 8 6 4 2

Copyright © S. G. Hartnell 2025

The moral right of the author has been asserted.

All characters and events in this publication, other than those clearly in the public domain, are fictitious and any resemblance to real persons, living or dead, is purely coincidental.

All rights reserved.
No part of this publication may be reproduced, stored in a retrieval system, or transmitted, in any form or by any means, without the prior permission in writing of the publisher, nor be otherwise circulated in any form of binding or cover other than that in which it is published and without a similar condition including this condition being imposed on the subsequent purchaser.

A CIP catalogue record for this book
is available from the British Library.

Hardback ISBN 978-1-4087-3163-5
Trade paperback ISBN 978-1-4087-3164-2

Typeset in Garamond by M Rules
Printed and bound in Great Britain by
Clays Ltd, Elcograf S.p.A.

Epigraphs on p vii taken from *Haunted* by James Herbert
(New York: Putnam, 1988) and *We Have Always Lived in the Castle*
by Shirley Jackson (New York: Viking Press, 1962).

Papers used by Sphere are from well-managed forests
and other responsible sources.

Sphere
An imprint of
Little, Brown Book Group
Carmelite House
50 Victoria Embankment
London EC4Y 0DZ

The authorised representative
in the EEA is
Hachette Ireland
8 Castlecourt Centre
Dublin 15, D15 XTP3, Ireland
(email: info@hbgi.ie)

An Hachette UK Company
www.hachette.co.uk

www.littlebrown.co.uk

For Meg

To be haunted is to glimpse a truth that might best be hidden.

JAMES HERBERT, *Haunted*

'I can't help it when people are frightened,' says Merricat. 'I always want to frighten them more.'

SHIRLEY JACKSON, *We Have Always Lived in the Castle*

Prologue

Everybody died that night. Everybody in that small row of houses, part of a tiny village in the Scottish Highlands. Everybody except one. The deaths of so many people, all in one go, caused a lot of rumours and head-scratching in the press at the time, but eventually a collection of police officers, medics and scientists came up with an explanation: a combination of freak weather and a particularly aggressive strain of influenza. Whether Mary Macdonald got the flu and recovered, managed to avoid it or was simply naturally immune, nobody really knew. But it was a miracle she survived, having spent over a day and a night alone in her house's underground cellar, wrapped up in blankets as the town became submerged in snow.

The spread of the virus was blamed on a couple of village meetings held at the local barn to discuss the impending treacherous weather. Most of the attendees began to suffer the next day from soaring temperatures within their own bodies and plummeting temperatures on the streets outside. Then the snow came, and everyone was shut up inside their houses, spreading the illness around their friends and family members. The situation would become a phenomenon studied for years to come. But the sole survivor, young Mary Macdonald, only ten years old, would never be studied or interviewed in the way scientists at the time would have preferred. Indeed, just six months after that dreadful night, Mary Macdonald would barely exist herself.

Chapter 1

An Introduction

Natalie

She fusses around when I walk in. She has a lot to be doing, apparently, but the day has already tired her out before it's begun.

'Do sit down, my dear,' she urges me as she goes over to make me a cup of tea. I do as she says, sitting at the table and watching her as she puts the kettle on. 'This old AGA needs some maintenance,' she mutters, more to herself than to me.

While the kettle boils, she sits opposite me. 'I must say, I'm so relieved to see you. Part of me thought we'd never be able to find a new governess for Master Rupert – though they're probably not called that now, are they?'

I'm thrown by this, but manage to get my words together. 'No, I'd probably say "tutor" these days. "Governess" sounds more than a little old-fashioned, I think.'

'Well, regardless, I'm so pleased you've chosen to come here to Marwood ... especially after all that's happened. I shouldn't really talk about it, of course, we were told not to. And for a while, I didn't want to. But it feels so raw, part of me wonders whether it hurts even more to keep it all bottled up – locked away in here.' She taps her head, looking wistfully at the surface of the table.

This is all a bit more intense than I bargained for, but I'm rather compelled by how freely she's talking, mere minutes after I've walked into her home. After a few seconds of silence have passed, she snaps her eyes back to meet mine. Hers are green-grey and have a piercing quality that makes me feel exposed, as if she can see right inside me. 'I'm so sorry, my dear, your name, it escapes me. Natalie, is that right?'

I nod. 'Yes, that's right.'

She smiles. 'I'm pleased I got that right, at least. And you can call me Mrs Medlock. Everyone does, even though I'm not married. Housekeepers are always "Mrs", or rather they were before the country did away with decorum and politeness.' Her eyes examine me once again, roving up and down, taking all of me in. 'We've seen quite a few girls recently, but nobody has been suitable. We'd almost abandoned all hope and sent Master Rupert off to Eton, although his father would prefer that to be a last resort. Thinks home-schooling would be best, at least at the present time. One of the young girls I interviewed rather fancied herself as an artist and suggested teaching Master Rupert through the means of "artistic expression". Paintings and collages and the like. Utter nonsense, if you ask me. Not that I underestimate the value of art and culture. Everything has its place. But in its place it should remain. You're a bit older than her, though. For the best, I think. Life experience is so important. And I gather from your accent that you're from the United States?'

Again, I nod, 'Yes, I'm from South Carolina.' I wonder about going into some of my back story, but decide it's probably not the best time.

She doesn't seem particularly interested anyway. 'I've never been to America,' she says offhandedly, 'never travelled. I don't much like change, so I feel crossing an ocean would be asking for trouble.' Her gaze goes distant once again, to a spot slightly above my shoulder. 'Lord Ashton used to travel to the US a great deal, though. Not so much any more ... '

The mention of the name catches my attention at once, 'Oh, so Lord Ashton still owns the manor?'

Mrs Medlock looks like I've slapped her. 'Well of course he does, my dear. The house has been in his family for generations. He isn't here much. Even though he rarely goes abroad, he and Lady Ashton spend so much time in their London home on Thurloe Square these days, it's quite likely you'll never see him. He trusts my opinion when it comes to his son's education. My advice is that if his lordship ever does speak to you, only tell him the good bits. He doesn't like too much information, you see. He's a very disciplined, time-conscious man. Always says the right thing, does the right thing. Always knows what to do in a crisis.'

Once again, I feel her attention wane, like a radio going in and out of signal. Then, to my surprise, I see a tear fall from her eye, followed by another. She raises her hands to catch them and lets out a half-gasp, half-sob. 'Oh goodness, how embarrassing. It's just ... there are so many reminders ... '

I lean in closer across the table and gently lay a hand on hers. 'Reminders of what?'

She takes in a deep breath, sniffs a little, then says, 'Of all the terrible things that happened here. My memory is not what it was, but some things never fade. So much of it is my fault.'

I'm finding all of this slightly awkward, but I can't help it – my interest is more than piqued. 'Do you want to talk about it?'

Her face twists, as if holding back more tears, then she gives a small nod.

'Good. Why don't you start at the beginning,' I prompt, gently.

Another deep breath. A hand goes up to her hair, as if to check it's still in its tight bun. 'It all began with Mary Macdonald,' she says. 'The day the orphan came to Marwood Manor. Nothing was the same after that. Of course, I don't blame her. But I can't help but feel Marwood Manor was for ever cursed from the day Mary Macdonald came to stay.'

Chapter 2

The Arrival

Mrs Medlock, December 1978

Mary Macdonald was delivered to Marwood Manor on Christmas Eve. Why on earth they chose one of the busiest days of the year, I have no idea. I think perhaps the Scottish authorities were keen to be rid of her. Lord Ashton wasn't even her proper uncle – she was his deceased cousin's estranged daughter's daughter. He was hardly ever in touch with that side of the family; they were several rungs below him in terms of class. I know Lady Ashton never encouraged him to keep in contact – if they didn't have property on a garden square in London and a large estate somewhere rural, they weren't worth knowing in her books. But in spite of all this, they apparently agreed to take the child in, at least temporarily.

When she arrived, Lord Ashton was away in New York – he'd been delayed flying back due to poor weather, which meant he and Lady Ashton were to be separated over the Christmas period. She decided the best way to cope with this was by throwing a lavish Christmas Eve party, then booked a car to drive her directly to Claridge's the next day for Christmas dinner with some Jewish film star who didn't really celebrate the season. Being ten years younger than her husband, she was still very much of the 'party' frame of mind – which was probably why she forgot to mention to me the arrival of a disturbed Scottish orphan. The first we knew of the child was when she arrived on the doorstep.

'Oh my gosh, it's Marigold. Or Martina. Or ... oh yes, *Mary*, that's it,' Lady Ashton said, slurring her words slightly as she bent down to pat the little girl on the head. 'Remember, Mrs Medlock – I told you she was on the way.'

I gritted my teeth, trying to keep calm. 'You didn't actually say anything of the kind.'

She looked puzzled. 'Oh, I'm sure I did. Didn't I? It doesn't really matter. In short, little Mary here has lost both her parents – flu, wasn't it? – and she's been sent to live here for the time being. She's my husband's ... er ... niece ... cousin ... second cousin ... something like that.' She flung her hands in the air in a *who-knows* gesture, sending some of the clear liquid of the cocktail she was holding onto the floor. Unaware of the spillage, she carried on with her instructions. 'Could you take Mary up to one of the bedrooms and make her comfortable? We should probably find her a drink or food.' She looked around, as if one of the hired-for-the-day cocktail waiters would be able to supply something child-friendly at a second's notice.

'How about I get her upstairs and into bed, then Bessie will make her some hot buttered toast and warm milk?' I suggested, trying to take on board this sudden rush of information and the resulting extra work it would lead to.

'Oh, that sounds perfect, simply divine,' Lady Ashton said, sending another splash of drink onto the floor. I made a mental note to ask Bessie to mop up the mess before someone broke their neck on their way out later.

'Linda, darling! Where have you got to?' shouted a high-pitched female voice from inside the living room.

'Here I come,' the glittering hostess replied, teetering on her ridiculously high heels as she walked around the large Christmas tree in the front hall and returned to her guests. I watched her go, still livid at her for not notifying me of all this sooner. A girl – a random girl, and an orphan to boot – foisted upon us late at night with no warning. It was liberties like this that at times got me thinking that all those socialists with their workers' unions might have had a point.

The little girl said nothing as she followed me up the stairs, and still nothing when I led her into a dark, chilly bedroom on the second floor. It was perhaps too large and grand for a child of her age, but I knew it to be clean and tidy, with newer linen than the other options. I unpacked her suitcase of clothes, an odd jumble of cardigans, shabby dresses and mismatched socks, eventually finding some pyjamas folded at the bottom, which I instructed her to put on. Still she said and did nothing. I must admit, I got a bit impatient then, telling her I wanted to see her in the pyjamas and tucked up in bed by the time I returned. I set the little suitcase down on the chest of drawers, then went down the back stairs to the kitchen.

'Who was at the door?' asked Bessie, piling up the trays that had held the canapés so they could be wiped down in the morning.

I sat down on the first available chair and sighed. 'A child. A bloody orphan, at that, poor wretch. Did *her ladyship* say anything to you about her coming?'

Her ladyship was heavily laden with sarcasm, even though it was, technically, the correct formal address (although she was always telling us to call her Linda). Maybe I'm old-fashioned, but for a housekeeper to be on first-name terms with the lady of the house – well, it just felt wrong to me.

If only Lord Ashton were here, I thought to myself as Bessie set about making toast and putting the kettle on the AGA. He'd have a clear idea as to what was going on. I decided to go back up myself, instead of sending Bessie. The girl's silence and disobedience so early on in her stay unnerved me. Of course, I'm not a monster, I realised that losing one's parents at such a young age must be distressing for a little one like her, but all the same, it didn't bode well for the future. Start as you mean to go on, that's been my motto for life, and it's always done me right. Nearly always.

I didn't bother knocking on the bedroom door, I just marched in with the tray. My earlier frustrations immediately resurfaced when I saw that Mary was neither in her pyjamas nor in bed. Instead she was looking out of the window. It had started to snow outside, and the guests were making a move down the front steps. I could hear their jolly, half-drunken calls of 'Merry Christmas!' as they bade their hostess goodnight.

'Come away from the window,' I told her. 'You'll catch a chill.'

Mary didn't move, so after a few seconds I marched over. 'Come on, do as I say.'

She remained silent and almost as limp as a ragdoll as I pulled her out of her clothes and put her pyjamas on her. 'Come on, get in,' I said sharply, tugging the covers back so she could climb into the big four-poster. She seemed so tiny in the middle of it, surrounded by the quilt and pillows, as if she were in danger of being submerged. As I turned back to the door and made to leave, I heard a rustle of sheets and turned to see the girl standing once more at the window, staring out at the falling snow.

Then, to my surprise, she spoke. Her question shook me from the inside out.

'Will I be dead by morning?'

I took in a breath, then let it out again, unsure how to respond. I presumed this was something to do with her parents' sudden demise. If they'd both had influenza, maybe they'd died together the same night, leaving the girl all alone with their corpses. I shuddered at the thought, then said, 'I think that's unlikely. Now go to sleep.'

I closed the door, wondering if my words were too harsh. All those years in the job, I'd forgotten how to be kind. I found the brisk, no-nonsense approach usually the best way forward. That's how you run a household. That's how you survive what the world throws at you. But there was something in that quiet little voice, and those bleak, horrible words she had uttered, that really rattled me. And somehow I knew her arrival was the start of a strange and worrying time. I could feel it in my bones.

Chapter 3

Orphaned

Mary, December 1978

I was very cold when I arrived at the big old house. I'd been cold for a long while, although in the hospital it was warm and cosy for a bit. There I was shown into a little room – a 'family room', they called it – with sofas and animals and some bourbon biscuits. But I didn't get to stay there long. They told me I was to live with my uncle, instead of an orphanage. They seemed to think this was a better choice because my uncle was rich – even though he wasn't really my uncle. I didn't know whether to be pleased or not. Dad once told me he'd never met a happy rich person in all his life, and I worried I was going to a sad house filled with unhappy people.

When they told me my new home was called Marwood Manor, I'd imagined a palace from the books me and Mum read by the fire in the lounge at home. Palaces where princesses lived, waiting for princes to come and take them away and make them queens. I thought this cousin-uncle would be waiting for me on the steps, dressed either like a duke or an old-fashioned soldier, and would tell me about the kingdom he had been put in charge of. But when we arrived, it was nothing like that. The house wasn't one of those glittering, magical places. It was an enormous, hulking beast in the night, like an animal waiting to pounce, towering above us as we walked up the steps. Everything felt dark and strange, and behind the great wooden front door was an angry-looking woman. Maybe it *was* a fairy tale. But not one of the good ones.

I didn't say goodbye to the social worker, Nadine, when she dropped me off. She seemed annoyed she had to work on Christmas Eve, and I got the feeling she blamed me for this. I also didn't say anything when the angry lady started talking to a younger, more beautiful woman about me. The beautiful woman was wearing a dress that looked like it was made from diamonds. Everything glittered from the light of the enormous Christmas tree in the front hall. I tried to think of the Christmas tree as a good sign.

The angry-looking lady didn't introduce herself, but I heard the beautiful one call her 'Mrs Medlock'. I was then taken by the arm and led up a big, creaking old staircase, onto a landing with a patchy, fraying carpet, and then up some more stairs. All along the walls were paintings, some of people, some of country houses and lakes, and one of them with a woman leaning over a goat that was bleeding from its neck. I didn't like the look of it at all, and the hope I'd felt after seeing the Christmas tree started to disappear. Why would someone put up such a horrible picture in their home?

My feeling of strangeness carried on all the way to the cold, dark bedroom Mrs Medlock showed me into. My bedroom at home had been warm and cosy, before the power got cut off in the storm and the heating stopped working. This room felt just as chilly as the rest of the house – though not the same as the fierce, needle-like freeze that had filled our whole town just as everyone was getting the flu. That was like pain, pain so tight around your chest you couldn't breathe.

I was instructed to put my pyjamas on and get into bed, but the sky outside the window caught my attention. I hadn't realised how high up we were, but I could see now how the lawn stretched out, neat and tidy, with a light layer of snow starting to settle on it. I felt like the snow had followed me down from Scotland all the way to Oxford. A movement made me look over to the side of the lawn. For a second I thought I saw someone walk just out of sight around the side of the building: a woman, I think. But when I leaned forward to see more, there was nothing there. Perhaps it was a guest from the party, having a night-time stroll before going home. Or maybe it had been something else. Maybe I had been sent away to a haunted building, alive with spirits that were at that very moment planning to carry me off to the afterlife. They'd tell me that surviving was a mistake and I should have died with everyone else back home.

Due to the fear that gripped me inside and out, my voice disappeared and I was unable to answer Mrs Medlock when she spoke to me crossly. The words just weren't there. It was like the cold had frozen them out of me. Only when she came back up with some food and a hot drink could I say the thing that was most frightening in my head: 'Will I be dead by morning?'

She didn't seem happy with these words, and replied that it was 'unlikely'. I didn't know what to believe. Mum and Dad had told me everything would be OK when they bundled me up and said that when the storm arrived I should go to the cellar and leave them in their beds. Away from their illness. Away from the wind and ice outside that was breaking our windows and chilling our little house as each hour went by. So I did what they said and hid in the cellar. But I wish I hadn't heard what Dad said to Mum just as I closed the trapdoor and began to go down the steps into the darkness: *We'll all be dead by morning.*

Chapter 4

A Very Strange Christmas

Mrs Medlock, December 1978

That Christmas at Marwood was a very strange one. Normally, Lord and Lady Ashton would have a big dinner with friends who lived across the globe and would visit England, especially for the season. I usually regarded that as a stress, but in truth I did miss it.

On Christmas morning, nursing a predictable hangover, Lady Ashton followed through with her plan of going to Claridge's, and the car picked her up at 11.30.

Bessie and I spent most of our Christmas Day clearing up after the party guests the night before, tutting at the spilled drinks and cigarette burns we found as we loaded up trays and re-plumped cushions. Our reward was a meagre dinner for the two of us, with some child-sized leftover plates taken upstairs.

Mary Macdonald's silence continued throughout Christmas Day, into Boxing Day and then the run-up to New Year's Eve. Nothing I could say or do seemed to encourage her to speak or even come out of her room.

At dusk on 29 December, I found Lady Ashton sitting in the

living room, cross-legged by the Christmas tree, reading the gossip pages of a magazine. Anyone would have thought she was in her teens, rather than her thirties. I decided it was time to ask her about the Macdonald child, since she had neither mentioned her nor, as far as I was aware, gone to see her since she arrived.

'Oh, she's probably just a bit down, poor lamb,' her ladyship said, flicking through the glossy pages that reflected the warm glow of the fairy lights on the tree. 'It must be so dreadful to lose one's family like that. I had influenza once and I was utterly convinced I would die.' Suddenly she looked up and clapped a hand to her mouth, looking panicked. 'Oh my gosh, you don't think she's got flu herself, do you? If so, isolation is *absolutely* necessary. Quarantine her right now. I can't believe I didn't think of this before. Especially with my little New Year's Eve gathering in a couple of days' time, not to mention the Twelfth Night ball.'

I told her infection seemed unlikely, since the girl was exhibiting no symptoms of illness and anyway was keeping to her own room most of the time.

'That is a relief.' Lady Ashton nodded. 'Well, I shan't go in and see her, just in case she's harbouring anything catching. It's probably best if you and Bessie take up her meals.' I told her this was what we had been doing already. 'Oh, splendid. And if she must come out of her room, do accompany her. A bracing walk round the garden or something. Maybe that will make her happier.' I was given one of her teeth-filled smiles as a form of dismissal, so I took myself away.

The next day, when Bessie returned from Mary's room with a breakfast tray containing the remains of food she'd picked at, she remarked how the girl was still sitting on her bed in silence. 'It's like there's nobody there, behind the eyes,' she said, clattering about the kitchen as I tried to work out the butcher's account payments for that month. 'It's like she's from that film, the one with Gregory Peck. *The Omen*. Have you seen it?'

I tutted as I closed the accounts book, 'No, I have not.' I got up, feeling my back click as I straightened, and then came to a decision. 'Right. Exercise. That's what Lady Ashton suggested. I'll tell Mary she is to take a walk around the grounds.'

Bessie shook her head, 'The child just wants her parents back, I think. Dragging her around a field isn't going to do that.'

'No, it won't bring them back. But it might take her mind off things. Then I'll suggest some quiet study – copying out interesting words from the *Oxford English Dictionary*, perhaps. That was my father's advice when one needed mental occupation.'

I thought I saw Bessie roll her eyes at this, but she'd turned her back before I could admonish her for it.

Mary didn't seem immediately taken with the idea of going outside, but she didn't object as I pulled her coat around her and found some mittens from her suitcase. The snow had stopped falling on Boxing Day, but a thaw hadn't yet set in and the entire grounds were still covered in a blanket of white. I saw Mary tremble as she lifted her foot off the ledge of the servants' entrance door and into the powdery crunch outside. Perhaps her experience in the frozen village in Scotland had given her a mortal fear of snow, I thought as she paused statue-still, her face closed up and tight as if she might cry.

'Come on, it's not that bad,' I said, sighing. If I'd known it would be this difficult, I'd have got Bessie to take her out.

Eventually I got her walking at a pace to match mine through a combination of dragging and coaxing. Being honest with myself, I hadn't quite anticipated the biting chill of the cold, and I suspected the grey skies weighing down upon us from above would drop another layer of snow before long.

'Oh, Mrs Medlock,' called a voice to my left. I turned back to the house, where Lady Ashton was leaning out of a window, a fur of Arctic fox slung around her neck. 'Could you come back inside so I can go through some of the details of the Twelfth Night ball?' She smiled and watched me as if she expected me to drop everything in order to listen to her go through her guest list, say nasty things about people she pretended to like and demand obscure alcoholic concoctions that would remain untouched on the drinks trolley for years to come. But of course I was a housekeeper, and it was my duty to do my mistress's bidding. Although where possible, I tried to assert a bit of independence – just to keep her on her toes.

'Certainly. I'll just finish little Mary's walk, since it was your suggestion the girl got some exercise, then I'll be right with you.'

She looked slightly annoyed. 'Oh, I really don't think you should walk the girl too far. Her constitution is probably very poor. I mean, well, she is from *Scotland*, and as we said the other day, she's probably harbouring all manner of viruses. You haven't allowed her to see ... I mean, she hasn't ...'

Her face appeared suddenly stricken, and I hurried to quash her fears in case they led to further demands on my time, like disinfecting the entire house. 'She's been nowhere but her room. Everything's in hand.'

Lady Ashton clutched at her fox fur in relief. 'Thank goodness for that. Oh, by the way, Mrs Medlock, could you track down a new writing pen for me – the one on the desk in the library has a very bad nib that makes it impossible to write smoothly.'

I felt myself grow tense again, certain that this was just another way of asserting herself over me. Finding me little jobs to do that she could easily do herself. It was a game she played for the simple entertainment it gave her.

'Of course. I'll have a look as soon as I'm able. In the meantime, you could try the writing desk in the first Lady Ashton's suite.' I felt myself growing tense, my voice getting tighter, especially on those last few words, but I pressed on. 'I fancy she had a rather nice collection of pens, and I'm sure Lord Ashton wouldn't mind you putting them to good use.'

This had the result I'd expected, although I became instantly cross with myself for stooping so low. Any reference to Lord Ashton's first wife was difficult for both of us, though for different reasons. I saw her smile vanish, replaced with a cold, distant look she generally reserved for postal workers or tradespeople. 'I'll meet you in the library in five minutes. Oh, by the way, it looks like your charge has escaped you.'

I turned to see Mary strolling down the lawn, quite far from me now, going at a remarkably confident speed considering how hesitant she'd been just moments earlier. I looked back at the window, but Lady Ashton was pulling it shut, flashing me a glare before she disappeared from view.

I hurried away, trying to catch up with Mary as she pressed on through the thick snow, seemingly more determined than ever. 'Slow down, young missy,' I called after her, but she ignored me, taking a left by an old overhanging oak tree towards a winding path; one that led to a long stone wall. 'No,' I said, shaking my head, speaking more to myself, feeling a flutter of panic rise within me. I picked up speed. 'Stay where you are,' I shouted, gaining on her as she slowed, clearly intrigued by the wall's length. Of course, I can understand why she found the sight quite arresting: the wall did look almost never-ending as it snaked through the trees, disappearing out of sight into an overgrown thicket of bushes, brambles and fallen branches. But as I got closer, I realised Mary wasn't looking that way. She was staring straight ahead at the large wooden door built into the wall.

'I said, stay where you are,' I snapped again, although she hadn't moved for a number of seconds, apparently under some kind of spell. I took hold of her shoulder to turn her around, but she raised her arm in a quick movement and pointed at the door. Her meaning was obvious.

'Oh no you don't,' I said firmly. 'You're not allowed in there.' I could feel my breathing becoming tighter and more shallow, an effect I knew had nothing to do with my hurried arrival at the scene.

She looked at me and screwed her face up, clearly angered by my refusal. But she still didn't say anything.

'Besides, there's no way in. It's ... it's locked.'

She turned her attention back to the door, as if her eyes had the power to burn it down with perseverance alone.

'Come on, back up to the house. Her ladyship needs my help in planning her next inane little social gathering.'

I cursed myself for letting the situation flummox me. I shouldn't have been so critical of Lady Ashton in front of her. Children should learn respect for their superiors, and she wasn't going to take that on board any time soon if she heard me getting mouthy about my employer. But still, I wasn't happy about being left at the mercy of whatever whim took her ladyship's fancy while her husband was away. I tried not to start muttering under my breath as I led Mary by the arm, her feet struggling to match the fast march I'd set for us both. And it didn't escape my notice that all the way back, she kept trying to turn her head to get another look at the sight behind us. The sight of the door in the long stone wall.

Chapter 5

Twelfth Night

Mary, January 1979

I thought about the door in the wall for days after that. It started to appear in my dreams at night, when I huddled up into a little ball in my bed and tried to remember what it was like to be in the arms of my mum and dad. They held me close to them as we sat on the sofa during the first night of the snowstorm, with Mum saying we should have left when we had the chance. But when they became ill, they told me to stay away from them. To go in the other room. Stay out of their bedroom. Then, eventually, go down to the cellar and pull the trapdoor shut on top of me. In my dreams, it felt as if that door in the wall in the garden was like the trapdoor to the cellar. A door that closed me off to one world from another.

I sat on my bed for most of the next day, listening to the sounds of the house as it creaked around me. Sometimes I overheard Mrs Medlock on the stairs talking to Bessie and complaining about 'her ladyship'. At other times the ladyship woman was telling Mrs Medlock what to do. They didn't seem to like each other. *That pot will one day boil* – that was what my mum used to say when she could tell people didn't get on. One day their problems would boil over and they'd say something they could never take back.

Later in the afternoon, when the snow had started to fall again in big white chunks outside the window, Bessie came into my room and told me she'd brought some things for me to 'entertain' myself with while everyone was busy downstairs for the New Year's Eve celebrations. I didn't know there were any celebrations, so I just stared back at her as she put down a tray holding a plate of biscuits, some blank paper and a set of crayons that looked a bit scuffed and dusty. I thought about telling her that I wasn't five years old, but the idea of speaking still felt like being asked to push over a great big building with just my hands. So I said nothing. 'I thought something new to do might cheer you up,' she said, and patted my head as if I were a pet.

I was actually pleased to have the crayons and the drawing paper. I made pictures of my family – pictures of how we used to be, pictures of how we would have been if the storm hadn't come. The wind howled as I drew, and as I completed picture after picture, I could hear something buried within the scream of the wind. Something that sounded like someone crying.

The flurry of snow and wind outside calmed down during the first few days of January. 'A new year brings with it new weather,' Mrs Medlock said to me one morning, bringing with her more paper and crayons, along with some books for me to read. She'd obviously spotted that I'd used up all the other blank sheets of paper with my drawings, although she didn't say anything about the pictures I'd made. But I saw her eyes stay for quite a long time on the one with my parents lying in coffins. She told me that tonight was the night of Lady Ashton's Twelfth Night ball, the final part of the Christmas season. I'd forgotten there was a

Christmas season, but I didn't say this to her. I just stared at the patchy carpet in my cold, grey-brown bedroom and kept quiet.

Later that night, guests arrived at the house, like on New Year's Eve, although even more this time. More people than our village ever had. The big trees lining the driveway were all lit up, like massive Christmas trees, and people laughed and called out to each other as they poured into the house. I watched them from my window, feeling odd about having all these strangers so near me without them even knowing I existed. Their laughter and chatter echoed through the house, up the stairs from the hallway, until it sounded like a pack of dogs getting excited over a new box of their favourite food. And then, within the laughing and chattering, I started to hear another sound. The sound of a cry. A long, high-pitched cry. And then a sob – clearer than the muffled noises downstairs, but with its own sort of strange echo. It took me a moment to realise that the sound wasn't coming from downstairs, but from the air around me. Was it the wind, threading itself through the gaps in the window? Or was it something else? Something much, much worse. A spirit, lost and alone, hoping someone would one day find it. The spirit of someone like me.

I scared myself into hiding under the blanket on the bed and holding tight to my knees. Then the strange crying-moaning became louder all of a sudden, and I jumped up, terrified and desperate to get out of the room, grabbing my dressing gown from the hook on the door as I went. Out on the landing, I wasn't sure where to go or what to do next. Relieved that I could no longer hear the moaning cries, I decided to go downstairs to see what all the people had come to the house to do. Mrs Medlock kept talking about 'the party', but I wasn't too sure what adult parties were really about. At my birthday parties I played hopscotch in the garden with the other children from the village, and pass-the-parcel with jelly sweets. I didn't expect to find things like that here.

I walked along the landing until I came to a little door at the end, which revealed a small staircase leading to another landing-balcony area. From there I could see down into the room I remembered Bessie had said was the library – there were certainly a lot of books on the shelves. Nobody noticed me staring down, and I quite enjoyed watching them all. All the women were wearing long, flowing dresses in silver and greys, and the men were dressed in dark smart suits with bow ties. They all had drinks in their hands, and many of the men had their other hands round the waists of the women.

I sat up there in the little balcony for quite some time, until Lady Ashton came into the library, laughing and waving her hands, 'Everyone help yourself to a fur and come out into the garden for a big surprise!'

She gestured to two piles of soft-looking fur coats on two trolleys, with young men handing them out to the guests – silver-white fur for the women, and dark for the men. I waited until everyone left and the men were wheeling the trolleys away before making my way downstairs and sneaking to the doorway that led to the lawn area, near where Mrs Medlock had taken me for a walk a few days before. Everyone was outside, standing on the snow-covered grass, watching something that caused a bright white light to flicker in the darkness and then burst into a shower of sparks and flashes. 'Behold the largest Catherine wheel ever seen in the whole of England!' called out Lady Ashton from somewhere near the front of the crowd. Everyone made 'ooh' and 'wow' noises as the light and sparks grew brighter.

I was keen to get a better look at the Catherine wheel but worried I'd be spotted and sent back up to bed. So I kept to the shadows, making sure most of the people had their backs to me as I walked past them down the lawn and deeper into the darkness. They looked like a herd of beasts with their wolfish coats on, breathing hot clouds of steam into the frozen air. The flashing lights made their shadows sway and twist on the ground behind them. I paused in the darkness for a few seconds, watching the sparks fly, but then one of the women towards the back of the group turned around and I was afraid she'd see me. I ran off quickly, down the lawn towards the trees.

At first, I didn't know where I was going. Then, as I arrived at a dip in the ground, I realised where I was headed. In the darkness, I began to make out the long, curved stone wall that snaked along the far side of the lawn and deep into the trees. A few more steps took me up to the door. The big, wooden door that had floated in and out of my dreams ever since I first saw it. I reached up and could just about get my fingers around the rusty metal handle that hung in its centre, but no matter how hard I pulled, it wouldn't open. I tried kicking the door with my shoes, but aside from a loud thud, nothing happened.

Disheartened, I started to turn away, ready to sneak back up to the house, but then I heard a low scraping noise, like metal being dragged across a blackboard. Something made me stand completely still, my already frozen body now locked and impossible to move. The door was opening. Slowly, and with an enormous groan, it swung towards me, revealing the most intense darkness I had ever experienced. It made me feel tiny and terrified, so enveloping was the blackness. And then, to my horror, I saw movement from within the dark. Someone – or something – had been released from behind the wall. And they were about to come out and find me.

Chapter 6

Without Permission

Mrs Medlock, January 1979

I spent most of Lady Ashton's Twelfth Night ball the way I did all of her parties: treating the below-stairs like a war room, organising the caterers and waiters, hired in for the day through a regular local firm we used. I've never felt at home surrounded by large groups of people, so I only ventured up to the main rooms if Lady Ashton requested it. Unlike New Year's Eve (when she had spilled wine down her dress and demanded I start treating the stain while she changed), the Twelfth Night gathering passed by without the lady of the house bothering me. What did happen, though, was far more stressful.

It was Bessie, with her too-soft-for-her-own-good heart, who convinced me that it might be nice to take some cocoa upstairs. 'It's sad when you're a child, alone when there's a party going on downstairs. Missing out on all the excitement must be tough.' Her imploring West Country accent and wide eyes caused me to roll mine and say very well, she could take up some cocoa provided the guests didn't see her. 'I'll use the back stairs,' she said, then scurried off.

I was halfway through getting used glasses cleared away and back down to the kitchen, with the help of some of the hired lads, when Bessie came racing into the room, clearly out of breath. 'She's gone!' she yelled to the kitchen in general, making one of the waiter boys jump so violently he dropped a wine glass on the floor. Ignoring the mess, I walked round the table to face Bessie properly. 'What are you talking about? Gone? What do you mean, gone?'

Bessie clasped at her chest, getting her breath back. 'Little Mary. She's not in her room. It's empty.'

I let out an exasperated sigh. This was just what I needed – some mute, insubordinate little orphan running rings round us in the middle of a party. 'She's probably playing silly beggars. Search the bedrooms near her room. If not, she might have come down here to find some food.' Part of me knew this wasn't likely, though. Mary didn't have a strong appetite, and although she did eat, she always left scraps of the toast or cereal we took up to her.

I joined Bessie in her search of a number of the bedrooms, then we reconvened downstairs. I wondered if perhaps we were foolish not to venture further up, deeper into the rafters of the house, but Bessie was keen to head to the library. 'She'll have gone where the people are,' she said, nodding adamantly. 'Poor little wretch, lonely and scared. She won't have gone into those dark corridors alone.'

But the library was empty, with a terrible chill passing through it from the open French windows. I saw the mass of huddled spectators on the lawn outside – Lady Ashton's odd choice of having a large Catherine wheel display at a Twelfth Night party seemed to be bewitching everyone. I tutted as I went to close the doors, frustrated that they'd been open for so long. The house was a nightmare to heat at the best of times. As I pulled the glass towards me, something off to the side, away from the guests, caught my eye. A large shadow was striding towards the house with something clasped in its arms. I let out a gasp and swung the doors back open to step outside.

'Oh my word,' I heard one of the male guests remark to his partner as he and a number of others turned round to stare at the extremely tall man walking purposefully through the snow and passing them without saying a word.

When he saw me, he spoke in the low but urgent voice that I knew so well. 'She was trying to get in. When I opened the door, she fainted.'

More of the guests were craning to get a look at what was happening, then Lady Ashton's voice cut through the night air. 'Mrs Medlock, Mr Oakwood, what on earth is going on here?'

I beckoned him into the house as her ladyship approached, looking both confused and annoyed. 'It's just little Mary – she ran off into the snow, but she's been found now.'

Lady Ashton peered into the library, where Mr Oakwood was laying Mary down on one of the sofas. 'Is she quite all right?' she asked, 'Because I don't think she should rest there – bed is probably the best thing.'

Well aware that she was more concerned about her guests filing past the unconscious child than the poor wretch's actual welfare, I decided not to reply to her – I just turned to Mr Oakwood and requested more details on what had been going on.

'She was trying to shift the door to the garden. Kicking at it, she was. I heard her and opened it, then she just went all rigid.'

I felt again that tightening in my breathing, just like the moment when I had steered Mary away from the door. I swallowed and pushed away any feelings of panic as best I could.

Though he looked worried, Mr Oakwood spoke in his steady, methodical way. 'Her ladyship is right, we should probably get her into bed.'

I considered, then nodded. 'Are you all right to take her upstairs?'

Without saying anything further, he scooped her up as if she were a leaf floating on pond water. He carried her up the stairs and I followed, joined by Bessie, then moved to lead the way when we got to the second-floor landing. 'In here,' I said, motioning to Mary's bedroom, and watched as he laid her down on the crumpled covers.

As her head rested on the pillows, she opened her eyes, blinking; then, to my surprise, she spoke: 'Who are you?'

'This is Mr Oakwood, Mary,' I replied, trying to keep the stress out of my voice. 'He works in the grounds. He picked you up when you were out wandering around the garden without permission . . .'

Mr Oakwood laid a hand on my arm. 'Shall we just give her the night to get some rest. Then I'm sure you can question her to your heart's content in the morning.'

I closed my mouth and nodded. He was right, of course. Although I was keen to impress on Mary how stupid it was to go out into the snow with nowt but her dressing gown, it was probably best I let her sleep for now. I looked back at the girl to see her eyes had closed once again, and Bessie walked round the other side of the bed to pull the covers up over her.

'Her ladyship is going to blame me for all this, I can just feel it,' I said as the three of us left the bedroom. I led the way down the back stairs to the servants' quarters.

'I'll tell her it was my fault,' Bessie said. 'It probably was too – I should have known the little missy was going to be curious, bless her.'

I shook my head. 'No, no, don't go taking any blame. Her ladyship could sack you if the whim took her.'

As I held the door in the stairwell open for Bessie, I saw her frown, confused. 'But surely she could sack you too.'

I walked purposefully into the kitchen and stretched out my hands over the AGA, feeling the heat start to bring feeling back into my fingers once more. 'She'll never get her way on that score.'

Bessie let out a sharp laugh. 'Why are you so special?'

I spun round to face her. 'Remember your place, young lady,' I snapped. Bessie looked stung and gave a shrug before going over to clear up some of the empty wine bottles at the far end of the kitchen.

As I turned back to the AGA, I felt the warm, solid frame of Mr Oakwood come up close to me. Then he laid a hand once again on my arm. 'I think perhaps you should call it a night too,' he said in his gentle voice. 'I can tell her ladyship you're settling Mary if she asks for you.'

I let out a hollow laugh. 'Oh, she'd love that, you traipsing around all them smart guests in your gardening gear and muddy boots.' In spite of my scornful tone, I was aware of how comforting his hand on my arm felt. And how I wanted him to stand even closer.

'She likes me, I think. She won't react badly.'

I tutted. 'That's because you fulfil some of her Lady Chatterley fantasies. Shameless flirt, she is.'

He took his hand off my arm, and I suddenly felt very cold and alone. 'I don't know what all that means,' he said. He did this sometimes, if I made a reference to something he hadn't encountered. He was a kind soul, Mr Oakwood, but I wondered if he was a bit intimidated by educated folk. Especially an educated woman. Of course, I had no degree to show off about or any other lofty qualifications. But I'd studied hard as a girl and knew my books, my arithmetic, my history – all of it came naturally to me.

There was a time when a teacher back in school, Mrs Dale, said I might think about trying for university. She had been a great supporter of higher education for women, believing that it was a mark of scandalous unfairness in the world that half the human race had university closed off to them simply due to drawing 'nature's short straw'. I remember her telling me how upsetting she found it that as soon as the midwife pulled a baby out of its mother and told her she'd given birth to a girl, she wasn't just stating a simple fact: she was also saying 'limited choices, less potential, second-class education' and so on. So she pinned her hopes on her students, with the view that every young woman who defied these odds – and there really were very few – would make it easier for the next generation of girls. But my mother had been in service, back when it was a more common career choice for a young woman, and she said it was a much better job than skulking around a university campus pretending to be as good as a man. So I ignored my teacher's encouragement. Instead of being Mrs Dale's shining light, I became her disappointment. Gave up my books. And started a new life at Marwood Manor. A tragedy, that was what she called it when she heard I wouldn't be applying for university. A tragedy. I never forgot that, nor the sad but unsurprised look she gave me when I told her.

'You shouldn't talk that way about her ladyship,' Mr Oakwood said, pulling me back to the problems at hand. 'It ain't right.'

'Suit yourself.' I sighed. 'But just tell me this: what sort of person doesn't go to see a child on Christmas morning? Just zoomed off to her fancy lunch in London. The first Lady Ashton would never have been so neglectful, so distant, so—'

'I do wish you'd call her by her first name. You always used to. Calling her "the first Lady Ashton" – it's like you never knew her at all.'

Even though he said it quietly, his words hit me with a force I wasn't expecting.

'I can't . . . I can't say her name. You know full well . . . I have my own ways of—'

I stopped when Mr Oakwood turned around suddenly, and looked over to see him staring at a little figure at the door. Mary was standing by the entrance to the kitchen, watching us. And I got the strange feeling that she had been listening to every word I'd been saying.

'Mary, for the love of God, what are you doing down here? We've only just got you settled in bed.' I strode over towards her and grabbed her by the hand. I was about to drag her back up the servants' staircase to the second floor when she spoke for the second time that night.

'Who's the first Lady Ashton?'

Chapter 7

The Face at the Window

Mary, January 1979

I was taken from the kitchen rather roughly by Mrs Medlock. She ignored my question, but that didn't stop me wondering about the answer. Was there another Lady Ashton apart from the posh sparkly lady who wore nice dresses?

As I got into bed, Mrs Medlock told me I was being a naughty girl. She closed the door hard, making it rattle, and I burrowed under the covers. I wondered if I was going to cry. I hadn't cried since before my parents died. I remembered Mum crying when she was sick and she saw Dad was starting to get ill too, even though he was trying to hide it. And I think I may have cried when I first went down into the cellar alone, with my parents telling me they couldn't kiss or hug me goodbye. That was what had happened to little Burnie, the baker's son, two days before, they said. His mum and brother were ill, and he hugged them and became ill himself. After I came out of the cellar, once everyone was dead, I didn't cry. It was all so strange, crying felt like too much of an ordinary thing to do.

In bed, my memory kept looping back to what Mrs Medlock

had said to the man who carried me back to the house. *I can't ... I can't say her name.*

Who *was* the first Lady Ashton? Was she somewhere in this house? If so, why hadn't I seen her, or been told about her? Was she locked up somewhere? Alone? I felt cold, suddenly, thinking about the noises I'd heard – moans and cries, sometimes far-off wailing. They sounded so sad. So real. Almost like they could be mine, but coming from a place far away.

As I felt myself drop off to sleep, I heard them again – a mixture of wails and sobs – and I couldn't tell what I was hearing in my dreams and what I was hearing in real life. Eventually the wails merged into the wind, and I was lost in the spinning darkness.

The next days passed with nothing very interesting happening. I didn't hear any more of the cries from upstairs, and I decided not to ask about them. Even though saying words out loud didn't seem as frightening as it had when I first came here, I wasn't really sure I wanted to start asking a lot of questions – especially after Mrs Medlock's reaction when I asked about the first Lady Ashton. I spent most mornings in my room, drawing and reading books. I'd done a lot of pictures of the trees outside my window and the falling snow. The ones I'd done of my old house and me and Mum and Dad made me sad, so I stopped. And anyway, I couldn't do people very well – they looked babyish and silly.

In the afternoons, Bessie took me out to play. Maybe she did this because she thought I should go outside more, or perhaps Mrs Medlock had told her to, but hers was the only kindness I experienced in that house, and I was grateful for it. She chattered away to me without stopping as we walked across the snow-covered lawn, avoiding the deeper drifts. With the sky still so grey, everything had a strange light to it, like you get before a thunderstorm, with the white fields stretching off for miles and miles in nearly every direction. Apart from down the bottom of the lawn, where the cluster of trees hid the big stone wall. And whatever lay beyond it.

All the Christmas decorations had come down now – they disappeared suddenly after Twelfth Night, as if by magic – and the house felt even darker and colder without the glowing tree. On the fourth afternoon after my night-time adventure, we walked back to the house through the snow a bit later than usual, with Bessie commenting on how dark it was getting and how we'd be in need of some tea as soon as we got in. The huge shape of the house in the dying light felt so threatening, it was as if the darkness was seeping out of the building itself and staining the sky and the snow, throwing the world into endless shadow. It reminded me of the total black behind the door in the wall, and I shivered at the thought.

Maybe I did it to make the house feel less scary, or maybe I felt that some white snow on its dark walls would brighten it up a bit; I don't know. But whatever made me start throwing snowballs, it certainly didn't impress Bessie.

'If you throw one more of them, Miss Mary, Mrs Medlock will spot you and you'll get sent to bed with no supper, no cocoa, no nothing.' She grabbed my hand and shook it, making me drop the snowball I was going to throw at one of the windows. I bent down to scoop up some more, but she said, 'I'm watching you, little madam,' and steered me round past the steps of the main entrance and towards the servants' door at the back. As we walked along the side of the house, I remembered the small snowball I had clamped in my other hand, and hurled it up at one of the top windows. It exploded with a small *pop*. I was pleased with my aim, but Bessie noticed and marched back towards me. 'Hey, what did I just tell you!'

I didn't answer. I didn't even look at her. Because I'd just seen something up at the window. I hadn't realised the curtains had been drawn until they twitched back. Then a flash of something pale came into view before vanishing again into the gloom. A face. The anguished face of a little boy.

Chapter 8

You Have No Clue

Natalie

The afternoon light, so bright when I arrived, has grown fainter, although it's still early in the afternoon. I'm conscious, though, that Mrs Medlock has been talking for some time and might want a break in our conversation. She goes over to a small lamp and turns it on, then comes back to sit opposite me.

'I'm sorry, my dear, I don't usually start rabbiting on like this to strangers. I like to keep busy, keep the house running, but if I'm honest, there isn't *that* much to do these days.'

I nod politely, then say, 'Do you get out to the shops much?' I thought a fairly neutral question would be a good way to ease us back into conversation, but Mrs Medlock has her gaze settled on the table once more.

'No, no ... deliveries, of course. I've never been one for shopping.'

I realise that I need to be more forthright. 'So ... the orphan, Mary ... she was a troublesome child when she was here?'

Mrs Medlock nods. 'Oh yes. Goodness me, yes. She was a right little madam and no mistake. Danced rings around us, even during her quiet patch. You're lucky you won't have to teach her.' I can tell her mind has dragged her back elsewhere, back into her memories, because what she says next chills me to the bone. 'Of course, during that time, when things started to get ... difficult ... well, she became the least of our worries.'

I raise my eyebrows. 'Difficult? More difficult than they were already?'

She looks up at me properly now, and I think, in the dull lamplight, I can see the glisten of tears in her eyes. 'Oh my dear, you have no clue, do you. No clue at all. How terrible things can get ... '

I lean forwards, compelled by her words. 'Why did things become so terrible?'

She takes a breath, lets it out slowly, then says, 'When Mary discovered Master Rupert up in his bedroom. Perhaps if the two of them had never met, none of what came next would have happened at all.'

Chapter 9

It's Quite Upsetting to Watch

Mrs Medlock, January 1979

'Get off me!'

I was deep inside the larder when I heard the shout. I was in there doing stock checks of the food, but came out immediately when I heard the commotion from outside the house.

'What on earth is all that racket?' I called out, while more shouts and protests were yelled into the cold afternoon air. At the door I saw Bessie struggling with Mary, doing her best to drag her along the frozen ground and into the house, but the girl was resisting.

'I told her to stop throwing them bleedin' snowballs,' Bessie said, evidently out of breath, 'but she didn't bloody listen and now she's refusing to come inside into the warm.' Her grip on the girl failed, which sent Mary falling back into the snow as she tried to get away.

I marched out of the door and over to Mary, grabbing the hood of her coat and tugging her to her feet. 'Get inside, now,' I said sharply, but she replied with such a firm 'No!' that it momentarily took the wind out of my sails. It was so odd to finally hear her talking, and with such vehemence, after weeks of silence, that I didn't know quite how to react to it. It was going to take some getting used to.

Instead of continuing to manhandle the girl, I put my hands on my hips and stared her down until her defiant gaze crumbled and slid to the floor. 'So, what's caused all this fuss?'

Bessie started to reply, gabbling again about snowballs, but I raised a hand to shush her. I continued to stare at Mary until at last she spoke. And just like on the night of the party, her words certainly had an impact: 'Who's the boy at the window?'

I instinctively looked over at Bessie. I intended no accusation with my gaze, but she evidently took it as such and started to defend herself. Again I told her to be quiet.

'I saw him at the window,' Mary said. 'His face was at the window. Not for long, but I saw him. I promise I saw him.'

I had no idea what to tell her, other than the truth, and I was cold and too rattled for that. Instead, I turned on my heel and said, 'Bring her inside, Bessie – and drag her if you have to.'

Thankfully Mary didn't require dragging, and Bessie managed to deposit her in her room without too much of a fuss. Perhaps the little madam had exhausted herself by that point. I met Bessie coming down the stairs, and she started again with her explanation of the whole brouhaha.

'It's fine, I don't blame you,' I said, rubbing at my tired eyes. 'It was inevitable, I suppose, that she'd discover him at some point. I just hoped we'd be able to keep them entirely separate for longer. But not all is lost. She might know about him, but *he* doesn't have to know about her.'

Bessie didn't look comforted by this. 'Well, I rather fancy he got a look at her from the window. I know he shouldn't have – although it were pretty gloomy by that point. Probably why he thought he'd risk a peep out from between the curtains, there being not much light an' all ...' She trailed off, and I simply nodded, resigned to the further complications all this would no doubt bring.

Our conversation was cut short, however, by a light cut-glass voice from somewhere up towards the gallery. 'Ah, there you both are,' Lady Ashton said as she began to descend the stairs in her oh-so-graceful manner. 'I've been looking for you, Mrs Medlock.'

I tried to stop myself sighing in exasperation. 'Yes, what can I do for you? I was just discussing Master Rupert with Bessie, and—'

'Oh, don't worry about little Rupsie. I've just been to see him to say goodbye.'

This made me close my mouth in surprise. 'Oh, are you—'

'Yes,' she said, cutting me off again. 'I came to tell you I have decided to join my husband at our Manhattan apartment. I may spend some time in Long Island too, although it might be a bit cold for that. It's not as if I can sun myself in the Hamptons. But I can do some shopping and catch up with my acquaintances there.'

I was disconcerted by this. I had always believed the plan was for the master of the house to return home shortly after Christmas. The idea of neither of them being in residence while Bessie and I were left with two children to look after – well, I wasn't impressed, and that's putting it mildly. 'So you're going to New York?'

'Yes,' she said, a flicker of irritation passing across her face. 'Manhattan is indeed in New York, Mrs Medlock – as ever, your geography is impeccable.' I noticed she was starting to look rattled, and I saw her lips pinch together – something she always did when she was trying to keep calm. We were both liable to bring out a wasp-chewing expression in the other before most of our conversations had finished. 'I'm going to spend the rest of the afternoon trying on some new dresses I've had sent over from

Selfridges. We've got several cocktail parties and other events booked in, and I want to be well prepared. Please could you bring the dresses up when they arrive and assist me.'

I did as I was told. I took up four bags over two trips to her bedroom, and tried to nod and say 'yes', 'certainly', 'very nice' in all the right places while she flitted about like a silk-clad insect, wittering on about how apparently Paul Newman was going to be at one of the parties she was attending. 'I was almost in a film with him once, back when I acted, but it didn't work out – I was tied in to a frothy little play on Shaftesbury Avenue and couldn't make the schedule work.' When it got too much for me, I dropped a well-timed remark about how one of the Chanel dresses she was posing in was very similar to an outfit the first Lady Ashton had worn at one of her last public outings. That shut her up. The dress got bundled back into the bag and I was told to go and see to the dinner arrangements.

At the door, she said something that made me turn around. 'Don't think you'll be able to carry on like this for much longer, *Dolores*.' The use of my first name was particularly stark, especially the strange emphasis she gave it. 'I know my husband is quite set in his ways. Likes continuity, likes the staff to remain the same, likes his house in order, but I've gone through enough years of agreeing with it all, and soon it will be time for me to have my say. And I *will* have my say. About who works here. And who should leave.'

She said all this while pulling on a particularly vibrant blue dress, then selected a white fur to throw over her shoulders. I felt a constricting of my throat, and my mouth went dry. Suddenly I had a burning desire to rush in and rip the fur from her back, wrap it round her head and smother her with it – hold it to her mouth as her thin little arms and legs flailed like a spider pinned upside down. But I didn't do this, of course. I didn't do anything of the kind. Instead, I just looked back at her and, keeping my voice steady, replied, 'There were never any complaints when Lady Ashton was alive.'

She met my stare in the mirror. And I saw the dislike writ large in her eyes, like a bloom of poison within a pool of glittering green. 'But you see, Honoria is dead. I'm Lady Ashton now. I have been for quite a long time, and if you carry on saying things like that, I'm going to start to think you're ... well, getting a bit confused. After all, you did serve me tea with ice-cold water yesterday. Not to mention the dresses. I specifically asked you to keep them downstairs, packed up in their bags, but you brought them up here against my instructions.'

A rush of prickling unease fizzed over me. 'I ... I've never served you tea with cold water ... and you just asked for these dresses to be brought up to you ... you're trying them on *right now*!' I couldn't stop myself from snapping these last words. Lady Ashton didn't flinch. She just shook her head sadly.

'It's quite upsetting to watch, I must confess,' she said. 'I had an aunt who was the same. Started making mistakes here and there, until one day she could barely dress herself or string a simple sentence together. And to think, you're only in your forties. If it's this bad now, one can only imagine how advanced your condition will become as you get older. We might even have to think about getting you some help. Psychiatric help.'

I was used to us not getting along. Used to us stinging each other with the odd choice word, the occasional passive-aggressive dig. But this was something else. This sent my mind spinning, making me feel weak at the knees and suddenly desperate to get out of that room, away from this strange, cruel woman. It was as if a docile though irritating pet had suddenly revealed fangs. I stood there for a few seconds unspeaking, then the words came to me. In that instant, I knew exactly what I needed to say.

'I'm sorry to disappoint you, your ladyship. But I could serve you mugs of lambs' blood with your morning toast, and still I would remain. Your husband is never getting rid of me. Not so long as I'm alive.'

I didn't wait to see how she took these words. Or to hear what nasty retort she'd offer up next. I walked out of the room, across the landing and down the stairs, all the while trying to stop my hands from shaking.

Chapter 10

Everything Changed

Mary, January 1979

The floaty woman, Lady Ashton, left the house. From the window I watched her get into a car with lots of suitcases. I didn't care much. She never properly spoke to me anyway.

A couple of days passed, during which time I mainly sat on my bed and drew, watched the snow falling and thought about what me, Mum and Dad would have been doing if they were still here. We'd probably have made a snowman, or gone to look out over the frozen lake, with Dad bringing his camera. But there was no frozen lake at Marwood Manor. And after what happened outside last time with the snowballs, I didn't think they'd let me build a snowman.

They hadn't told me I wasn't allowed to go outside again, but I got the feeling they wouldn't like it if I tried. Things changed, though, when Bessie came to bring me a boiled egg a few nights later and said, 'Mrs Medlock mentioned earlier about playing out of doors again tomorrow, so long as you make two promises.'

I crammed one of the strips of toast on the plate into my mouth and asked, 'What promises?'

Bessie sat on the bed with a sigh. 'Number one: you're not to go throwing any more snowballs up at windows, you understand me, young missy?'

I chewed on the toast, then nodded. She seemed OK with this.

'And second, you're not to go down the pathway beyond the lawn and try to get through that big old door into the garden behind the wall.'

I started to nod, raising the spoon to tap on my boiled egg, then realised what she'd just said.

'Garden?'

Bessie had got up from the bed and was now tidying up around the room, picking up my dressing gown off the threadbare carpet and putting it on top of the dusty old chest of drawers. 'What's that?' She turned back to face me.

'You said the garden. The garden behind the wall. Is there really a garden there? A proper garden? Not like the plain fields, an *actual* garden?'

Even in the low light, I could see Bessie's face start to go red. She picked up some more clothes off the floor and started to fold them, but I could tell she was just pretending to be busy. Eventually she said, 'You know, little Miss Mary, I rather preferred it when you didn't speak. You're going to get me into a whole lot of bother, and no mistake.' She put the folded pile on top of the drawers and left the room, closing the door behind her.

Later on, I managed to upset Mrs Medlock too. Maybe Bessie was annoyed with me, or perhaps they were now sharing their trips upstairs, but it was Mrs Medlock who came to take away the tray. Normally she would have left it for the morning, if Bessie hadn't come, but instead she marched through the door, put her hands on her hips and stared at me. 'You've been bothering Bessie. I've told you before, young lady, keep your questions to yourself and do as you're told. You've caused enough trouble in this house already. I don't need you poking your nose in where it's not wanted.'

At another time, this might have made me cry, but I found that tears still didn't come, and I wasn't ready to stop my questioning. Earlier, as I'd sat in the dark, eating my boiled egg and thinking about what Bessie had said about the garden, I'd heard it again. A high, echoey wail, like someone was crying far away. On and on it went, then I'd heard footsteps on the stairs, disappearing into another part of the house. But at least now I knew what the sound was. They were keeping someone else here. The face I'd seen at the window earlier.

'Who's been crying?' I asked.

I saw her lip tremble at this as she opened her mouth and paused, apparently not sure what to say. Then she said, simply, 'Nobody's been crying.'

I frowned at her. 'There was. There *was* someone crying. And it wasn't a grown-up person.'

Mrs Medlock did a similar thing to Bessie: she started clearing things up, clattering the tray and the plate, pretending to be involved with what she was doing rather than listening to me properly. 'You didn't hear anything of the sort,' she said. 'And if I get any more nonsense from you on the subject, I'll write to Lord Ashton and tell him you'd be better off in an orphanage.'

She left after that, and I sat and waited for the house to go quiet and still. Then, once again, the moans began. And I knew what I needed to do. I got up off the bed and pulled on my fluffy dressing gown. Really carefully, so as not to let the floorboards creak, I tiptoed along the landing to the far end, following the corridor round, and then round again. I walked for ages – the house was huge, with every hallway leading to another staircase, some winding, some straight, each corridor leading to more rooms and passageways, some small and tight, some open and airy. I wondered if I was ever going to find my way back to my room again. But I pushed that worry out of my mind as I carried on through the darkness, stopping every now and then to check if the cries were becoming louder or quieter. Finally, after a long time spent searching, I reached a corridor with a door at the end that seemed to be glowing around the edges. It was locked, but the key was on the outside, so I turned it, very carefully and quietly.

The key unlocked the door. But I didn't go in straight away. Even though the memory was different – it had been daytime when I'd opened the door to the cellar and gone back inside the house after the snowstorm – I still felt as if I had returned to that moment. Like I had slipped through a little crack in time and tumbled back to the very worst day. It was as though I knew that opening this door would change everything, like it had done before. I thought about this for a long time, standing there in the darkness. But I still went inside.

Behind the door was a room lit by a lamp on a table. The space around it was filled with all sorts of things. It was like an old antique shop Mum once took me to when we'd visited a town down towards one of the lochs. There was a pram, and a rocking horse, and long things made of poles with clothes hanging off them. There was a big chest overflowing with toys. Puppets and little cars and boxes of puzzles that looked like they'd never been played with. And at the end of the room was a staircase that wound round in a loop, leading up to a balcony. It was like the one downstairs in the library, although this one was smaller and glittered in the lamplight. As I walked closer, my bare feet making a slightly rasping sound on the patterned carpet, I saw that the winding staircase was encrusted with ruby-like stones and bits of coloured glass. Maybe they were gems, I thought to myself, as I put my foot on the first metal step and started to climb, up and round, up and round, until I got to the little balcony and saw before me another door, again with a key on the outside. As I reached out, about to turn it in the lock, I heard the sound again. I knew I'd reached the right place. The sound of a child crying was so clear.

Taking a deep breath, I stepped inside the room.

Chapter 11

The Boy

Mary, January 1979

I was not alone.

In front of me was a large room lit by two small lamps and two large candles. The whole place was piled high with books – hundreds of them, everywhere, in stacks that I was worried I might knock over if I went too close or moved too quickly. In the middle of the room was a large bed, with a roof thing like mine, but even bigger. And in the middle of the bed was ...

'Who are you?' the boy shouted. He was already crying, but now he started to shriek, pointing at me. Without thinking, I ran across the room and hurled myself at him, leaping onto the bed, sending books flying as I went. I pressed my hand to his mouth, trying to stop his yells. Maybe he was surprised by the suddenness of it all, but he went limp and silent almost straight away, his eyes wide and terrified.

'Keep quiet!' I hissed at him. 'Or she'll hear us.' I kept my hand there until the boy finally blinked at me, then nodded.

As soon as I removed it, he started talking. 'Who will hear?'

I was still sitting on top of him, pinning him down, and he didn't try to push me off. '*She* will. Mrs Medlock.'

He looked at me, frowning, his light brown hair covering the front of his face a bit. 'That old witch? She's nothing to be scared of. She's just a grumpy so-and-so.'

I frowned and climbed off him, suddenly feeling a bit strange about sitting on top of someone who wasn't fighting back. 'She's been very cross with me,' I said, settling myself on the side of the bed, watching him. I guessed he was slightly older than me, but not much. Maybe eleven or twelve. He was wearing pyjama bottoms, but instead of a pyjama top he had a thick dark-red jumper with a gold-orange 'R' on the front of it. He drew his knees up and leaned forward so that he was sitting cross-legged in front of me, sniffing and wiping his tears away.

'She's always cross. My mother calls her "Old Hatchet Face". Even though she isn't that old.'

I stared at him. 'Your mother ...' I said, then all at once everything made sense. He was Lady Ashton's son. And if Lord Ashton was my cousin, or something like that, then this boy must be part of my family too.

'She's gone. Gone to America.'

I nodded. 'I know, I saw her leave. Why has she left you here? Why can't you go with her?'

He reached for what looked like a T-shirt and used it to dab at his eyes. 'I'm not supposed to go out. I'm very weak.'

I looked at him again, sitting there cross-legged, the duvet bunched around his bare feet. He didn't look weak. There was a boy at the church in our village, where my mum used to do the flowers, who couldn't run around because of brittle bones. He was tiny and wiry. And although *this* boy wasn't big and strong, he just looked normal. Maybe a bit paler, but apart from that like any other boy.

'What's wrong with you?' I asked.

'I'm very sensitive to daylight, that's what the doctors say.

Doctors my parents speak to. If I were to spend too long in the sun, I would burn all over and my skin would scar and go red.'

I nodded, even though none of this made sense to me. Why would he burn, especially when there had barely been any sun here for ages?

'Also,' he said, carrying on and straightening up a bit, as if quite enjoying telling me about his problems, 'the doctors suspect I have a low imm ... immune system. Immune something. It means I might catch illnesses.'

This made me look away from him. 'My parents died of illnesses.'

After a few seconds, he asked, 'What illnesses?'

'They said it was flu.' I looked back up at him, and he seemed confused.

'I wasn't aware that normal people died of influenza.' The way he said the word made him sound even posher than his mum.

As if he could read my mind, he said, 'You sound Scottish. Are you Scottish?'

I nodded. 'From the Highlands.'

'I've never been to Scotland, although naturally I've read *Kidnapped* by Robert Louis Stevenson.'

I didn't know what he was talking about, so I just stared at him, my mouth open.

'*Kidnapped*,' he said again. 'You must have read it, considering you're from there. If you haven't, you should right away.'

'OK,' I said.

'I did have a copy somewhere around here, but it's probably lost. I have so many books, they do sometimes go missing.'

As I got up to look more closely at the stacks of books, I brushed against one of the piles and sent it toppling.

'Sorry,' I said, feeling grateful that Mrs Medlock wasn't there to tell me off.

'It's all right,' the boy said, 'They fall over all the time.'

One had fallen onto my foot, though it was a little soft-cover book so it hadn't hurt me. I reached out to pick it up and looked at its cover. 'Agatha Christie,' I read out loud. I was going to say that was an author I *had* heard of and I was sure my parents had had a couple of books with that name on at home, on our shelves under the stairs. But something about the cover made me stop. It was an orangey-red colour and I saw instantly it was fire. Fire with a shadow in the background. At the front was a creature. A bat, opened out. And its little body had been stuck with pins. This wasn't the only horrible thing. Down the edge of the picture was a long hand, with arching fingers. I brought the book closer to my face, looking at the fingers, and as I did, I saw they weren't really fingers. It was more like a claw.

'I've got heaps of hers,' the boy said.

'It doesn't look very nice,' I said, my voice quiet and small.

He leaned towards me to peer at the book's spine. 'Oh, that one . . . yes, that one's . . . interesting. Most of her books are about detectives. There are detectives in that one too, but there are . . . other things.'

I glanced at him. 'Like what?'

He looked back at me for a moment. Then he said, 'Witches.'

Something about the way he said the word made me drop the book. I suddenly had a shiver down my spine.

He pulled a face. 'You're not scared, are you?'

'Of witches . . . aren't you?'

He shrugged. 'Well, it depends. I've been reading a lot about them. People think they're just stories or no longer exist, but it wouldn't surprise me . . . ' he lowered his voice, 'if that's just what they *want* us to think.'

I nodded as if I agreed, even though I wasn't sure I did or even wanted to think about it. I put the book down on top of another pile near me, carefully, so it wouldn't topple over like the last.

'I imagine you might have stumbled across the odd ceremony or ritual in the Highlands? I think that sort of thing happens a lot there.'

I shook my head slowly, feeling unsure and a bit confused. 'I don't know ... I don't think I saw things like that.'

He let out a sigh. 'I long to see the Highlands, but I doubt it will ever happen.'

I frowned at him. 'Why not? You're rich, aren't you?'

He sighed, a bit dramatically. 'I *told* you. I'm not well. I can't travel. If I were to exert myself in such a way, it's likely I'd keel over dead in an instant, if I didn't burn all over first. I'm not even supposed to walk around this room much – just once or twice a day to stop my bones seizing up. Sometimes I do cheat, though, and go over to the window to take a peek at the outside just before it's getting dark.'

'I know,' I said. 'I saw you.'

He didn't look pleased. 'Oh, well, I didn't see you. I try to be quick, in case the old witch Medlock sees me. I keep complaining to my father about her, when he's here. But he won't sack her.'

I thought about telling this boy about how much I missed my parents, and how strange and odd these past weeks had been, but I didn't. I just sat there quietly, staring at the thick, expensive-looking white bedsheets and trying to think about something else.

'So what have you been doing here, if you're not allowed to read books?' he asked. 'That's all I have to do, so I can't think what else could possibly occupy you in this old place. Are they going to send you to school?'

'I am allowed to read books,' I corrected him. 'And they haven't mentioned school. But no, I haven't done much really. I've been outside a bit. I even tried ... ' I stopped, wondering whether to tell him about the big door in the long stone wall. Perhaps talking about it more would get me into trouble. If this boy had never been outside, maybe he didn't even know about it.

'Yes? Spit it out,' he said eagerly.

'I tried to get through a door at the bottom of the lawn, but the tall Mr Oakwood man stopped me and brought me back up to the house. Bessie said there's a garden down there. Hidden away, behind a wall.'

Suddenly the boy seemed quite excited. He sat up straight and said, wide-eyed, 'Yes, I've heard there is too. We had another woman working here once. Miss Jessel. She used to teach me arithmetic and Latin and stuff, you know the sort of thing.'

I didn't know about that sort of thing, but I just nodded.

'Well,' he carried on, 'she once told me about the door in the wall and the garden beyond it. I think she said she'd seen it. But it was all ... a bit strange. She wasn't herself that day. Maybe she was unwell. That's what everyone said after she'd gone – that she was unwell. She said something like "If things carry on the way they're going, I'll end up in the garden behind the wall just like the first ... "'

He stopped himself. Instead of looking excited, he now seemed nervous. But even without him saying any more, his words began to make some sense to me. 'The first Lady Ashton?' I asked, quietly. I don't know why I half whispered it, but I felt it needed to be said softly, like a secret or something you say to people when they're sad.

'Be careful,' he hissed, raising a finger to his lips. 'Or she'll hear.'

I felt my eyes widen as I stared at him. 'What ... what do you mean?'

He leaned towards me conspiratorially, his eyes flicking to the door. 'My old tutor ... she didn't last, a very unreliable woman ... she said once that the ghost of the first Lady Ashton probably walks the house and grounds at night. She said she'd heard rumours about her down in the village. I was getting cross about something and wouldn't pay attention, and she told me that if I wasn't a good boy, the first Lady Ashton would come and take me in the night. And probably carry me off to the garden behind the wall.' He stopped and bit his lip, then glanced to the door. 'Maybe she was just saying it to get me to behave. I've got cross lots of times since, even after my tutor left, and I've never been carried off in the night. But I do hear creaking and other noises sometimes. It makes me think she's here but waiting. Waiting for her moment.'

I was scared by this. But even so, I still wanted to hear more. I didn't know what to say, so I just stayed silent, waiting to see if he was going to tell me anything else. But then abruptly he said, 'I think I need to go to sleep now. I need my sleep, otherwise I might catch diseases.'

'OK,' I said, and got off the bed. I watched as he pulled the duvet over his legs and settled back onto the thick pillows behind him. I found myself wishing my bed was this soft and comfortable, with the room cosy in the low lamplight. 'Can I visit you again?' I asked. I didn't know why I sought permission, but he nodded. 'If you like. Go and find *Kidnapped* in the library downstairs and read it. Then we'll talk about it.'

I told him I would, and made my way around the piles of books towards the door. Just as I had my hand on the handle, he spoke again, and I turned round.

'You haven't told me your name. I'm Rupert. What's yours?'

'I'm Mary,' I said.

He gave a slow nod of his head. I thought he was finished, but then he said something I wasn't expecting. 'There's a key. A big iron key. On Mrs Medlock's ring that she carries with her everywhere. All the house ones look the same, but that one – it's different. If you're able to steal it, you could try to get through the door in the wall with it. Just let me know what you find in there.'

I stared back at him, silently, until I noticed that his eyes had started to close as he drifted off to sleep. Then I turned back to the door and left, walking carefully down the little spiral staircase and through the creaking house back to my room. And with every step, I prayed the spirit of the first Lady Ashton wouldn't hear me.

Chapter 12

Everything Changed

Mrs Medlock, February 1979

At that point, I didn't have a clue that Mary had discovered Master Rupert. I think some weeks went by before I realised, and anyway, I had bigger fish to fry. It all started with a phone call from Lady Ashton on a cold Sunday at the start of February. I'd allowed Mary to put on some music on the cassette player in the living room (it was a relatively new piece of equipment, given to the house by one of Lady Ashton's former acting friends). When both her ladyship and Lord Ashton were out of the house, I usually enjoyed a bit of music on Sunday afternoons, although I liked to keep the tone sombre. I didn't approve of needless merriment and generally discouraged the noisy tunes that seemed to be so popular. Listening to the radio was nigh-on impossible by that point, with pop groups and drug-addled rock stars competing to see who could out-debauch the other. Once Mary's cassette had come to an end, Bessie wanted to put on 'something lively' and suggested fetching her soundtrack to the recent film *Grease*, but I soon nipped that in the bud, taking down a recording of Beethoven's 7th and telling her to put it on and keep the volume quiet. She grumbled a bit, but she was soon humming along tunelessly as she dusted the corners of the room.

I was just pouring a cup of tea when I heard the telephone ring. Signalling to Bessie to turn down the music, I walked into the hallway and held the receiver to my ear: 'Marwood Manor,' I said, without enthusiasm.

'Mrs Medlock, please, we have spoken about this. If you answer the phone like that, people will think we're some dowdy National Trust property, or even worse, a shabby little B&B with net curtains and a damp problem.' Lady Ashton's voice came from the phone with remarkable clarity, considering she was halfway across the world.

'I'm sorry, your ladyship, that wasn't my intention. I've never stayed in such an establishment, so I definitely wouldn't want people to think of Marwood in such a way. Perhaps those sorts of places are more common in Walthamstow.'

A few beats of silence passed between us. I knew a reference to her place of birth would rile her, and I took a moment of sadistic pleasure in imagining her going white with fury. I was ready for her games. I wasn't going to let her shake me up any more.

'I'm sorry, Mrs Medlock. I think we must have a bad line, or your Yorkshire accent seems to be getting thicker.' She placed a disgusted sort of emphasis on that last word, left a pointed pause, then continued. 'Could you repeat for me what you said? Slowly, please, so I can make a note of it and pass it on to Lord Ashton.'

I didn't dignify this with a proper answer. 'What do you want?' I said, my jaw tightening and my teeth clenched.

'Now, now, Mrs Medlock, there's no need to be like that. As a matter of fact, I have a job for you, and if you do it well, I'm sure we'll be able to forget our little disagreement the other day. To cut a long and frankly rather dull story short, our dear friends the Kellmans have had a spot of bother with their eldest child, Ernest.

I imagine he probably gets a bit sick of the Oscar Wilde references. Or maybe he finds it hard, having a rather controversial MP for a father. He's been ... well ... asked to leave his school, temporarily we hope, because of some difficulty with a member of staff. I won't go into the details, but the Kellmans think some solitary confinement away from their home in Chester Square would do him good. They were thinking of packing him off with a tutor to Switzerland – apparently the Swiss are good at that sort of thing, ironing out even the most troubling attributes in young minds – but I said he's welcome to come and stay at Marwood for the rest of the term if he needs a quiet place to study alone.'

I felt my blood starting to boil within me. 'Did you indeed? And who is to take care of this young ruffian while you and Lord Ashton are in America?'

She gave a light laugh, 'Oh, little Ernie isn't a ruffian – he hasn't been violent, as such, just ... misunderstood, I presume. And yes, you and Bessie will need to take care of him on a day-to-day basis, but don't worry, you won't be responsible for his education. No, the Kellmans have employed a very nice young man named Mr Quint, who will be accompanying the boy and home-schooling him.'

I sighed heavily, and didn't bother to hide it. 'Right. And will this Mr Quint be coming to the house every day?'

'He'll be staying at Marwood too. I thought it would be easier that way.'

'Easier for who?'

'For "whom", Mrs Medlock.'

I ignored the correction. 'So we *are* a B&B then?'

I thought I had gone too far and expected to receive more threats about my position, but instead she said with ice-cold simplicity, 'Just do it, Mrs Medlock. Expect them tomorrow.'

The rest of the day was manic. I sent Bessie upstairs to prepare two guest rooms on the first floor, away from Mary on the second and Master Rupert on the fourth. Hopefully I'd be able to keep them all at arm's length and from fraternising with each other. The last thing I wanted was the three children to form a pack, making me some sort of schoolmistress. No, simpler to keep them separated. Lady Ashton had given me no information on how old this boy was. He could be a seven-year-old, or a great tall burly teenager, eating me out of house and home. Hollow legs, my mother used to say of my older brother, before he passed away at just twenty-one, God rest his soul. He could eat an army's worth of food in one sitting.

When Mr Oakwood came to the kitchen to bring firewood, he found me in a flap. 'What's going on?' he asked, setting the wood down and putting his hands on his hips. I tried not to look at the way his muscles pressed to his shirt, or the slim curve of his waist as he stood there looking quizzically at the mass of paperwork on the table.

'Her *ladyship*, that's what's going on. She's only gone and turned this place into a hotel.' I explained to him about the unexpected guests, and he listened and sympathised in his usual single-word way. In the end, I allowed him to encourage me to take the air with him outside to give myself a break, leaving the account books and order forms on the kitchen table. Next to them I'd also left my large ring of keys, which usually went everywhere with me. In the midst of the palaver (and, I admit, the distraction of Mr Oakwood's attentions), I didn't notice until later that I didn't have them. Nor did I notice the absence of one particular key when I returned.

Chapter 13

The Young Man

Mrs Medlock, February 1979

Even though I tried to get everything sorted before their arrival, I still felt unprepared the next day when I saw the car winding its way up the drive. Two passengers got out, each carrying a suitcase. A man who looked around thirty, and a boy who could only have been around thirteen or fourteen at the most.

I noticed the boy's body language first. It was clear he wasn't happy about this situation. He kicked each step as he climbed the stairs to the entrance, prompting the man with him to nudge his shoulder and remark 'Walk properly.' When they reached the top step, I left the living room, from where I'd been watching them, and opened the door before the bell was rung.

'Oh, hello there,' the young man said. I'd expected that a private tutor would have one of those painfully tight posh accents, but his voice was more open and less reserved. Educated, certainly, but there was something about the way he said those three words. You could tell he had charisma. Yes, that was it. Charisma.

'You must be Mrs Medlam?' he said. Without waiting for an

answer, he breezed on, 'I'm Alan Quint, and this is my surly charge, young Ernest.'

'Medlock,' I said, without smiling. *Medlam* was a little too close to *Bedlam* for my liking.

'Sorry?'

'Mrs Medlock.'

He twigged then what I was on about. 'Oh yes, so sorry, must have misremembered. Anyway, shall we go in and get settled? I'm famished. I suppose we're a bit late for luncheon, but I trust it won't be long till supper?'

Again I inwardly cursed Lady Ashton for turning Marwood into a hotel for guests she was not even here to receive. Who did this man think he was, dictating to me when meals should be served?

'I dare say our housemaid, Bessie, will be able to find something for you on a tray,' I said, turning to go back inside, leaving the door swinging open for them.

'Oh, I'm so sorry, but is there someone to help us with our bags?' Mr Quint called after me.

'No, there isn't,' I said bluntly. 'Follow me. I'll show you where you're sleeping.'

I walked quite a way ahead of them up the stairs and across the landing, with the two males trying to keep up while weighed down with their suitcases. I opened the door to one of the bedrooms and said to the boy, 'This one's for you.' He walked in and dropped his suitcase on the floor by the wardrobe. It clattered open, spilling out clothes and books. He gave no suggestion that he was going to pick it up – he just sat down on the bed with a huff. I looked at him, keen to set a precedent. 'Don't go thinking we're here to tidy up around you, my lad. Get your things all neat and put away into the wardrobe, then I'll see about a snack for you.' He glared back at me. If it hadn't been for his seemingly eternal scowl, he'd have been a sweet-looking boy, all blond hair and blue eyes. But his angry expression made him look harsh and severe. Cruel, even.

He continued to sit in silence, so I left him there and led Mr Quint to the room next door. 'Here you go. This should be comfortable enough.' It was identical to the boy's room, but Mr Quint didn't seem to mind.

'I'm sure it will be more than adequate Mrs *Medlock*,' he said, walking around, tapping one of the posts of the bed and brushing his fingers along the folded-up curtain. There was something about the way he said my name that I didn't quite like. I suspected he was mocking me, but I wasn't in the mood to waste too much energy getting riled by it. 'May I ask how long Lord and Lady Ashton are planning to be away for?'

'I don't know,' I said.

'Interesting.' He spoke absent-mindedly, scratching the side of his neck as he looked around the room, then out of the window, peering at the grounds. 'Very interesting. But their return isn't imminent?'

I knew it was unlikely, but still I repeated my answer.

'I thought housekeepers were supposed to know everything? Isn't it built into the breed?' he said, smiling. It wasn't a nice smile.

'I'm sorry to disappoint you. And I don't consider my job to be my *breed*.'

He raised his eyebrows. 'I'm sorry if I've touched a nerve. I forget sometimes what a delicate, sensitive sex you are. So different to men.' He paused, his eyes settling on me for an uncomfortable amount of time. Then he looked away. 'But everyone has their place in the world, Mrs Medlock, and I'm sure you do too, in your own way.'

'And what is your place in this world, Mr. Quint?' I said.

He made a sound of amusement and turned back to me, still

with that same smile on his lips. 'To seize opportunities when they come along. I'm quite fluid when it comes to my lifestyle and living arrangements. I think this teaching post will suit me very well. For the time being.'

I had no idea what he was trying to say with all this, but I sensed some sort of power performance was afoot. I had endured various psychological games from Lady Ashton, but to be put through my paces like this by a guest was even more unsettling.

'I'll let you get unpacked,' I said, deciding it was time to leave. He said nothing further, but watched as I walked out of the room.

Back down in the kitchen, I instructed Bessie to make cheese sandwiches for our guests and take them up on a tray. She did this while rabbiting away about some play she'd been listening to on the radio, causing me to zone out, but when she returned, she was so flushed and flustered I was forced to give her my full attention.

'What's wrong?' I asked, narrowing my eyes. 'What did he say to you?'

'Nothing's wrong,' she said, with a slight giggle. 'He didn't say anything. Well, nothing bad, in any case.'

I guessed that she found Mr Quint handsome, and I wondered if he'd flirted with her – a more likely situation when it came to Bessie. I didn't press for details; however, I did remark a little later on how moody and rude his young student appeared to be.

Bessie waved her hands. 'Oh, ignore him, lads get stroppy around that age. I imagine Master Rupert will – although he can get quite stroppy already. Maybe the new boy will calm down a bit once he's into his studies and whatnot.'

I tutted. 'Well, I think Mr Quint's likely to have his hands full trying to educate him.'

Bessie sighed. 'That's true. Lucky he doesn't have a teenage girl as a student. I doubt she'd be able to focus on her studies.' She said this last sentence dreamily, as if to herself, with a wistful sigh at the end that I found disproportionately irritating.

'I don't like him,' I replied, gathering up my cup and saucer and taking them to the sink. 'And you watch yourself. If he says anything ... *ungentlemanly*, you let me know. If he's under this roof, he needs to be upstanding and respectful.'

Bessie made some comment about the word 'ungentlemanly' – apparently she found it amusing – but I felt too weary to pull her up on it. Instead, I asked, 'Have you looked in on little Miss Mary at all?'

To my surprise, Bessie gasped. 'Oh my gosh, with Mr Quint's arrival and everything, I clean forgot. She's not there.'

I turned to face her. 'What do you mean, she's not there?'

Bessie shrugged. 'Just that. Her room was empty. She was looking at things in the library earlier, and I saw her pick up a little box that had a letter opener in it, which I didn't think was safe for her to play with. I left it out in the hallway on the telephone table; I'll go and put it back later. Anyway, I told her sharply that she wasn't to mess about with things that weren't hers, and sent her to her room. But when I went to see her later, she had gone.'

This was unusual. Mary rarely ventured out of her bedroom, and when she did, it was under the instruction and supervision of me or Bessie. Apart from on Twelfth Night. Thinking back to that evening, and where she had attempted to go, made my skin prickle.

'Perhaps she's playing outside,' Bessie said. 'I'll go and have a look for her now.'

'You do that,' I said. 'And if she's up to mischief again, we're going to have a serious conversation about her behaviour.' Bessie had gone before I'd finished my sentence. But I still finished it, quietly to myself: 'I'll lock her in her room if I have to.'

Chapter 14

Worrying Recollections

Natalie

'You must have been worried about losing all those children in such a big old house,' I say, as Mrs Medlock nudges a teaspoon absent-mindedly across the tabletop.

'Worried?' she says, as if the word doesn't quite make sense to her. 'Well, it was never really my job, so it's hard to get worried about something that you don't see as your responsibility. Although as time went by, the more I realised that "child wrangler" had been unofficially added to my list of duties. I'd always known I was to care for Master Rupert. Not in a medical sense, of course, just with getting him dressed and in the bath and organising his meals. Things like that. Not that he needs help with all that now. Strapping boy, he is. I think you'll like him when you meet him. But anyway, when the other children descended upon us, the place was like an orphanage.'

I nod. 'I can imagine how that would be a bit ... well, a bit tricky. For a housekeeper.'

She lets out a low, mirthless laugh. 'Housekeeper barely covers it. The staff's been so whittled down, I've practically become the cook and the cleaner too. But now you're here, I'll at least know Master Rupert is being kept occupied and cared for.'

I'm not quite sure what to say to this, so I say nothing. Mrs Medlock seems to think my silence is a sign of concern, and she hurries to reassure me that I won't be expected to see to the more 'household' tasks where the boy is concerned: 'Master Rupert's too old a lad now to want a young woman assisting with things like getting dressed and bathing. Of course, in the old days, a young aristocrat would have had a valet or at least some other kind of servant to look after him. How things have changed.'

I can't argue with that. But I'm keen for Mrs Medlock to stay on track rather than wistfully drifting off into vague nostalgia. 'So it was quite a crowd, back when the new boy joined with his tutor?' I ask.

She rolls her eyes, as if still annoyed by the whole thing. 'To start with it was irritating. Later, though, everything became hellish. Truly hellish. Perhaps I should have spotted things sooner. Stopped my grumbling and seen what was going on under my nose quick enough to do something about it. I was certainly too caught up to see what little Mary was doing.'

I lean forward, with interest. 'What *was* she doing?'

Mrs Medlock lets out a heavy sigh. 'All the time we were getting ourselves in a flap about the son of an MP coming to stay with his tutor, little Miss Mary was letting herself into the forbidden garden. With a key she'd stolen from me.'

Chapter 15

The Garden

Mary, February 1979

I recognised the key straight away. It was just how Rupert had described it. Mrs Medlock had left it lying on the table, giving me the chance to quickly remove it when she was bustling about talking about 'the visitors'. I wasn't sure who these visitors were, but I thought they'd be the same as all the others who had come to the house since I arrived: posh people dressed in sparkly dresses and black suits with bow ties who laughed a lot and drank while standing around. That sort.

It turned out I was wrong. The visitors were a boy and a man. The man was dressed in a brown suit-like jacket and a shirt, and the boy in a jumper and creamy-white trousers. He looked very neat and tidy; the sort of boy who wouldn't enjoy rough play or outdoor games. I watched from the window as he and the man walked up the steps together, the boy kicking at them as he trudged towards the front door. I only got one proper glimpse of his face, and he looked angry. Very angry.

I stayed in my room while Mrs Medlock spoke to them, then I heard them start to come upstairs. I decided it would be better to leave the house while she was busy sorting out the newcomers, so I went down the stairs very, very quietly to the floor below, and peeked over the old, gnarly wooden banisters to watch Mrs Medlock go into one of the rooms with the man. I took my chance and ran down the remaining steps onto the landing as quietly as I could. But not quietly enough. From one of the doors on the landing, a head poked out to see what the noise was. The blond head of a boy. He stared at me, and I back at him. He looked slightly older than me. I didn't know what he was going to do, and I didn't really want to find out, so I just put one finger to my lips in a 'shh' sign and then carried on, down the last flight of stairs to the main hallway below, not waiting to see if the boy did anything to alert the other two adults.

I decided to go through the library and out of the window doors, like I did during the party. Outside looked different now the snow had melted. I'd been watching it disappear over the past weeks from my bedroom window, although little white patches remained dotted around the long lawn, like bits on a drawing someone had forgotten to colour in.

When I got to the big stone wall down near the trees, a strange thought popped into my head: what if, after last time, Mrs Medlock and that big, tall man, Mr Oakwood, had removed the door, and I ended up walking along this little pathway for miles and miles, never able to get inside. I was pleased when this didn't happen and the door appeared, just beyond a bend in the path, the same as before. It was so old and lined, like the trunk of a tree, just straighter and smoother. I took the key out of my coat pocket and reached up high to fit it into the lock. That time, no dark, terrifying shapes came through the door toward me and made me faint to the ground. All that happened was a small click, and I grabbed hold of the rusty iron handle and pulled the door towards me.

I stepped through straight away and stared around. It was a garden, just like Bessie had said, with walls all around it, but in front of me there was another part of the wall that curved in, with a door in its centre, open and inviting, and beyond it another that led through into another. I walked through them all, looking at the old stone covered in what I thought was ivy. I ended up facing a large hedge, with a winding pathway going in both right and left. I chose the left path, and more hedges were suddenly all around me, with pathways jutting off and criss-crossing. I noticed there were spaces for flower beds, which were filled with plain green plants, although no actual flowers. Without colour, the garden felt strangely bare and ugly.

The sky was grey and getting darker, and it felt as if the bushes and walls were closing in on me. But I didn't find this scary. It was actually rather nice, like the garden was protecting me, keeping me safe, as if it *knew* what had happened to me. Knew that closed-in spaces could keep you safe while everyone you loved on the outside left this earth and went to a faraway place where they wouldn't be ill any more. For the first time in a long time, I didn't feel lonely at all. All that bothered me was the dull, muted feel of the garden. Now that I had found it, I wanted it to be a brighter, happier place, a place that was safe but also where I could, maybe sometime soon, be happy. Properly happy. I wondered if all the flowers had died, or if perhaps some of them had survived the winter and might send out bright red buds when the weather got warmer. But perhaps not. Maybe it would always be a quiet, dead garden. Neat and cared for, but forever slightly sad.

The pathway opened up into a circle, in the middle of which was what looked like a fountain. There was certainly water inside it, but it was brown and murky, with leaves floating in it, and nothing was coming out of the spout at the top. The concrete part of the fountain, above the bowl where the water sat, was dirty and cracked, although I could see what it was meant to show. It was the shape of two hands, held together, with the nozzle of the fountain coming out from the gap between their palms. I couldn't tell if it was supposed to be the hands of one person or two, but whatever it was, it made me feel strange and trembly.

I went over to a nearby bench and sat down, feeling some flakes of paint peel away as I scuffed it with my legs. For some reason, my own hands were starting to pulse and burn, as if I was holding on to something very warm. It was like Mum's hands were in mine, back when she was becoming ill and her fever was growing and she was starting to realise that she shouldn't be touching me but didn't want to stop. She wanted to hold my hands one more time and tell me it would all be OK. Then Dad came in and broke us apart and told me I had to keep away from them. It was the last time she touched me. There was probably a last hug and kiss too, although I didn't remember that so well. It came before we realised saying goodbye was necessary.

By the time I came out of the cellar, it was too late for goodbyes. Too late for anything. I hoped Mum and Dad had been able to say goodbye to each other. Because when I walked through the house after the storm, when everything was still and quiet like it was in the garden around me now, I found them lying together on their bed, holding hands, as if ready to face the unknown together.

I wasn't sure when I'd begun to cry. But when I started, it all came in a rush. Tears I hadn't allowed out before. And I only stopped when someone tapped me on the shoulder and said, 'What's this all about then?'

Chapter 16

Poor Lamb

Mrs Medlock, February 1979

'This is becoming a bit of a pattern,' Mr Oakwood said as he arrived in the kitchen with little Mary holding onto one of his large hands.

I almost dropped the tray of eggs I was carrying. I'd been just about to help Bessie search for the girl when I'd noticed they were sitting on the edge of the kitchen countertop and thought they'd best be put away before someone sent them flying. Feeling my body stiffen with anger, I put the eggs down safely on the table and marched round to take Mary by the shoulder. 'Tell me you weren't disobeying me ... tell me you didn't go ... '

The girl pulled a poisonous face at me and tugged herself free. 'I just wanted to see the garden!' she shouted.

I took a deep breath, rage starting to course through me like lava in a volcano. 'You wicked little girl. I told you *explicitly* not to go anywhere near that place. And you wilfully disobeyed me. Right – you're going to your room and you're not coming out again, not for a long, long time ... '

My anger roared within me, and with a rush of energy, I seized the girl and half led, half dragged her out into the corridor and towards the staircase at the front of the house. But Mr Oakwood was close behind me, and after a few strides, I felt his hand on my shoulder.

'Can I have a word? Before you banish the young lass to her room, let's just have a chat. Please.' His soft, calm voice made me pause. I glanced down at Mary, still looking as if she'd like to spit blood at me, then made up my mind.

'In here,' I said, pushing her through the doorway of the library. 'Sit on the sofa and *do not move*. Understand?'

She didn't reply, but she at least obeyed by marching over to one of the sofas and sitting on it with a thud, her arms crossed, eyes still glowering. I closed the door so I was alone with Mr Oakwood in the dark, slightly chilly hallway. 'I won't have this,' I hissed at him. 'What with everything happening, with them two upstairs I've got to look after, I can't have her wilfully disregarding my instructions ...'

He breathed in slowly, his lips pressed together as if he were thinking about something. 'Don't you reckon,' he said slowly, 'it might be a weight off your mind if Mary were occupied. She clearly has an interest in the garden. What harm is there in her playing in there? I can keep an eye on her while I'm doing my work. It's not like she can go anywhere – it is walled, after all. And I can deliver her back for tea each evening. I might join you all, if it's not an imposition. It does get lonely sometimes in my little cabin.' His mouth now twitched, making it clear his self-pity was partly in jest. I think he also knew very well I'd enjoy seeing him more often.

'I ... I don't want her going in there. It's ... it's ...' I struggled to find the right words. It's a bad place, I wanted to say. A dark, terrible place. Cursed, even, although I was aware of how strange that would sound. 'It's just not ... feasible.'

'It wouldn't be any trouble, I promise you,' he said, his voice growing even softer, the slight Yorkshire lilt to his accent making me think of my own northern roots, and the family I hadn't seen for so long. 'And forbidding a child from something only makes it seem more exciting than it actually is. Maybe if you just said, "Fine, do as you wish, girl," she'd soon get bored of it and do something else. For now, I think she just needs some sort of distraction. She was terribly upset when I found her, crying by the fountain. She's lost her parents, poor lamb. Surely this wouldn't be such a bad way to get a bit of life back in her?'

I stayed silent while I tried to order my thoughts. But try as I might, order would not come. Everything was awful. The unexpected guests, Lady Ashton's threats against me, and now this obstinate and ungrateful girl poking her nose into things she couldn't understand.

Some tears slipped down my face and I felt myself tremble. I closed my eyes and let myself tip sideways a little to rest on the wall in order to stop myself falling, and inevitably a strong male hand was placed once again on my shoulder.

'Are you all right?' he said, 'Do you need anything... can I do anything?'

I opened my eyes, letting my vision swim back into focus until I could properly make out the depth of his grey-green eyes, and the lines on his square, handsome face. He was younger than me – not yet forty – but his skin was roughened by his years of work in the elements. I felt a pang of sadness as I forced back the feelings within me – feelings that arose every time I looked at him. I steadied my breathing, blinked, then thanked him for his concern. 'I'm fine. I'm in no need of assistance. The orphan girl can play in the garden to her heart's content, for all I care. She can do as she chooses.'

With that, I turned my back on him, walked away towards

the staircase and began my ascent upwards, not sure where I was going. Perhaps to check on Master Rupert, or see if the guests were settling in OK, or maybe just to scream into the vacuum of three pillows pressed tightly together so nobody could hear my world breaking inside me. In spite of all these muddled, desperate feelings, I still regretted leaving him down there in the corridor, alone, my distant, oddly formal words to him still echoing around my head. He deserved much better than that. But after everything that had happened, I had forgotten how to be kind. And the sooner he realised that I was a lost cause, the better.

Chapter 17

The New Boy

Mary, February 1979

They banished me to the library. Well, Mrs Medlock did. She shoved me inside and told me to sit on a sofa, so I did, but made it clear I wasn't happy about it. Although I knew Lord and Lady Ashton must be very grand and rich, their sofas weren't very comfortable, and I could feel a spring digging into me as I waited. Then something made everything else in my mind vanish. A voice. A boy's voice.

'Are you in trouble?'

I spun round. The blond boy I'd seen on my way down to the garden was sitting at the shiny reddish-brown wooden table at the end of the room. Mrs Medlock had thrown me in here so fast, she hadn't realised someone was already here.

I explained that I wasn't in trouble, I was just cross at everyone because they wouldn't let me do what I wanted.

'I'm much the same,' he said, getting up from his chair and wandering slowly round the library, pushing his hands into the pockets of his smart cream trousers. 'They all told me I'd done bad things, had let everyone down. But they just stopped me doing what I wanted. It was all much ado about nothing, really.'

I frowned at him. He talked in a very grown-up way, and walked around like he was someone in a play or a film I'd see on the telly, not a real boy in real life. He was posh, like the boy upstairs in the attic, but in a different way. He stretched words out as if he was bored and almost couldn't be bothered to say them.

'What did you do?' It was the only thing I could think to ask.

He looked at me, and a strange smile started to spread across his face. 'That would be telling, little mouse.'

This made me frown even more. 'Who's little mouse?'

'You are,' he said, his smile now a smirk. 'It's what you look like. A little field mouse. A little Scottish field mouse, from the sound of your voice.'

I turned away from him and faced the door. 'I don't want to talk to you. I don't think you're a nice boy.'

He didn't seem too put out about this, and was still smiling when he walked round to my other side and faced me properly. 'I'm *not* a nice boy. Nice boys are dull. We do all kinds of things to the nice boys at my school, just to teach them a lesson. Hide their books, steal their clothes when they're in the showers, mix up their essays so they can't find the right one. Or change the names on them before they hand them in so they get the wrong grades. It's dreadfully good fun to watch them flapping around and trying not to cry.'

I hadn't heard anyone talking so calmly about nastiness before. 'That's horrible,' I said, staring at him. 'Why would you be so mean? I'd be really upset if someone did that to me.'

He stared back at me and nodded slowly. 'Yes. I can very well imagine that.'

I didn't know what he meant, but I didn't think I wanted to anyway, and I was just about to tell him this when the door opened and Mr Oakwood walked in. I saw him open his mouth, as if he were about to speak to me, then close it again when he saw the boy standing there.

'Oh, hello, who's this then?' the boy said, looking at Mr Oakwood as if a strange animal had just walked into the room.

'I'd like to ask you the same question, young man,' Mr Oakwood said, his eyes flicking over him. 'Or I would if I didn't already know. I believe you're here to study. I don't see much studying going on at the moment, though.' He nodded towards the desk at the far end of the room, 'Maybe you should go and work quietly over there while I talk to Miss Mary here.'

The boy raised his eyebrows. 'I can't study if I don't have anything *to* study,' he replied, talking to Mr Oakwood as if he was stupid. 'And anyway, my tutor, Mr Quint, is taking a bath, though I'm not sure what it's got to do with you. Are you some sort of servant? You look like someone who should work in the fields.'

I saw Mr Oakwood's eyes widen, but apart from this he didn't show any sign of getting angry at such rudeness. Instead, he turned to me and said, 'Mary, Mrs Medlock says it's OK for you to be in the garden while I'm working in there. I'm heading back there now, if you'd like to come.'

I did want to go, but I was also keen to sneak up to the attic to tell Rupert about my success and how his plan with the key had worked. I thought about it for a moment, then said, 'Can I come down a bit later? I'm hungry.'

'Yes, I am too,' the boy said, sounding bored again and dropping himself onto one of the other sofas with a thud. 'The sandwich that maid brought up earlier wasn't quite sufficient. Can you fetch us something? Maybe some muffins or tea or something.'

I was amazed he dared ask this of Mr Oakwood, as the thought of this tall, strong man, with mud and bits of garden on his shirt and arms, carrying in tea and cakes seemed so strange it almost made me laugh. Again, Mr Oakwood ignored him and spoke to me instead. 'You can come down when you're ready.'

He gave me a nod, then left the room.

'Well, I didn't care much for him,' the boy said, once the door had closed.

I wasn't sure if I wanted to carry on talking to him, so I stood up. 'I've got to go now.'

'Yes, to get some food,' he said, sounding more enthusiastic. 'I'll join you.'

I frowned at him. 'No, I'm not going to get food. I'm going somewhere you can't go, so just stay here.' I tried to make those last three words sound strict and strong like Mrs Medlock, but I wasn't sure I managed it.

Like Mr Oakwood, I left the room trying not to look at the boy, and ran across the hall and up the stairs before he could call after me. It took me a bit longer to find the room high at the top of the building this time. Perhaps it was because I didn't have the sound of Rupert's cries to guide me, or because the corridors were lit with pale daylight – at least the ones that had windows were. Everything looked different when it was dark, so being able to see properly actually made things more difficult.

Eventually I found the corridor with one door right at the end, leading to the room with the rocking horse and the toys. There was no daylight, the curtains pulled closed like they were up in Rupert's bedroom, and although the lamp was on, I almost sent a box of Scrabble crashing down as I wound around a stack of games, but managed to save it, steadying myself with my other hand on a pile of jigsaw puzzles. Just as I was about to start my climb up the winding staircase into the connecting room, I heard a noise behind me. Was someone in the corridor? Or worse, in the room? I couldn't see into the darker areas around me. What if someone or something was there? Watching me.

I thought back to what Rupert had said during my first visit. How he thought the first Lady Ashton might be waiting, biding her time, choosing her moment to carry him off into the night. For a moment I thought I could almost feel the icy grip of fingers sliding over my shoulders, pressing into me. But when I reached up with my own hands, I couldn't feel anything. I gave my head a little shake and carried on up the metal staircase.

I opened the door to the bedroom without knocking. Rupert was sitting cross-legged on his bed, once again in his pyjamas and a jumper, reading a book, with a few others opened and scattered around him. His face seemed to brighten when he saw me. 'I was wondering when you'd come to see me again,' he said, sounding much happier than before.

I walked over to his big bed, which was made quite tidily, although I saw that on its surface there were lots of different things along with the books: two magazines with cars on the front of them, a model aeroplane, and a notebook.

'Guess what I've been reading,' he said. He held up the cover and I saw the word *Kidnapped*. 'I found my copy after we spoke last time, and I thought I'd read it again.'

I got the feeling he wanted this to make me happy, so I did my best to smile, although I was impatient to get to the thing I'd come to tell him about. 'That's nice,' I said, nodding.

'Have you found the copy in the library downstairs? I think it's in the set of green-bound hardbacks with silver edges.'

Again I nodded, though I'd forgotten to look for the book. Then a picture in one of the other open books caught my eye. It was a strange drawing or painting showing a goat with long black horns standing in the centre of a circle of women. They weren't the sort of beautiful naked women I'd sometimes seen in the paintings on the walls in the house. They were wearing cloaks and looked very ugly. Their faces were all bunched up and I couldn't tell if they were frightened by the goat or happy to see him. One of them was carrying something that looked like a skeleton. The skeleton of a baby.

Rupert saw where I was looking and said enthusiastically, 'Horrible, isn't it? But still amazing. It's strange how some things can be scary and beautiful at the same time.' When I didn't speak, he carried on. 'It's called *Witches' Sabbath*. It's by a painter named Francisco Goya and was bought by a rich Spanish lady, the Duchess of Osuna, who collected paintings about witchcraft. She also created a garden, El Capricho or something like that. It's in Madrid. She was a very interesting woman.'

The more I stared at the painting, the stranger I felt, reminding me of the unsettling image on the cover of the book I'd seen during my first visit. Rupert's mention of a garden helped me pull my attention away from it and back to what I'd come to tell him. 'I've been inside the garden,' I said in a loud whisper.

He looked a bit puzzled at first, as if he thought I meant the Spanish one he'd been speaking about, then he understood. 'Oh goodness! How did you . . . ?'

'The key,' I said, getting up on the bed to face him properly. 'It worked. The big old one on Mrs Medlock's chain.'

Rupert was wide-eyed, his mouth open, his attention focused upon me. 'Where is it now? Do you still have it?'

I shook my head. 'Mr Oakwood took it off me.'

I saw the disappointment in his eyes. 'So you got caught?'

'Sort of,' I said, then launched into describing the whole thing – how I'd snuck off down there when the guests arrived, how Mr Oakwood had found me and brought me back up to the house, and how after chatting to Mrs Medlock, he had told me I was allowed back in.

Rupert listened to all this, his face showing surprise, alarm and delight as the story went on. Then he said, 'Did ... did you see anything ... anything like ...' he lowered his voice, '*you know?*'

I frowned at him. 'Like what?'

'The first Lady Ashton?' he whispered.

I shook my head.

He looked disappointed. Then he frowned and said, 'You said guests; what guests?'

'Hasn't Mrs Medlock told you? Two people have come to stay. A schoolboy and his tutor. The boy was kicked out of his school for doing something truly *terrible*. But I don't know what. He wouldn't tell me.'

Rupert leaned forward, seeming very interested. 'You've spoken to him?'

I nodded.

'Do you think he'd come up here? I'd love to meet him.'

I wasn't sure about this. 'Why? He doesn't seem very nice. Rather bossy.'

Rupert looked sad all of a sudden and closed the book that had been lying open on his lap. 'You see ... I'm not like other children. Well, I haven't met many others. Hardly any, in fact. You're one of the first girls I've ever spoken to. I think there may have been one other, when I was very young – the daughter of a cleaner who's left now. And I've only ever seen other boys on TV.' He pointed to a small television I hadn't noticed before, sitting on a chest of drawers at the other end of the room.

'You're allowed a TV in your room?' I asked. I was impressed and jealous. I'd never been allowed one back home. We'd just had a small set – even smaller than Rupert's – in the corner of the lounge, and it didn't always get signal. I enjoyed watching *Mr Benn* and *The Famous Five*, but Mum and Dad usually preferred me to do other things, like playing outdoors or drawing and reading.

'You mean ... you've never played with other kids?' I stared at him, amazed.

'I told you.' He looked a bit cross now, and pulled his legs in closer to him. 'I've always been too poorly to go out and play. And anyway, there aren't any other children here. At least not usually.'

I was still staring. 'So, what, you've spent ten years in this room? And *that's it*?'

His frown grew deeper. 'I'm not ten, I'm nearly twelve, I'll have you know.' He sounded very annoyed.

'Sorry,' I said quickly. 'You just ... I thought you were ten like me.'

'Well I'm not,' he snapped.

'The other boy is the same age as you, then, I think, maybe slightly older,' I said, trying to cheer him up a bit. 'So he might be a nice friend for you.'

I let my voice go quiet and then stopped altogether, because I suddenly felt a bit sad. I had hoped Rupert would be a friend for me. But maybe, now this boy had arrived, he wouldn't want to talk to me. They'd have a club, just the two of them, like some of the sillier boys at my old school, who used to joke that girls were either poisonous or didn't know what games were fun.

'He probably wouldn't want to be friends with me,' Rupert said, a little grumpily.

'Well I suppose that remains to be seen,' said a voice from the doorway.

Both of us spun round. Standing there was the boy we'd been speaking about, leaning casually up against the side of the door frame as if he'd been there for ages. He didn't seem particularly interested in the room, or the fact that he'd come up a little winding staircase into a secret part of the house. He sighed lazily and began to wander around, like he had done downstairs.

'You followed me!' I half shouted at him, cross that he'd managed to be so sneaky and quiet.

'It wasn't hard. You scurry around like a little mouse, completely unaware of what's happening behind you. I think I might call you Mousy.'

'My name,' I said, through clenched teeth, 'is Mary.'

'What's *your* name?' he asked, walking to the side of the bed and looking at Rupert. 'I'm Ernest, although you're welcome to call me Ernie.' He held out his hand. I was jealous I didn't get a handshake.

Rupert stared at the hand in front of him like he'd never seen anything so strange and didn't know what to do with it. At last he took it and said, 'Rupert. I'm Rupert.'

Ernest nodded, looking at him in a way that seemed a bit too smug for someone making a new friend. 'So you're the invalid in the attic, are you? I've heard about you, of course. Mother's mentioned you a few times, but somehow I never quite believed it all to be true. But here you are, flesh and blood.'

Rupert looked very confused by this, and a bit hurt. 'You mean ... people have been talking about me?'

Ernest let out a little laugh that didn't sound that nice. 'My dear chap, you don't think the son of a lord who never sees the light of day could ever remain a secret? No, you're gossip. People like the sense of mystery, I rather fancy. They probably imagine you as a cross between Prince John and Bertha Mason. But I knew it would be something a lot more ordinary than that.'

I didn't understand what he was on about, and I couldn't work out if Rupert did or if he was just upset about the idea of people talking about him. He flushed red and looked down at the bed covers.

'So what is actually *wrong* with you?' Ernest asked.

Rupert frowned. 'That's a rather insensitive way of putting it.'

Ernest shrugged. 'Sorry,' he said, not sounding like he actually meant it. 'I'll rephrase it: what affliction do you suffer from?'

There was something about the way these boys spoke that made my head swim – so many different words, such an odd way of saying things. It reminded me of old films Dad and I used to watch on the sofa at Christmas.

'I'm sensitive to light,' Rupert explained, 'And my heart mustn't be taxed, else I might pass out.'

I saw Ernest's eyebrows rise. 'Is that why it's so dark in here? And you mean ... well ... you can't play rugby or cricket or run around at all? I'm surprised you're not overweight. We have an old uncle who's morbidly obese because he doesn't get any exercise.'

Now it was Rupert who shrugged. 'I don't get given too much food, I suppose.'

'Do they starve you?' I asked, wondering if he had to live off boiled eggs and soup like me.

'No, I wouldn't say starve,' he said. 'But I don't really get sweets or cake ... only at special times like—'

Ernest cut him off. 'Well, I'm rather starving now. I say we go down and raid the larder.'

Rupert and I just stared at him. I didn't know if he expected us to leap up and join in the fun, but neither of us moved, and he looked a bit disappointed.

'I wanted to talk to Rupert *alone* about something,' I said, in a small voice.

'Oh yes,' Rupert said, more animated now. 'You were going to tell me about the garden.'

'What garden?' Ernest asked. 'Is this the garden that coarse servant man said you were allowed to play in?' Without being invited up, he kicked off his shoes, dropped himself onto the bed and sat cross-legged like Rupert. I felt a bit shy with the two boys staring expectantly at me, waiting to hear what I had to say, and suddenly I didn't want to talk about the garden and the strange way it made me feel. How it made me feel safe and sad all at once and how Mr Oakwood had had to hold me close to stop me crying. When I didn't answer, Rupert took over.

'It's hidden behind a large stone wall in the grounds, a little away from the house, down the lawn and towards the fields. I've never been in there, or at least I don't think I have, but I have heard rumours from the staff about it over the years.'

'Why is it hidden? Is it to make sure the plants can grow without animals trampling them?'

Rupert rolled his eyes. 'There aren't any animals like that – this isn't a jungle or a farm. No, it's all because of . . .' He looked around as though suddenly afraid. I guessed why.

'The first Lady Ashton,' I said quietly.

'Yes.'

I decided to ask some questions I hadn't thought I should ask until now. 'What was she like? How old was she?'

Rupert still looked nervous. 'Well, obviously I never met her, but from what I've heard from listening to people talk, she was apparently a great beauty, but very young, just nineteen when my father married her. I don't think he was much older. But then she died.'

Ernest looked excited. 'Was she murdered?' I wasn't sure I liked how keen and interested he was. I felt we were sharing too much with him, but now that we'd started, there was no way of stopping.

Rupert shook his head. 'No, I think she might have had an illness when she was pregnant. A psychiatric illness or something. A couple of years ago, a man and a woman came up here at a party. They were guests. They didn't know I was here; I think they just came upstairs to find somewhere to be alone and kiss or something. But I could hear them, and when they were leaving I heard the man say how some of the paintings on the walls in the house were collected by the first Lady Ashton, and how she'd met a tragic end and was "clearly quite deranged" to do that while she was pregnant.'

Ernest made a noise to show he wasn't convinced. 'Do what? That all seems a bit vague.'

Rupert put his palms upwards to show he didn't know. 'But it's interesting. I don't know what she did, but it seems she died when she was about to have a child. And my old governess certainly seemed to think the garden had something to do with her. She said as much, before she suddenly had to leave us.'

Ernest's reply was hushed, almost reverent. 'Do you think your governess was bumped off because she found something out? Maybe she's buried in the garden along with your father's first wife.'

I was surprised he could talk so calmly about these things, and I was even more surprised that Rupert seemed OK to share them with this complete stranger. Then Ernest turned to me: 'You're allowed to play in this garden, right? Well, why don't you take us both down there? If anyone has a problem, you can say you just wanted to show us around.'

I thought about the fuss between Mrs Medlock and Mr Oakwood about just allowing me inside. I didn't want to make things even trickier, but Ernest seemed determined.

'In fact, let's all go now.' He jumped off the bed.

Rupert stared at him as if he were talking a made-up language. 'I told you, I can't leave. I'm sensitive to the light, I'll burn up in an instant.'

Ernest waved a hand. 'Oh pish. I think it's all nonsense, if you ask me. Doctors are always talking rubbish, my father says so. I doubt there's anything the matter with you. It's probably just worry and hysteria on your parents' part. They're afraid that because there's been one tragic death in the family, there might be another. They need to be more realistic. I think it's all silliness and hysterics.'

I rather liked this word, hysterics, even though I hadn't heard it before, and there was something a bit comforting in how certain Ernest sounded about everything. Rupert looked torn. I could tell he liked the idea of us all going out on an adventure. There probably wasn't a boy anywhere who wouldn't like that, especially one who had been stuck up in a room all day, every day for most of his life. But at the same time, he was clearly scared. 'I don't want to burn,' he said, rubbing at the skin on his neck as if he was afraid of finding scorch marks already covering him.

Ernest sighed impatiently and marched over to the curtains. With one big tug he tore them open and daylight rushed into the room, making the whole place look shabbier and more downtrodden than it had appeared in the semi-darkness.

'No!' Rupert shrieked.

Ernest pounced on him like some wild bobcat or wolf, tugging at his jumper and pyjamas. 'Hold his other arm, little mouse,' he commanded me, and I was so shocked at what was happening I did as I was told. Ernest continued to tug at the flailing, writhing Rupert until he'd got his jumper and pyjama top off and the boy's skin came into view. He was so bright and pale, like a sheet of fresh paper.

'It hurts! I can feel it,' Rupert sobbed, tears pouring from his eyes as he wrestled to get free. 'I can feel the burns. Please, let me go, I don't want to die, I don't want to die, it's hurting . . .'

'Is it?' Ernest asked, breathing hard with the effort to hold Rupert still. 'Or are you just being silly? Where are these burns, then? Where?' He clambered properly on top of him now, pinning him to the bed with both his arms and his knees. And then Rupert did something so surprising, it made me scream. He pulled himself round with all his strength and punched Ernest in the face – not hard, but it made Ernest let go, stunned.

'Get off me,' Rupert shouted, then with one last huge heave, he sent Ernest tumbling off the bed. Pushing me to the side, he got to his feet, leaving the sheet and pillows all a-jumble, then froze like a statue when a booming voice rang out from the doorway.

'Stop this at once!'

Mrs Medlock was standing there, looking horrified. She stared at Rupert, his skin bare for all to see, the full beam of daylight making him almost sparkle. Then she turned to Ernest, his hand clamped to his nose where he'd been punched, blood starting to drip down his chin. Finally she moved her gaze to me, on the ground with Rupert's pyjama top clasped in my hand like a trophy. I hadn't even realised I'd picked it up.

'What in God's name is going on here?' she said, her lip trembling with fury.

Chapter 18

Things Begin to Change

Mrs Medlock, February 1979

I was almost paralysed with shock as I took in the sight before me. All three children in the same room, wrestling like animals. I wasn't sure at first what was going on, but it looked savage. That strange visitor, Ernest, pinning Master Rupert down on the bed and pulling off his clothes, and Mary helping him. I couldn't speak at first – my chest constricted and I thought I was going to faint. Then, when Rupert broke free of them both and jumped off the bed, I managed to shout. I was so worried he'd hurt himself, so worried he wouldn't be able to cope with whatever those two horrible children were doing to him. It was like something from *Lord of the Flies*.

Upon hearing my shout, they all stood still. I asked them what in God's name was going on, and they just blinked at me, apparently unaware that their shrieks and shouts had carried through the house, like a gaggle of restless spirits were haunting its rafters.

Far too late, I realised what was most startling about the room: the curtains were open, bathing everything in the dull white afternoon sunlight. 'Close them!' I shouted, running towards the curtains and trying to pull them shut. But I didn't succeed in my actions, as a hand shot out and stopped me.

'No, wait,' a boy's voice said. I turned to see Master Rupert standing there, his face marked with tears, staring out at the view of the lawn and the fields and distant trees.

'Get away from the window,' I barked at him, but then another hand was on me – Ernest had stepped forward and was stopping me from tugging the curtain cord.

'Leave him be,' he said. 'The light hasn't hurt him.'

I pushed the boy off me. 'I will not tolerate this – I will not be manhandled by a bunch of children! I cannot allow . . .'

But I found I couldn't say any more. Because Master Rupert had walked towards the window so that his nose was almost pressed against the glass. Then he looked down at himself, running his hands along his thin, flat torso, up to his neck and his face.

'It doesn't hurt. All this time I thought it would hurt . . . but it doesn't.'

He turned to me, and I saw the confusion and amazement clearly written in his eyes.

'Please, Master Rupert . . . this isn't safe. Just come away.' I tried to move towards him, but he held out his hand, motioning me to stay back. Normally I wouldn't dream of obeying such a command from a child; I'd have just dragged him back to the bed myself. But there was an aura about him now that I couldn't explain. I'm not a religious woman – not any more, after everything – but it was as if I could truly sense something *other* about him in that moment. Like he was made fresh, anew. Born again. And for the first time, I saw him not just as a child – small and weak – but as the man he would one day be. A boy who had the potential for manhood in a way I'd never envisaged for him.

Eventually, after some moments of us all standing there in silence, Ernest's belligerent voice cut through.

'I knew it. I knew all of it was hysterics and nonsense.'

That brought me back to Planet Earth. I swung round and glared at him. 'You've been in this house all of a couple of hours and have already caused all this ... this ... It's no wonder they kicked you out of that school if this is how you carry on.'

I wanted him to be cowed by my reprimand, but he just smiled – no, smirked. 'Oh, what I did at school was far worse than this.'

There was something genuinely chilling in his tone, and I drew in a deep breath. 'If you utter one more word, I will strike you. And that's a promise, young man. Now get downstairs to the library. I'll send for your tutor to begin your studies. And you, Master Rupert,' I turned back to him, still standing by the window, staring out as if mesmerised, 'I don't know what's going on here, or how safe any of this is, but if you insist on keeping those curtains open against my advice, at least put some clothes over you. It's not suitable you standing there like that – goodness knows what damage it's done already.'

I shot a look over at Mary, who seemed to shrink away from my gaze. 'As for you, little madam, you seem incapable of behaving yourself. Come with me.' I stepped forward and took hold of her arm, and with the other hand gave the Ernest boy a rough push towards the doorway. He didn't complain, but led the way down the staircase, then out into the corridor.

I kept such a close watch on those children during the weeks that followed, they weren't able to fraternise for one moment without either me or Bessie descending upon them and dragging them back to their respective bedrooms. Most of Ernest's time was spent in the library with Mr Quint, a man I had decided I disliked almost as much as his young student. There was something distasteful about the way he looked at Bessie, and on more than one occasion I rather fancied I caught him flirting with her quite shamelessly – along with vulgar innuendo about buns when she served him and Ernest some cakes with their tea. He was the type of man who was well aware of his good looks and how to use them to his advantage among young women, often rendering Bessie a giggling mess when she came back to the kitchen after speaking with him.

'You need to watch yourself with that man,' I said disapprovingly one night a couple of weeks into their stay.

'Oh, he's all talk,' Bessie said. 'There's no harm in him.'

I wish so much I'd been more careful, back in the early days. If I'd only seen what he was doing under our roof. And what he was planning to do, perhaps. I don't know how far in advance everything was arranged, or if he just took advantage of a situation and seized the moment when he saw it. I'll probably never know. But aside from being far too friendly towards Bessie in a mild sort of way, there wasn't too much to find fault with. He kept Ernest occupied, went for a run in the evening, usually choosing to stick to the country roads rather than explore the grounds, and stayed in his room the rest of the time. Ernest, who became even more sullen and morose, barely said two words to me, apart from when I caught him trying to sneak upstairs in the direction of Master Rupert's room, upon which he muttered a few choice four-letter words under his breath.

Mary, too, seemed to think silence was the way forward, and had reverted to the near-mute state in which she'd arrived at Marwood. The only time I heard her speak was when Mr Oakwood occasionally came to the house for lunch and took her back down to the garden with him. As they set off across the lawn, I could hear them chatting away to each other. It surprised me to discover I felt strangely isolated by this. Almost like I had done at school when other girls went off to the shops or cinema without me. I told myself I was being silly – that being jealous of a little orphan girl and the gardener was preposterous. I had made myself into the villain in that child's eyes, and I doubted there was anything I could do to change that.

As soon as I felt we'd settled into a routine, I became concerned again – and Mr Quint was the source of my anxiety. The days were getting milder and the sun occasionally peeking through the thick white cloud that had filled the sky since the previous autumn. When we tipped into the start of March, the temperature noticeably took a jump upwards, and all of a sudden we were leaving doors open by choice to let in a breeze, rather than rushing to shut them to keep out the cold. The warm weather led to more socialising between Bessie and the oh-so-charismatic tutor. The evenings began to feel like summer, rather than early spring, and on more than a few occasions she was late back from an 'evening walk', rushing up to run Master Rupert his bath or attend to her other duties. It was obvious she was meeting Mr Quint. That they had some sort of routine rendezvous planned, either in the grounds or out in the Oxfordshire countryside. I disapproved, and made this perfectly plain to Bessie, but she just brushed off my barbed comments with the naivety and disapproval girls in their twenties are unfortunately cursed with.

I didn't know if the pair of them were involved in a ... well, shall we say 'biblical' way. In truth, I didn't *want* to know. But I was unsettled by the idea of her spending time with him. I felt protective of her.

Things took a turn for the worse during the second week of March. The peace had been shattered by a blazing row between myself and Master Rupert. He demanded to be allowed to walk around the rest of the house in the daytime, since he had suffered no ill-effects from the curtains remaining open in his room. I suspected he wanted to visit Mary or Ernest, and I was still dead set against it. I told him he wasn't to leave his room, and he hurled a pillow at me. It didn't hurt me, of course, but I became quite rattled and took myself off to bed earlier than normal.

I woke just before midnight to the sound of a car approaching the house. For a moment, I was convinced it was Lord and Lady Ashton returning without notice, and rushed to the window. Of course, it wasn't them. It was Mr Quint. I recognised his tall, slim frame as he stepped out of the taxi, then opened the back door to help out a young woman. Had Bessie gone out with him this late? Maybe he had taken her into the centre of Oxford to the pictures, or drinking in some pub? But as I watched, another young woman got out of the other side of the car. And neither of them was Bessie. One had bright blonde hair styled into a voluminous feathered cut; the other was darker and more discreet, although I couldn't properly tell without much light. Both wore dresses that looked colourful and unseasonably summery in a garish, polyester sort of way, and they were laughing as they trotted up the steps with Mr Quint between them. I was horrified. This man was bringing two unknown young women to Marwood – two strangers – without consulting me or anyone else as far as I knew. To a house where children were sleeping. This was unacceptable.

I heard them downstairs, starting their ascent to the landing, and then the closing of a door. They'd gone to his room. All three of them. My heart was pounding with shock. I was aware what young men could be like, and what some women got up to, but the thought of such a thing happening here, at Marwood, while I was in charge, was unthinkable.

I threw my dressing gown around me, tied it tight, and set off down the servants' staircase to the first-floor landing. There I stood very still, aware that the floorboards creaked loudly under the fraying carpet. A few minutes passed, and I was close to abandoning the whole thing and going back to bed when I heard a sound. The sound of a woman. Breathless. Excited. I risked the floorboards, taking a few steps forward. I could hear more at this distance. High female notes and a low male grunt. They were at it – fornicating like animals on heat. In a room right next to where the Ernest boy was sleeping. I got closer to the door, unsure what to do, and for a moment I thought I heard movement from inside Ernest's room. But no, I must be imagining it. The sounds from Mr Quint and his guests were now filling the corridor, and I couldn't bear to stand there any longer. I took the main staircase back upstairs, deciding to confront the tutor in the morning about his appalling behaviour and then make a complaint to Lady Ashton over the phone. She could contact the boy's parents and get them to dismiss the tutor and replace him, or even better, take their son home and school him themselves.

Just before I reached my bedroom, a thought struck me. Maybe I *had* heard a noise from inside Ernest's room. Perhaps the children were disregarding my instructions to stay in their own rooms and were out and about after dark. It wouldn't be the first time with little Miss Mary. And if shenanigans were indeed occurring in Mr Quint's room, I definitely didn't want the girl wandering around the house.

I turned on my heel, descended the stairs again to the floor below, and walked through the darkness along the corridor. My fears were vindicated within seconds: Mary's room was empty, and the dressing gown that usually hung on the wardrobe door was gone. I was about to go back down to Ernest's room to see if she was inside, chatting to him at this late hour, when I heard her voice. It was echoing, distorted, like a ghost or a memory. In those few seconds, it was so strange and disorienting I couldn't understand what was happening. Then I looked up and realised. It was coming from the air vent above her bed. Suddenly I realised how she had known of Rupert's existence in his secluded part of the house. She had heard his cries through the air vent and had tracked him down herself.

She was in there, of course. In Rupert's bedroom. The two of them were sitting on his bed, a half-completed puzzle between them. And, oddly, a pot plant. A shrub-like thing in a scratched and scuffed terracotta container. The two children had the grace to look sheepish as I approached them, my anger probably writ large on my face. 'What,' I said, stretching out my hand, pointing, 'is *that*?' These words were all I could manage, and part of me knew the answer well before Mary delivered it in a small, wavering voice.

'It's ... er ... a plant.'

I kept my stare on her, raising my eyebrows to show that more information was expected. And so she continued.

'It's from the garden. Mr Oakwood said I could take a little gift up to Rupert. Since he's not allowed to go outside.'

Rupert seemed to think this was his cue to speak. 'I want to go and see the garden with Mary the next time she goes there. It's not fair me being shut up when I don't need to be.'

I brought my hands up to my face, trying to stop tears of stress and frustration from falling. 'It's midnight. You should be asleep,' I hissed at them.

'I want to go to the garden. Tomorrow!' Rupert shouted at me.

'Enough!' I shrieked. Both children looked properly scared now, but not enough to deprive them of words.

'Why are you so weird about the garden?' Rupert asked. 'What's wrong with you all? What's so secret about it?'

Mary piped up, 'Is it to do with the first Lady Ashton? Is it a secret? About her? And why she haunts this house?'

There was a hammering in my chest so hard I was convinced I'd die of a heart attack before the dawn. 'Get back to your bed ... right now ... ' I said, gasping for breath.

Mary chose defiance in the face of my obvious distress. 'Not until you let Rupert come out and play like any other boy.'

I looked at them both, stony-faced, determined. And then I turned away. I'd had enough.

'Fine,' I said, heading out of the room. 'Stay here all night for all I care.'

I slammed the door behind me, then walked down the winding staircase and back out into the dark corridor. I didn't go to my room. I descended the main staircase, past the floor where Mr Quint and his guests were causing thudding and groans, and down to the hallway, then through the house into the kitchen. Once by the stove, I made myself a mug of cocoa and sat down at the table. I wept for hours, until finally, at about three in the morning, I decided I couldn't take it any more. I rose from my chair, checking I had my ring of keys with me, opened the back door, stepped out into the darkness and began to walk. In the direction of the garden.

Chapter 19

The Spectre in the Moonlight

Mary, March 1979

I was furious with Mrs Medlock for days after she barged in and interrupted my conversation with Rupert and Ernest. I understood she was worried we were hurting him, but we weren't. We were helping him. I knew he must have got mixed up about feeling ill and had talked himself into it. My mum used to say that about a cut finger. 'Don't tell yourself it hurts,' she'd said. 'Just carry on with something else and you'll soon find it goes.' That was Rupert's problem. He'd thought about being ill too much and talked himself into thinking he actually was. I was sure of it. And Mrs Medlock and his parents and Bessie and everyone hadn't helped, all going along with the nonsense.

I talked to Ernest about this. I'd seen him on the landing the next day and he'd wandered into my room, looking at my things, kicking the furniture, acting like everything in the world bored him. 'Can't believe I've been shut up in this place,' he said. 'Though I suppose at least I have more freedom than him up there.' He raised his eyes to the ceiling, so I knew he was talking about Rupert. 'It's outrageous they've had a boy cooped up like that. I've read books about this sort of thing. It's quite plain what's happened.'

'Books about ill children who aren't ill?' I asked, confused.

He rolled his eyes. 'No, no. Delusions. Or people believing things that just aren't true because others have gone along with it and that makes them feel like they should too. In this case, a child has said something like "I feel ill", and then an adult somewhere has regarded that as fact and a sign of something far more serious than it is, then they've told another adult, then before you know it there's this belief in place, like a system, and they all believe it, all of their assumptions feeding off each other. So the child believes it to be true even more. And then none of them want to admit there's been a massive mistake, because that would mean admitting their own participation in the delusion. There's a book about this sort of phenomena. Gustave Le Bon, I think the author was. Crowd psychology, that sort of thing, you know?'

I didn't know, and didn't understand a lot of the words Ernest had said, but I thought I'd better nod in case he thought I was stupid and stopped talking to me. He then went on to tell me a bit about Mr Quint. He said he'd decided he had originally been wrong about him, and how he was actually a 'capital fellow' who knew a lot of interesting things.

'What sort of interesting things?' I asked, though I was sure I probably wouldn't understand those either.

'Oh, just stuff about growing up. The position of boys and men in the world. The roles of women and girls. How one discovers one's true self. Things you need to do in life to find that within you. I consider myself quite well read, of course, but I'm aware I'm still young and learning, and I'm grateful I've got such a wise teacher. He's told me things I've never really thought about. Things I never knew before.'

I watched Ernest nod to himself for a bit. Even though he'd just said he knew he was still young, I got the feeling he was doing his best to sound wise and grown-up. It reminded me a bit of how Rupert sometimes talked to me, although with Ernest it didn't make me like him anyway near as much. 'And you believe him?'

'What?' he said, frowning at me.

'You believe him? Mr Quint? You believe all the things he tells you?'

He looked annoyed. 'Well of course I do. He's my tutor and an adult.'

'But before that you said—'

I stopped talking. I'd heard something. A creak that made me startle. The definite sound of floorboards. And movement.

'Gosh, you're jumpy,' Ernest said scornfully just as Bessie walked into the room. He looked at Bessie, then at me. 'There, see? Not one of your ghostly imaginings.'

Bessie seemed puzzled by this and asked about my ghostly imaginings. I didn't want to tell her, especially the things Rupert and I had talked about, about the first Lady Ashton, and how every creak and noise I heard in the house might be a sign she was awakening, ready to take us. In daylight, especially on sunny days, as it was that afternoon, all of that seemed rather silly. But I knew that as soon as it was dark, I would worry about it again. That each sound the old house made felt like a rattling breath or approaching doom, coming for me in the darkness.

'Hello? Little Mary?' Bessie said, waving a hand at me.

'I wouldn't bother,' Ernest said, shaking his head, doing his I'm-a-grown-up look again. 'Away with the fairies.'

'Mr Quint's looking for *you*,' Bessie said. 'He said he's got a few more things to go over before you finish for the day.'

She led Ernest out of the room, throwing me a look that I didn't like, as though she suspected I was up to something. If it had been Mrs Medlock, I'd have worried about punishment, but Bessie had always been much kinder to me, like an older sister. She never seemed as angry as the housekeeper. Or as sad. I was surprised I thought this, as I'd never really thought of Mrs Medlock as sad before, but I knew I was right. She *was* sad. I just didn't know why.

Things got worse with Mrs Medlock when I brought the plant from the garden up to Rupert's room. I thought she'd had some time to get used to me going there. People did get used to things, I knew that; things that made them cross before started to make them less cross. I thought this was how Mrs Medlock was going to be about me going to the garden.

But when she noticed the plant, I saw something in her face that made me worry she was going to fall down dead in front of us. She was more shocked and upset than I'd seen her since arriving at the house. I'd tried being quiet and going along with things, but she still got angry, so I didn't think there was any reason to keep quiet any more. But when I mentioned the ghost of the first Lady Ashton, she really changed. Her eyes flew open so wide, I wondered if they might get stuck and she'd have to go through the rest of her life like that, with staring eyes like she was always shocked or afraid. Then she just left us. Told us we could stay there all night if we wanted to. For some reason, I found this scarier than anything I'd heard or seen in the house up to that moment. It was like we'd broken her. As though Rupert and I had finally pushed her to an edge and she'd fallen off it. We didn't know what to say to each other after that. So I'd told him I'd better go.

I left the plant with him and started my journey back through the house. My mind was on what had happened with Mrs Medlock, so I didn't worry about any ghostliness for most of my journey. But when I was at the bottom of one of the staircases, close to my room, I thought I heard a sound. It wasn't a make-me-jump sort of noise. Not the sort of thing that made me feel instantly cold and frightened. It was something quieter but in the distance. A thud. Then another thud. Then another. It carried on as I continued my journey. And with each step, I became more scared.

The noise was coming from Mr Quint's room. I could hear it as I got to the landing. A constant thudding. And then a gasp. A man saying something. He sounded like he was out of breath, perhaps in pain.

Something was happening. Something awful, I could just feel it. Then suddenly the landing was filled with cold silver light. It was coming from the window.

As I walked towards it, I could feel my heart beating. I felt as though I was going to be shown something, like some strange force from another world was breaking through.

I saw her straight away. A figure lit up by the moonlight that had broken through a gap in the clouds. A woman travelling across the grass, floating above the light mist on the ground.

She was drifting towards the garden. Perhaps the first Lady Ashton had visited and done something terrible to Mr Quint. He could be dying in there, chained up, struggling to free himself as the life faded from him.

I thought about trying to rescue him. I thought about running to fetch Mrs Medlock or Bessie or even Rupert or Ernest. But I didn't do any of these things. I ran to my room, pulled the duvet over my head, and prayed. Prayed that I would be spared, the same way I was spared the night my parents died with the flu and the cold took every other nearby soul. Prayed that I would wake to see the dawn. Prayed that I would live.

Chapter 20

The Night in the Cabin

Mrs Medlock, March 1979

Even though there had been very little light as I set out, the clouds parted overhead as I crossed the lawn, offering a shaft of moonlight to illuminate my way. To be honest, I could have walked it blindfolded. The pathway down by the trees might have scared some, but not me. Even as I heard night-time creatures scurry from the undergrowth or bats flutter above me, I didn't falter. I followed the stone wall round until I found the door, raised the key to the lock and let myself in, the big oak doorway creaking and groaning as I pulled its heavy frame closed again and set off through the hushed stillness of the garden within the walls.

It didn't take me long to find what I was looking for. I walked along the winding pathways, past the hedges and trees, until I came to a little alcove. Although I couldn't see properly in the darkness, I knew there wasn't much there apart from some nondescript shrubs. There had been some flowers there once, but that was long ago, and when they died, they weren't replaced. I stood there and cried silently until the light wind dried my tears and I lost all sense of place and time. And then I heard him behind me, talking softly, taking care not to startle me.

'You shouldn't be out in the cold in the middle of the night,' he said, coming to stand next to me.

'How did you know I was here?' I asked, not looking at him. Still keeping my eyes on the ground in front of me.

He took a few seconds to reply, and when he did, it was accompanied by a hand on my arm. 'I heard you crying.'

I turned to look at him at that point, and I could just make out his tall frame in a sliver of moonlight. He was wearing a vest and underwear, and had clearly been summoned from his bed by my cries. Had I really been that loud? I found myself gripping on to him, my face burrowing into the warm fabric, the only barrier between me and the skin of his chest and the beating heart beneath.

We went to his cabin without saying a word. I don't know whether he intended for me to spend the rest of the night in his bed while he sat in the chair by the fire, but I made it clear to him what I wanted. What I needed. I pulled him to me, feeling his strong frame press close, holding on to it like a life raft. His lips on mine. Then on my neck. I had both dreaded and ached for that sensation for so long. I hadn't appreciated how dead inside I had become until that night, but with a rush of excitement something ignited within me and I was filled with energy and urgency. He didn't waver or argue as I tugged at his vest, nor as I cried out with both pain and pleasure as he started, strong and confident and earnest in his task, like he had been when he first came here just over twenty years ago, when I was twenty and he just sixteen. Back then, I watched him from afar, walking about the grounds with his spade and wheelbarrow. Watched him work topless in the summer sun. Watched him shed his clothes and shower himself at the old pump tap round the other side of the wall. Watched him tend so carefully to the flowers in this garden, back when flowers were allowed to bloom. Before the garden became something else. Before I found I couldn't visit it any longer.

I woke in his arms, his naked body pressed against mine, with morning light falling onto my face from the cabin's little window. There was a slight awkwardness between us during that first half-hour, as he made me some toast and brought over a cup of tea. The cabin was only one room, but it felt like he was already miles away from me. Our actions during the night had done something to us. Changed something within us. Perhaps because we had dared to revisit a moment in our past when we were young and foolish. Because for a few moments last night, I *was* young again, and so was he, as if the brink of middle age was so far off in the distance it didn't warrant a moment's thought. Back when we didn't have the weight of the world upon our shoulders. Before secrets and trauma caused a distance between us.

I was pulled out of my rumination when he got back into the bed. His arms came close around me, and I found the same comfort in them as I had during the night. It felt right and good and soothingly simple. And for a few fleeting seconds, I was happy. Then I thought of what I'd heard the night before from inside Mr Quint's room. And Mary and Rupert, chatting away in his bedroom, a plant taken from this very garden between them, the two of them plotting, no doubt, how to disobey me, the scheming, insubordinate little . . .

'Are you OK?' Mr Oakwood's soft voice said in my ear. 'It's just . . . I'm starting to lose feeling in my arm.'

I looked and saw that I'd been gripping his wrist tightly, my hand bunched around it. I let him go and said sorry.

'Don't apologise,' he said. 'I just . . . Would it help if you told me what was wrong?'

He was holding me from behind, so he didn't see my eyes fill with tears, blurring my view of the old lined wood of the cabin wall. 'It's Mr Quint,' I said quietly.

I felt him shift. 'The tutor?' He was clearly surprised by my answer.

'Yes. It's hard to explain.' I extricated myself from his embrace and sat up. 'He and Bessie have been ... flirting.'

He sighed heavily next to me. 'I know. I caught them together down by the barns.'

My head jerked round, causing a painful click in my neck. 'What? When?'

He shrugged. 'Last week, the week before, maybe.'

'And what were they doing?' I asked.

'I'm not sure I should go into that ... It might not be proper conversation in the company of a lady.' A sly smile started to crease his mouth, but I wasn't in the mood for humour.

'You mean they were ... '

'After a fashion,' he said, shifting himself so he was sitting upright like I was. 'Why's it important?'

'Why is it important?' I repeated, aghast, 'You didn't think to tell me?'

He shrugged again. 'I didn't think they were doing any harm. I didn't want to get Bessie into trouble. And it's none of my business, is it, what people get up to. Is this what's got you in a state? Bessie and the tutor?'

My tears fell properly now, and he went to comfort me, but I shifted away from him. 'Even if it was ... it's hardly appropriate behaviour, is it? For him or her. But no, it's worse than that. Last night ... last night ... ' I put my hand up to dab at my tears, cross with myself for getting so upset when I was trying to explain. 'He went out – presumably to the village pub, or maybe to the centre of Oxford, I don't know. And he came back with these ... *women*.

Two young women. And took them to his room. I could hear them ... They were ... '

I looked over at him, his deep hazel eyes gazing back at me, processing the information. Eventually he let out a breath as though it were a silent whistle, and then stared at the ceiling. 'It's not for us to judge.'

'Judge!' I snapped the word at him. 'That's exactly what I'm doing. He was in a room next to the boy who is supposedly in his care. That isn't appropriate behaviour for a guest under someone else's roof, especially not when he is employed as an educator. It's appalling behaviour.'

He nodded slowly. 'Put like that, it doesn't sound too clever of him. And I agree, it's not right to carry on that way when he's sleeping in the room next to the boy. But you shouldn't let yourself get so worked up about something like this. Just speak to Lady Ashton and have him kicked out, if it will make things better.'

'Oh, I will,' I said. 'Make no mistake. But it wasn't just that. It's them blasted children. Mary and Master Rupert. She'd given him a plant in a pot taken from this garden. Said it was because he wasn't allowed to go outside. Is this because of you? Have you been encouraging it? When I said she could spend some time here, I didn't expect her to start bringing foliage and whatnot into the house and disrupting the routines of that poor sick boy.'

Mr Oakwood touched my knee, laying his hand over the quilt. 'Please. Let me explain. I gave the girl that little plant because it seemed to make her so happy, caring for something and watching it grow. I didn't know it would upset you. I'm sorry. As for Master Rupert ... well, I don't know ... It's not my place to say, but it can't be right keeping a boy his age cooped up in his room, tucked away from all of life.'

His description felt like a summary of his own existence, living quietly out here alone in his cabin, but if he spotted this connection he didn't comment on it.

'I just think,' he continued, still speaking slowly and carefully, 'that Lord and Lady Ashton, good people as I'm sure they are, might have been too quick to believe a single doctor's opinion on the lad, and since then everyone's got a bit ... stuck.'

'Stuck?' I asked, unsure where he was going with this.

'Yes, stuck. Stuck with the way things are. Afraid of things changing.'

I suspected he wasn't just talking about Master Rupert's medical condition any more, and there was some underlying implication about me in his words. But I had to admit, even if just to myself, that there might have been a nugget of truth in what he was saying. We had all muddled along in our set roles for a long time now. I needed a sense of order and normality. It kept me grounded. After the upheaval and trauma of the past, the idea of things remaining immune to change felt comforting, in a way. Perhaps, though, this had blinded me to certain things, especially where Master Rupert was concerned.

I sat thinking about this for a moment or two, then said quietly, 'I don't think Lady Ashton's a good person.'

Mr Oakwood inhaled, then breathed out heavily. 'I'm sure you see more of what goes on than I do, me being stuck down here and you up there in the middle of things.'

The small electric heater by the bed started whining, and he moved over to give it a nudge. The movement pulled me out of my thoughts and back down to earth, and all of a sudden I was very aware of the strangeness of all of this: I was sitting unclothed in a wooden cabin in the very place I'd been avoiding for years, next to a similarly naked man – a man I'd known for two decades but had never even felt comfortable referring to by his first name. Gabriel. The name was strange to me. Foreign, almost. I had called him that for a short time, long ago, when he was a lad. But then, after everything that happened, I felt the need to build up a wall between us. Assuming a false sense of formality was an easy way to do that, and it carried on so long it stopped feeling false. It felt normal.

I pulled myself over to the end of the bed and picked my clothes off the floor.

'I need to get back to the house. I've no idea what time it is . . . I don't know what's happening to me.'

'It's quarter to seven,' he said simply, watching me.

'Well, that means Bessie will be up and about and no doubt wondering where I've got to.'

Finally he moved, pulled back the duvet, swung his long legs out of the bed and stood up. He went over to the small chest of drawers in the corner and started to dress. 'Let me walk you back up to the house.'

'Don't be ridiculous. We can't do anything of the sort, you must know that.'

I looked up at his face in time to see a flicker of hurt cross it. 'So we're to remain a secret? This is to remain a secret?'

I couldn't have this conversation, not until I'd got my thoughts sorted. It was too much to digest all at once. Things had changed so quickly. 'I'm sorry – we can talk some other time,' I said, and still not meeting his eye, I tied my dressing grown tightly round me, stepped into my slippers and exited the cabin. As I walked back through the garden, I could feel his eyes on me from the doorway.

Chapter 21

Recollections

Natalie

Mrs Medlock suddenly turns to me, as if only just remembering I'm there. An expression of embarrassment appears on her face – a dawning realisation that she's just told me something quite personal and secret, something that perhaps she hasn't ever really described to anyone else, or at least not in a very long time. Then she looks away from me again, her expression full of sadness, along with something else, both wistful and harder to define.

'Umm, Mrs Medlock . . .' I say, trying to gently steer her back, hoping she'll carry on talking.

'Yes, my dear?' she says, looking at me, frowning.

'Could you go on about Mr Quint . . . about your concerns about what he . . . well, what he was doing at Marwood?'

Suddenly she seizes my hands, gripping them tightly between her palms. 'I will,' she says, staring at me, her eyes now intense and bright, fixed on mine as if silently pleading, willing me to understand something. 'But please promise me . . . no matter what I tell you, no matter what you hear . . . you won't leave. You won't leave me here, will you? It's been so long since we've had another tutor ... it's really important ... Rupert's education, you see ... such an intelligent boy ... I wouldn't want to frighten you away.'

I'm taken aback by this sudden change of tone, but I nod and try to smile, gently pulling my hands from her grasp. 'It's fine,' I say. 'Honestly, there's nothing you can say that will make me leave.'

Her eyes are still wide, but are now darting about the room, as if worried we could be overheard. 'I wouldn't be so sure,' she says in a half-whisper. 'I wouldn't be so sure.'

Chapter 22

The Morning After

Mrs Medlock, March 1979

'Oh Lord, there you are. I've been so worried,' Bessie said to me as soon as I walked into the kitchen. 'I was about to knock on your door. I thought you were ill or something – that perhaps little Mary had given you that deadly flu that took away her parents.'

I sighed as I set the kettle on the AGA. 'I'm no medic, Bessie, but I do think that if Mary were to have spread an infectious illness to us, we would have exhibited symptoms long before now.'

'Did you sleep in?' she asked, clattering about behind me in a way that made my head ache. It was as if I was drunk, or had indeed just recovered from a heavy bout of influenza. Life had suddenly flipped over and sent me spinning into a void. I didn't know which way was up and which way was down.

I told Bessie I had woken early and had gone outside for a walk before returning to my room to dress properly. She seemed understandably puzzled by this – I would never normally be seen in the house in just my nightclothes and dressing gown, let alone wandering around outside – but I didn't stay long enough to hear her views. I decided the time had come to take the bull by the horns when it came to Mr Quint and his behaviour.

Although I managed to march across the hallway and up the stairs with my normal stern sense of purpose, my confidence wavered ever so slightly, my hand trembling as I rapped on his door.

A very sleepy 'Wha ... What is it?' came from within.

'Breakfast,' I said, even though I was carrying no such thing, and without waiting for permission, I turned the door handle. On any other day, perhaps the image I was greeted with would have shocked me and sent me into a fury, but after the night I'd had, it was just one of many strange things that was happening in my life. The handsome young tutor was lying in the centre of the bed, with a young woman either side of him, their hair falling over their bare shoulders as they turned to see what was going on. The scent of tobacco and the edge of something else – perhaps marijuana – greeted me.

'I say,' Mr Quint said, sitting up quickly. 'It's really not on for you to just barge your way into a fellow's bedroom like this.'

'What isn't *on*,' I said, folding my arms over my chest and glaring at him, 'is you behaving as though this is some debauched party hosted by Stephen Ward rather than a respectable family home.'

Mr Quint, still bleary-eyed from sleep, blinked dumbly, as if I was speaking in an obscure foreign tongue, and flapped his hand towards the door. 'Just clear off, will you, and leave us in peace.'

One of the girls chuckled as she moved up to nuzzle into his neck like some little animal, while the other began to lazily kiss his cheek.

'Do not talk to me like that, young man. This is no way to conduct yourself when you are here as a guest and there are children about.'

Mr Quint yawned widely, perhaps just to show me how little he cared about what I thought. 'Oh for God's sake, just listen to me, Nurse Ratched—'

'No, you listen to me. You can try to insult me or call me names all you like, but I promise you, unless you sort out your behaviour right now, I'll personally see to it that you lose your position.'

I felt my hands starting to tremble, so I moved them behind my back as I continued to stare at him, trying not to blink. At least my anger seemed to have an impact, as he nodded and sighed. 'OK, OK, I understand. Things got a bit out of hand, but I'll make sure it doesn't happen again.'

One of the young women sat up too, her breasts clearly visible, and asked, 'Is there a shower I can use? Or a bath? I do fancy a long bath.'

I couldn't believe the cheek of her. But then again, maybe she didn't know where she was or why all of this was so shocking. Maybe Mr Quint had pretended he owned the place.

'There isn't. And I must ask you and your friend to leave right this minute. I will be back to check.'

I turned around and exited, letting the door slam loudly.

I briefly checked on Mary, who was just waking. 'Did the ghost take the tutor?' she muttered sleepily as I entered. I guessed this might have something to do with the upsetting nonsense she'd garbled at me last night, but I was more alarmed by the reference to Mr Quint. Had she seen something? Heard something?

'What do you mean?' I asked, keeping my voice as calm as I could.

The little girl sat up, rubbing her eyes. 'Did he die in the night? Was his soul carried off?'

'Unfortunately not,' I said grimly, deciding that brisk dismissal of the subject was the best way forward for now. 'Bessie will be up with your breakfast in a moment. You should stay in your room until you've finished it. And beyond that too. In fact, stay here until you're told otherwise. Understand?'

She nodded, blinking at me as I left. As I passed along the landing near Ernest's room, I had a sudden thought – what if the boy came out and saw the young women departing? Part of me wondered if that would really be so bad, considering he had probably heard them last night in the next room. But maybe he hadn't worked out the number of participants, and it would be preferable to keep that unfortunate aspect secret from him.

I didn't bother knocking – I just strolled in, walked straight over to the curtains and opened them. 'Good morning,' I said briskly to the room in general. 'It's time to wake up and have some breakfast.'

I turned away from the window so that I was facing the bed, looking down at the boy. Immediately I felt my heart start to race, and I took a step back, thudding my elbow against the wall. I took a deep breath, trying to make sense of everything ... and the more breaths I took, the more I was certain ... the more I was convinced ...

I needed to leave. But before I could get out, there was movement in the bed, then a bleary voice croaked, 'I want to sleep.'

I didn't argue with him. I just turned and left through the open door. I didn't want to be near that room or the landing or even the entire floor any longer. I just needed to get away from it. And whatever had happened there.

Chapter 23

I Make the Rules Here

Mrs Medlock, March 1979

Master Rupert had a bath every other day and it was never a smooth task. He usually had some sort of grievance or another with which he would berate either me or Bessie. But neither of us had seen him fly into such a fury as on that sunny day in March – the day that dealt yet another blow to the order of things.

I got him in the bathtub and was proceeding to scrub his back when he snatched the brush out of my hand and said, 'I can do this myself, you know.' Used to rudeness, I calmly took it back from him and told him he mustn't exert himself.

'Exert myself? I never exert myself!'

'Don't get yourself in a state,' I said. 'Now tip your head back so I can wash your hair.'

He folded his arms, refusing, so I just poured the jug of water over his head regardless. It unleashed a further wave of fury. 'I hate everyone here! It's not fair that Mary gets to go down to the garden during the day while I'm stuck inside. I can't believe you let her. You always said—'

'Things change, Master Rupert,' I told him. 'The sooner you

learn that, the sooner life will hold far less power over you.' I sounded wiser and more matter-of-fact than I felt, but it was the only weapon I had against his protests. Part of me was tired of being the authoritarian figure in all this, constantly having to chastise and scold.

'Well, things don't seem to change for the better, do they?' he said. He stood up to get out of the bath, so I hurried to fetch his towel before he could send a cascade of water over the floor, giving me yet another job to do.

'You're learning about life fast, it seems, Master Rupert,' I said as I started to dry him down.

'I'll do it,' he snapped, snatching the towel away from me. 'I'm not a child any more. I think I should start to bathe alone. Ernest does.'

I sighed as I picked up his freshly laundered pyjamas and handed them to him. 'Ernest is older than you, and he hasn't got the same complications as you.'

'*Complications?*' He looked outraged by the use of the word, as if I'd just described him as ugly. 'I haven't got complications. In fact, Ernest and Mary don't think there's anything wrong with me. They think my mother got scared by what one doctor said ages ago and kept me hidden away, afraid of what might happen. Or that my father was worried about losing me, the same way he lost his first wife.'

Something about what he said made a strange kind of sense to me, although the more I thought about it, the more I wondered if it wasn't neuroticism on her ladyship's part – a far more selfish reason. I'd be lying if I said the thought had never crossed my mind that she perhaps found Master Rupert's afflictions more convenient than worrying. But I hadn't said anything, and Lord Ashton always went along with it, so I'd just sort of accepted things as they were.

The discussion didn't end there – or at least for Master Rupert it didn't. He carried on and on all the way back to his room, half muttering at times then building to mini crescendos of outrage, about all the things he was missing and how he rather thought prisoners in jail cells had better lives than he did. I told him I very much doubted this, although I stopped my sentence halfway through when we reached his bedroom and I saw what he'd done to the place.

'When did you ... What ... Where have the curtains gone?' I stared up at the now empty rails, one of them lopsided, a cluster of metal rings down at the end and no actual curtains in sight. I was furious Bessie hadn't warned me of this when she'd delivered the boy to me for his bath. The danger that he could be in sent a jolt of panic through my bones, and I darted around the room, lifting up boxes and trunks. Eventually I found the dark red fabric folded up under the bed. 'When did you do this?' I said as I unfurled them, trying to get my breath back.

'Earlier today,' he said simply. 'I don't need them any more.'

I clutched the heavy cloth in my hands and shook them in front of him. 'If your mother knew what you had done ...'

He shrugged. 'Well she isn't here, is she.'

This was the first time I'd heard him sound annoyed with his mother. He'd been sad in the past when days went by without her visiting or if parties or social gatherings kept her away, but it always seemed like a natural childish longing for parental attention, rather than the resentment he seemed to be displaying now. Was this the influence of Ernest, perhaps, or even little Mary? Or maybe Master Rupert was growing up and starting to realise his mother had a choice when it came to planning cocktail parties and balls rather than spending time with her own child. And he was tired of coming second.

'It's dark now,' I said, trying to sound calmer and get us both on a more sensible, cordial level. 'The sky outside is no danger to you for one night. But I'm going to get Mr Oakwood here early tomorrow morning – at six o'clock, if needs must – to put these back up.'

Master Rupert made no comment on this. He just sat and glared. I thought he was done with the arguing and pleading, so I turned to leave. I hadn't set foot out of the doorway, however, before he started up again.

'I want to go out to play tomorrow.'

I looked back at him, feeling in that moment more exhausted than I had all week. 'Do we have to go through all this again?'

'No, we don't. But maybe I should say it a different way. I *am* going out to play tomorrow. And there's nothing you can do to stop me.'

I was taken aback by how clear and defiant he was being. 'Master Rupert, you seem to be confused. I make the rules here.'

'No, you don't, actually. I've always thought you did, Mrs Medlock, but recently I've realised that you're just staff. And since the master of the house isn't here, and my mother is away too, you're answerable to the only member of the family left inside it: me.'

I was astonished. Rudeness and protests were one thing, but actual orders were so unlike him, I could hardly splutter a response, and when I did, it didn't make much sense. 'I . . . you . . . a child . . . I tell you, right now . . . just do as you're told.'

He shook his head. 'No, Mrs Medlock. It's time for you to do as *you're* told. Tomorrow morning I shall instruct Bessie to dress me in a hat and coat and gloves. And she won't argue, because you'll have told her she must do as I say. And then she will take me outside to play with Mary and, when he's finished his studies, Ernest. That is what's going to happen. I . . . I command it.'

The last three words sounded oddly tacked on, and he seemed to realise this, as he hurried to offer an explanation.

'Ernest says that's what leaders and kings say, when they make speeches.'

I didn't speak for a few seconds, trying to gather my thoughts. On the one hand, I took my responsibility for the boy's safety very seriously, and if his parents thought that him exerting himself outside, away from his room, was too much of a risk, who was I to argue? But on the other hand, what he said wasn't entirely inaccurate. We *were* the servants and he was a member of the family we served. And if he commanded it, how much latitude did I have to continue disregarding his instructions?

'Half an hour. That's all you get. Half an hour, if it's a grey day and the sun isn't shining.' I said this with my eyes closed. I hadn't the energy to stare at his defiant, angry face any longer.

'Really?' he said, hopeful and excited, far closer to the Master Rupert I was used to.

I didn't reply. I'd given my answer. I was done. I exited, closing the door behind me, leaving the boy on the bed in front of the curtainless windows and the starless night sky.

Chapter 24

No Bones Will Be Broken

Mrs Medlock, March 1979

Master Rupert ended up going outside. Of course he did, with his new-found will of iron like that and my determination starting to disintegrate. It was only a matter of time. But that didn't stop me being furious with how it all turned out. Children just can't do as they're told. Part of me was tempted to alert Lord and Lady Ashton to the situation that their son was beginning to overrule me. But I couldn't help worrying that Lady Ashton in particular would view that as me throwing in the towel. Admitting that I had lost control, that my grip on how this place was managed was weakening even further. And I definitely didn't want that, especially after her thinly veiled threats before she left for the US.

I didn't have the energy to go and see Mr Oakwood after the tense conversation I'd had with Master Rupert, so I sent Bessie down to give him the message about the curtains. I did wonder if he'd take offence at being summoned, as it were, especially after ... well, after the time we'd spent together on that strange night. But I decided the best way forward was to go on as before and not let emotions cloud my judgement. I've always tried to be a strong, practical sort of person, and sudden whims and affairs of the heart are not my style.

He came as requested at 6.30 the following morning. After fetching him by proxy, I decided I should be the one to meet him at the kitchen door. He'd know I was up anyway, even if I avoided him, and I sincerely didn't wish to seem rude.

'Morning,' he said, with that slightly slanted smile of his. Seeing it was like familiarity and warmth and safety, all combined. I welcomed him in and explained what was needed, even though I was sure Bessie had probably told him already. He listened in his usual quiet way, nodding and not interrupting, and then we fell into silence for most of the journey upwards through the house. On our way past the bedrooms on the first landing, a door suddenly opened and out stepped a disgruntled-looking Ernest. He was wearing pyjamas, and his blond hair was sticking up. 'What's all this stomping around? It's so early.'

'Mr Oakwood has come to fix the curtains,' I said. He blinked at me, bleary-eyed and confused. Before further discussion could be had, I took the lad firmly by the shoulders and steered him back into his room. I cast a glance around it, but could spot nothing unusual or shocking. Nothing that raised concerns, unlike my previous, troubling visit to the room. I watched as he flung himself back down on top of the covers and closed his eyes, then went back out onto the landing.

'Everything all right in there?' Mr Oakwood asked.

'It is, this time at least,' I said, as he and I continued our march through the house.

'Wake up, Master Rupert,' I said, as I clattered open the door, not bothering to knock. I was still irritated that the whole situation had been caused by him in the first place. The boy had evidently been asleep, and he sat bolt upright as we entered, looking around with much the confusion Ernest had exhibited minutes before. 'What ... Oh, the curtains.'

'Yes, the *curtains*,' I said, making my displeasure clear. I checked Mr Oakwood had everything he needed, then told Master Rupert – who was pulling himself out of bed and stretching – that Bessie would be up with breakfast shortly. After that, we would set about finding him appropriate clothes for his excursion in the garden.

His head instantly swung round to look at me. 'You mean I'm still able to? I can go outside?'

I took in a deep breath, then looked over at the window. 'It looks like it's going to be a grey, cloudy day. So long as it doesn't rain, or the sun doesn't come out too strongly, then yes. I'm a woman of my word. But only for half an hour, as we agreed. And if your mother and father ask about this, you're to remind them of what you said to me yesterday. Or I will. This is all your doing, Master Rupert. And you can deal with the consequences.' I left the room before he could question me further on the terms and details of his trip outside.

I decided to take the main stairs back down to the kitchen, although I regretted this when I was ambushed once more by Ernest, now carrying a towel in his arms. 'I've decided to bathe before breakfast,' he said. It wasn't a question, but a statement, as if I had no say in the matter.

'Baths are taken in the evening in this house, young man. Morning bathing doesn't set one up for the day, and you have studies to do – not relaxation.'

He made a half-laughing, half-choking noise to express his disbelief. 'I don't see why it's any concern of yours when I decide to wash. And Mr Quint sometimes has baths in the morning. I realise you've probably been here a long time, but you don't have to cart buckets of hot water up the servants' stairs any more, you know. The advent of plumbing and hot water changed all that quite a while ago.'

Again I was struck by how his tone made him seem older than he was. His words commanded an edge of wisdom and experience, even if the young lips that spoke them hadn't seen more than thirteen years on this earth. I was about to argue, then decided it wasn't a battle worth fighting. 'Do as you please,' I said, moving past him.

'I shall,' he called after me. 'And while we're at it, Rupert will do as he pleases too. You can hang up his curtains all you like, you can mutter your dark warnings and threats, but you can't lock him up. Nor me, nor Mary.'

I forced myself to ignore his imperious, entitled voice as I continued my descent towards the main hallway.

Getting Master Rupert bundled up was an ordeal. He claimed he didn't need a scarf, mittens or thick padded coat, items he'd hardly ever worn, since he'd never really had need. He claimed it couldn't possibly be *that* cold in March. 'It's more to cover up your skin,' I said as I wound the scarf back round his neck after he'd dropped it on the floor. 'To be honest, if I'd known it would be this much of a struggle to get you to behave sensibly, I'm not sure I—'

'Fine, fine, fine,' he said, flapping his hand at my shoulder to stop me crowding him. He straightened up and surveyed himself in the mirror on the front of the wardrobe.

'You look like a parcel ready to be posted,' a small, Scottish-accented voice said from the doorway. I turned to see little Mary standing there, her own coat clasped in her hands.

'We don't need your assistance with this, young madam,' I said. 'And I've told you you're not to come to Master Rupert's private quarters.'

'Oh, let her stay,' Rupert said, walking towards the door. 'There's no fun in playing outside on my own anyway.'

I folded my arms. 'I can tell you right now, there will be no *playing* of any kind. The whole point is that you don't exert yourself. What if you fell and broke your arm? What would I tell your parents then?'

'No bones will be broken,' Master Rupert said confidently. 'But since this is my first excursion, and I appreciate you letting me do this, Mrs Medlock, I will do as you say and sit quietly enjoying the morning air.'

I was slightly flummoxed, but didn't argue. An amenable Master Rupert was a rare thing these days, so I had to take whatever victories I could. The three of us walked down the stairs, the two children whispering and laughing behind me as I led the way.

'Bessie's doing the weekly vacuuming of the library and dining room,' I explained as we arrived in the entrance hall, 'so I'll be keeping an eye on you.' I led them out through the front door and we set off round the back of the house.

Master Rupert's joy was apparent the moment he stepped onto the grass. 'It's so soft! But not like carpet, a different sort of soft!'

'You've stood on grass before,' I said. 'And you're wearing shoes, anyway.'

'But not since I was very young. This is the first time in years, and now I'm old enough to appreciate it.'

Unsure how grass was supposed to be 'appreciated', I decided to keep quiet as I directed them to a couple of chairs under a big oak tree that Bessie had left out at my instruction. I hadn't bargained on Mary being with us, and of course there was nowhere for her to sit, so I told her to return to the house and occupy herself quietly and not disturb anyone.

'Oh please, can't she stay?' Rupert asked, looking pleadingly at me. 'Who shall I have to talk to and play games with?' He must have seen my eyes flash with disapproval, as he hurried to correct himself. 'I mean calm, sitting-down games. The sort that don't involve running around.'

I sighed. 'All right. If the grass is dry enough, Mary may sit on the ground by your chair.'

She did so without even testing the lawn's dampness, and the two of them talked away to each other, apparently discussing some book Master Rupert had recommended about shipwrecks and treasure. I sat down in my own chair, allowing their childish chatter to murmur away like white noise, mingling with the sounds of the birds in the trees and the whispering sway of branches. Master Rupert had been right about the temperature; it wasn't cold at all. Very mild for March, and before long, without me realising, my eyes had closed and I drifted off to sleep.

I dreamed I was lying in a bed, being held in a man's arms. Mr Oakwood's, perhaps. Or a different man. With a different feel to him. Tense and firm, rather than relaxed and strong. And he was talking quietly in my ear, a flow of words I couldn't properly understand, only fragments landing like seeds in the fertile bed of my mind: *Not too deep beneath the surface. Not very deep underneath the ground.* Those sentences flicked and floated, neither defined nor ill-defined, until at last I realised I was in a bed made of earth and leaves and there were roots of plants and trees twisting around my legs and arms and throat until I couldn't breathe.

I awoke with a start, and perhaps a little cry. Not that anyone was there to hear or ask if I was all right. For when I looked over at the chair where Master Rupert had been seated, with little Mary by his feet, I saw that it was empty. With the horrible images of the dream still dancing in my head, I turned to look across the long stretch of grass towards the trees at the end and the stone wall beyond them. Unless I was very much mistaken, I had a pretty good idea where they had disappeared off to.

Chapter 25

Something Strange

Mrs Medlock, March 1979

I wasn't furious just with the children that day. Bessie caught the sharp end of my temper too. As I marched towards the garden, I heard giggling over near one of the greenhouses. For a moment I thought I'd been mistaken: that the children hadn't gone down to the forbidden garden after all and were messing around among the plants nearer the house. But a few seconds' detour made it clear what the noise had been. Bessie was standing with a mug in her hand, facing none other than Mr Quint, who was halfway through some anecdote or other. As I came into view, I caught the words 'Nobody should be guilty about pleasure, and I'm certainly not going to apologise for that particular vice.' I decided I would prefer not to know which vice he was referring to, and after pausing a moment for effect – which at least silenced them both – I directed my questioning to Bessie. 'What are you doing? Have you finished the vacuuming? And where are the children?'

She looked taken aback. 'The children?', she said, frowning, ignoring my other two questions. 'They're down in the garden. They said you had authorised it.'

'Did they indeed?' I said, not hiding my irritation, 'So you just took them at their word, did you? And if they ask for a trip to Disney World next and tell you I've given my approval, you'll do what? Book a flight?'

To the left of me, Mr Quint let out a laugh, although I got the distinct impression he was mocking my display of anger rather than crediting my words with wit. Bessie was going red, as she always did when she was put on the spot. 'I'm sorry ... I ... I think they're with Mr Oakwood.'

I rolled my eyes. 'Well, that's quite likely, isn't it, considering he lives down there.' I turned my attention to the now silent tutor. 'I take it, Mr Quint, that your presence here suggests young Ernest has finished his studies for the morning.'

His smile started to look more like a smirk. 'He's learned enough for the day,' he said. 'So I'm a man of leisure now.' He winked at Bessie.

'Well, perhaps you need to have a word with the family who are paying you,' I said. 'Perhaps this job isn't stimulating enough for you.'

I saw a glint in his eyes that I didn't like. 'Oh, I'm finding ... stimulation. Never fear.'

'Or maybe,' I said, trying to hold back from shouting at him, 'I should talk to *my* employers and discuss with them the appropriateness of having a man like you under their roof.'

Mr Quint shrugged, 'Do as you wish, Mrs Medlock. I'm sure they'll make their own assessments about your competency.'

My eyes widened in anger. Not trusting myself to keep my temper any longer, I left the greenhouse, deciding I was better off continuing in my search for Master Rupert. What if he'd collapsed on his way down to the garden? What would I say to his parents if I were to find his exhausted little body on the pathway under the trees, cold and alone? I tried to banish the thought from my mind, although it had distracted me from the other horror I was having to contend with: the thought of returning so soon to a place I had spent years avoiding.

Of course, there was no little body lying on the path. But the large wooden door was open, which suggested that young and distracted souls had passed through into the garden beyond. Mr Oakwood would never have left it like that. Taking a deep breath to calm myself, I stepped inside.

My mind instinctively carried me through the maze-like paths by memory, thoughts of the night I'd spent here with Mr Oakwood flooding back. It felt like a lifetime ago – a lifetime lived by another person.

I managed to find the children surprisingly quickly once I was inside. Mary spotted me first, her dark little eyes pinned on me for a good few seconds, before hurriedly turning back to what she was doing: sprinkling seeds in the ground. I looked around the clearing and saw Master Rupert handing a shovel to Ernest next to him.

'What on *earth* is going on here? I've been generous and understanding, I've tried to let you have some sense of ... of ... joy and freedom and allowed you to carry on here under Mr Oakwood's supervision, but you *knew*, Master Rupert, you *knew* you were supposed to just sit outside and not run about. You've betrayed my trust. You're forbidden to leave your room from this moment on.'

My little speech stopped everyone in their tracks, including Mr Oakwood, who had arrived in the clearing with a wheelbarrow loaded with what looked like dead tree branches. 'They told me you'd said it was allowed,' he said, as my eyes turned to him.

'Oh did they, now? It seems everyone just takes deceitful children at their word around here.'

He let go of the wheelbarrow. 'Why don't you come inside for a cup of tea,' he said, nodding towards his cabin, 'and we can talk it through.'

I ignored his suggestion. 'Lord Ashton ... this garden ...' I could hardly get the words out.

He came over to me, looking kind and calm. 'I know he doesn't like the garden to flourish in the way a normal garden would, after it was more or less sealed up after ... well, after all that.'

All that. If I hadn't already been so upset, I would have flared up at him for wording the horror of what we'd gone through – what *I* had gone through – so casually.

After an awkward pause, he carried on. 'I've tended to it well ever since. But don't you get tired of the grey? The dark greens, the lack of anything vibrant and colourful.' He moved closer to me and continued in a lower voice. 'Because the world is vibrant and colourful ... I think I've only just started to see that more clearly.'

He moved to touch me, but I backed away. I noticed, from behind Mr Oakwood, Mary's eyes upon me. While the boys had been planting and chatting to each other, she'd been listening and watching. It was too much. I walked away from them, through the trees and the bushes, until I came to the cabin. Inside I sat myself down on the chair and waited for him to follow me. He did as I expected, coming in through the door gentle and slow, like an animal trainer approaching a distressed and unpredictable creature.

Although there was no heater on or fire burning, the hut had a warmth and sense of familiarity about it that I found restorative. I hadn't realised how tense my body had become, how cold I felt – always a symptom of stress, whatever the weather outside – and I felt myself start to relax and unwind as I sat and watched him put the kettle on. I started to tell him that I felt undermined by his actions, but he cut across me before I could get too far with my protest.

'If it's any consolation, the children have been as good as gold since they got here, and Master Rupert hasn't suffered at all as a result.'

'Hmm,' I said, watching his back hunch and his long, strong legs bend as he poured hot water into two mugs. 'Well, you're no doctor. He could wake up tomorrow with charred skin and ... I don't know ...'

'You sound like one of those people in the village pub,' he said. He handed me my tea and sat on the edge of the bed, frowning slightly. 'They talk nonsense about this house. Ask me questions sometimes, if I go down there for a pint of an evening – not that I go regular, like. It's odd, isn't it, living in Oxfordshire these twenty years, and I still miss the Yorkshire pubs I went to as a lad. Probably shouldn't have been drinking that young, but there we go.'

I sipped at my tea. 'I don't think I'd know enough of public houses to draw a comparison between those found in Oxford and those found in Yorkshire.'

He chuckled. 'Public houses. You do speak in a funny way sometimes.'

I ignored this remark. 'Continue with what you were saying. About the local talk regarding this house.'

He too sipped at his tea, considered for a few moments, then said, 'As you can imagine, there are rumours about the first Lady Ashton. Rumours about her death. The ... um ... mysterious circumstances surrounding it.' He paused, looking at me as though to check I was all right, making sure his words hadn't caused any alarm. They might well have done if I had allowed myself to focus on them, but I was keen for him to get to the heart of whatever point he was making. 'Leaving that aside, they talk about Lord and Lady Ashton like they're this glamorous couple. I think it's because of Lady Ashton's connections to younger celebrity types in London. But the way they talk about Master Rupert isn't quite so ... respectful.'

I sat up sharply. 'What do you mean?'

He sighed. 'If a boy is tucked away for years, not seen by society, not seen by visitors, guests, tradesmen or anyone else in the village, people are going to talk. Chinese whispers, really. They tell stories to each other. Discuss theories about why he's kept locked up.'

I set my mug down on the little stool near me with a clatter, spilling some of the tea. 'Ignorant gossip will always just be ignorant gossip. And he's never been *locked up*. We've never once locked him in his room.'

Mr Oakwood held up a hand. 'I know, I know. But some say they've heard he's so close to death he might die at any moment. There've been a number of very silly and unkind descriptions of him as hunchbacked and helpless, or with extra limbs – always of course by people who have never seen him. And some say he's visited by a team of doctors every day, who have to administer twelve injections just to keep him awake.'

Hearing all this was upsetting me. 'I hope you tell them to mind their own business and not spread vicious lies.'

'What I'm saying,' he said, leaning forward, 'is that the opposite is true. You tell me now, when was the last time Lord or Lady Ashton requested he be seen by a doctor? He's seen tutors – or governesses, as you call them – even the occasional hairdresser, brought in from London, as you well know, but never anyone medical. Not for years. Bit strange, that, considering how ill the boy's supposed to be.'

I picked up my tea again, catching the drips as they fell with my other hand. 'I'm not paid to form conclusions,' I said. 'And neither are you.'

Mr Oakwood turned and looked out the window of the cabin,

towards the clearing where the three children were pottering about. 'Let them be happy. At least while Lord and Lady Ashton are out of the country. Let the poor lad know what it is to be a kid. Know what it's like to have friends.'

He looked so earnest and hopeful when he said this, I couldn't help but smile. 'You're a fine one to talk about friends. A borderline recluse, living here alone.'

He smiled back. 'Why would I need friends when I have you nearby?'

I felt myself blushing, and lowered my gaze to my tea. I was charmed, I have no qualms about admitting it. I just wish it had all ended differently. It was as if happiness had been ever so slightly within reach. But then a thought entered my head and Mr Oakwood spotted the change in my face.

'What's bothering you?' he asked.

'I'm worried,' I said quietly, not sure how I was going to word what I was thinking.

'About what? Little Rupert's health?' he prompted.

'No . . . well, yes, of course. But also about Mr Quint.'

I heard him sigh. 'I know, you told me about . . . his antics.'

I looked up at him. 'Yes, that, but there's more. It's . . . it's all so strange. I don't know if I'm imagining things or going mad, but there's . . . there's something *wrong*.'

Mr Oakwood frowned at me. 'I understand that he's behaved very poorly, but—'

'It's about the boy, Ernest.' I let the words out in a half-whisper, slightly scared of what I was saying. 'There's something . . . I think there's something strange going on.'

He was looking more worried now. 'Just tell me what happened.'

I took a deep breath, then said, 'I confronted Mr Quint and his . . . *guests*. Told him what I thought of the whole thing. Said the young women had to leave and that I might phone Lord and

Lady Ashton about it all. He was belligerent and dismissive. But after that, I went to get Ernest up. I was concerned the boy would be ... I don't know ... interested in what he'd heard in the room next to him throughout the night. I thought he'd make a thing of it, and decided to nip it in the bud there and then.'

'And was he?' Mr Oakwood asked.

'I don't know. I never found out. Because something ... When I walked in, I opened the curtains and found the boy asleep on top of his covers.'

Mr Oakwood looked confused. 'Why is that—'

'It was his *room*,' I said, still whispering. 'It felt like something had occurred in there. I thought I saw ... There was something light – perhaps pink – on the floor. I don't think the boy owns anything pink, I haven't seen him wearing anything of that colour. And in the air ... I could have sworn I could smell tobacco, perhaps even marijuana.'

Mr Oakwood seemed to be taking all this in. 'Well ... maybe he's been smoking on the quiet. He wouldn't be the first lad to sneak a crafty one from an adult and start the habit young. He is a teenager, after all. I don't know so much about marijuana. I'm not sure where he'd get it from. He could have brought it with him, I suppose. And as for what was on the floor ... maybe it was just a piece of clothing you haven't yet seen. A colourful T-shirt he doesn't wear around the house. Too proud. Listening to him lecture Miss Mary and Rupert, he seems to have enough pride to last a lifetime. Bloody superior and rude, one could say. I have to stop myself getting a bit sharp with him.'

I shook my head. 'Something strange had happened in that room. And I couldn't help but think ... I can barely consider it ... but what if Mr Quint didn't spend the night with *both* women. What if one of them went in ... '

I let myself trail off, but Mr Oakwood had understood. He

thought about it, then shook his head. 'I know the lad acts a bit high and mighty, but he's not old enough for all that yet. Surely a young woman would know that.' He too fell silent for a moment, clearly unsettled by the idea. 'They were both in the tutor's room when you went in, weren't they?'

I nodded. 'Yes, they were. But in a way, that's part of the problem. It's the feeling of not knowing ... there being something *wrong* about the whole thing.'

We sat there not speaking for a minute, then Mr Oakwood finally said, 'I think one thing's for sure. We need to keep a close eye on that Mr Quint. And perhaps telephone Lady Ashton in America and tell her your concerns.'

'No,' I said quickly. 'I don't want to speak to her.' I thought again of her veiled threats. *We might even have to think about getting you some help. Psychiatric help.*

'Well then, at least separate the two of them,' he urged. 'Move the boy to a different floor.'

I thought about this for a bit. 'Yes. I suppose that would be a start.' I rose from my seat and walked over to the window, where the children were just about visible. 'And as you say, we're going to have to keep a close eye on Mr Quint in future.'

Chapter 26

Eavesdropping

Mary, March 1979

Mrs Medlock wasn't happy when she found us in the hidden garden. We'd been helping Mr Oakwood plant things, and she had 'strong words' (that was how Rupert described it afterwards) with him in his little hut cabin thing. She was cross and felt 'undermined' – a word we heard when we were trying to eavesdrop.

But when they came out of the cabin, Mrs Medlock didn't look as angry as before. She watched us carry on with what we were doing – digging up little patches of ground and putting in the plants, like Mr Oakwood had shown us.

'I think it's time this place had some colour,' Mr Oakwood said. 'A feeling of new beginnings.' He smiled at Mrs Medlock when he said that. She didn't smile back. For a moment I thought there were tears in her eyes, but then she looked the other way before I could be sure.

Rupert said Mrs Medlock had always been weird about this garden, and he thought it was because she had much preferred his father's first wife. The first Lady Ashton. They'd been around the same age, apparently, and almost like friends, not that Rupert had been there, of course. He said he was just guessing from what he'd heard over the years. The garden had been the first Lady Ashton's special place. 'Do you think that's why her spirit returns here?' I asked him, thinking of the night when I'd seen the shape of a woman crossing the lawn in the moonlight, and the strange, shimmering way she'd disappeared into the growing mist. Rupert had told me he thought this was probably the case. He said he had read in his books about Wicca and witchcraft how spirits roamed and often had connections to nature, so her ghost returning to a place of plants, earth and water made sense. Especially if the garden meant a lot to her.

When the three of us were allowed to carry on visiting the garden, I thought it was just a special treat, and that Rupert would soon be sent back to his room. But I was surprised when Mrs Medlock ended up letting him go outside more and more as the weeks went on. It was almost like she'd given up. And even though she herself was so funny about the garden, she visited it a lot more often than she had before. There was one morning when I woke very early and went to find some water. When I looked out of the window on the stairwell towards the back of the house, she was out there, striding across the lawn in the morning mist, as if she'd just come from the hidden garden. I didn't mention to her that I'd seen her. I worried that if I did, the whole thing would become a 'problem'. That was what Ernest said, when he told us how he got away with all kinds of stuff with his parents: adults liked to obsess about 'problems'. The only thing you needed to do was to avoid something coming up too frequently, and they could be tricked into thinking it wasn't a problem at all.

Things carried on nicely for a while as the weather got warmer and the flowers Mr Oakwood had helped us plant started to appear amid the dull greys and greens of the garden. He said new life was like that, and in the summer the place would be bursting with colour for the first time in years. Rupert seemed as delighted as I was about this, but Ernest scoffed and said, 'Real men shouldn't get excited about flowers.' Mr Oakwood told him he was foolish, and asked, 'If I'm not a real man, what am I? A squirrel? A bear?' This made me and Rupert laugh and Ernest scowl.

Ernest was often unkind in the things he said, and made it obvious that he didn't think me and Rupert were very good company. It could be because we were a bit younger than him and he considered himself wiser. He missed his sister, he said, who had been sent away to boarding school, and he wished he could see his friends he'd left back in London. Even so, he carried on spending time with us – perhaps because he didn't have anyone else, apart from Mr Quint, who he had to see every morning anyway.

His attitude changed, though, when he was told his parents were coming to visit to see how he was getting on. This news sent Mrs Medlock and Bessie into a bit of a flap. They ran round cleaning things, dusting shelves and banisters, and sent off for a special meat order, with Mrs Medlock muttering about having to 'play the hostess' while her ladyship wasn't at home. She didn't sound very happy about this, but I'd have loved to have been allowed to play the hostess. I would have had great fun cutting neat slices of cake for the guests and making Ernest's parents feel welcome. I was looking forward to seeing them, even though I thought they would probably be as stuck-up and posh as their son.

Ernest, however, wasn't happy about the visit. 'Why do they feel the need to come down here and bother me?' he said, kicking at the side of Rupert's four-poster bed.

'At least they want to see you,' Rupert said, sounding sad.

'First they sent me to school, and now they've sent me here. What makes you think they want to see me?' Ernest shook his head, looking angrily first at Rupert, then at me, as if we were two idiots he was trying to convince of something completely obvious. 'Whatever the reason for their visit, it won't be anything to do with me.'

I thought this sounded silly. Of course it must be to do with him. Why else would they be coming all the way from London? The answer to that question became clear the following day, when the three of us snuck into the corridor, trying to eavesdrop on his parents' conversation with Mrs Medlock.

Chapter 27

She Doesn't Seem Insane

Mrs Medlock, April 1979

'A party? But ... well, Lord and Lady Ashton aren't at home.' I stared at Eliza Kellman and her husband as if they were insane, momentarily forgetting this wasn't polite or proper.

'I'm well aware of that, Mrs Medlock. In fact I dare say I'm more often in contact with them both than you are.'

That wouldn't be hard, I thought to myself. I reached forward and picked up the teapot, offering them both some more – a distraction while I digested what she'd just said.

I'd been on edge ever since Mr and Mrs Kellman had arrived, with the latter marching into the entrance hall and handing me her coat and gloves without saying a word, and then looking around like a visitor at a restaurant waiting to be shown to her table. She was a tall, severe-looking woman in her late forties, with prematurely greying hair that seemed to emphasise a sense of authority and wisdom. Her husband, Clive Kellman, was one of those men you could imagine being startlingly good-looking when he was young, but the cruel hand of time was taking its hold and his face was starting to look lined, his jaw less sharp.

I'd met them both on a number of occasions over the years, but this was the first instance where I had been made to spend an extended period of time with them.

'No more for me, thank you,' Mrs Kellman said, turning her nose up at my suggestion.

'I'll have another cup,' Mr Kellman said, smiling at me. I didn't trust his smile. It was the smile of a politician – which I suppose was appropriate, since he was the MP for some posh part of London. 'I'm afraid my wife may not have explained it as well as she ... Well, what I'm essentially saying is that we're sorry to impose, but it was Lord Ashton's suggestion. I spoke with him on the phone last week about this and he suggested using Marwood Manor for the party while he was away.'

I was gripping the sides of my chair. It needed re-upholstering, I could feel the fabric fraying under my fingers, and I was half tempted to seize it and tear it with my nails like a wild thing until nothing but the wooden frame remained. The selective expenditure on the household – both upkeep and staff – had been a frustration of mine for years. Lord Ashton didn't consider the subject a concern of his and would refer me to Lady Ashton. Any requests to hire more staff, even just a kitchen maid or an extra cleaner, fell on deaf ears. There were other spending priorities, apparently, like expensive dresses and travel abroad, and, of course, house parties. And now once again, I was being used – being made to play host to strangers I didn't like or care about, stretching my time and patience to breaking point. I would be more understanding if they were actually here to manage everything. I would help out and assist, like a housekeeper should. But this – this was taking it too far.

As if he could read my mind, Mr Kellman smiled at me again and said, 'We will do everything for you. Or rather, my wife will.' He glanced across at her. I imagined he thought himself well practised in achieving a look of love and adoration, but I noticed that no evidence of warmth met his eyes. His wife didn't bother to pretend. She stared back at him in her default stony way, apparently unimpressed with the way he'd worded this.

'Well, I'm sure Mrs Medlock has her own method of doing things, so I wouldn't want to interfere,' she said, shooting a look my way. 'But I do have some ideas when it comes to the caterers, the drinks I want served, the time the guests should arrive, not to mention the invitations. I'll sort out all those.'

'I see,' I said, deciding it would be best to say as little as possible in response to all this. 'And when did you envisage this party taking place?'

'I was thinking Saturday the twenty-first of April,' she said.

'That's less than three weeks away,' I replied.

'Very quick mathematics,' she said, slightly scathingly, reminding me of Lady Ashton at her worst. 'More than enough time to sort everything out.' She rose to her feet, causing her husband to put down his cup and do the same. 'And talking of mathematics, I think I should see my son and his tutor. I'd like an update on how his studies are going.'

To my surprise, Mr Quint was polite, gracious and sincere to both the Kellmans when they quizzed him about their son's progress. He laid out the exercise books young Ernest had filled, including a range of essays and projects on subjects as varied as the Spanish Armada, human biology, trigonometry and art history. I hadn't shown much interest in Ernest's education myself up until that point, but as I observed his work, I wondered if I'd perhaps underestimated Mr Quint. He was a clever one. A chameleon. And I hadn't forgotten that night when he'd brought those two women to the house. For a sudden moment, I thought about blurting out what I had seen and heard in front of the Kellmans, if only to enjoy seeing the ripples of shock and disapproval spread across their faces. I wasn't entirely sure why I didn't tell them, but something about the idea of disturbing the equilibrium sounded a warning bell in my head. As was so often the case for someone spending their life in service, it was best to just endure and persist. It had been that way since the beginning of time. I'm well aware I probably sound old-fashioned, but it is my firm belief that stoicism is far more powerful than protest.

'I can see my son is progressing well,' Mrs Kellman said, straightening up and turning to the boy, who was sitting in a corner of the library slightly away from us adults. He hadn't said one word since his parents had entered, nor had they to him. Instead he just sat like a blond-haired statue, his eyes on the floor.

'Do you feel your time here has been restorative, Ernest?' his father asked, walking around the desk towards him.

The boy said nothing at first, and for a moment I thought he was going to ignore his father altogether. But then he lifted his eyes from the carpet and stared at him with a look of challenge. 'Restorative? In what way?'

I looked back at Mr Kellman and saw his brow crease and his eyes narrow. 'In terms of behaviour, outlook, disposition. Your general demeanour.' There was a harder edge to his voice now. The charming politician act was waning, and I could sense impatience underneath his words. Perhaps even a dislike for his son.

Suddenly, like an animal that had been spooked by an approaching predator, Ernest stood up, snatched up his workbooks from the desk and threw them across the room. Then he stormed out of the library without waiting to see his parents' shocked reaction.

A pin-drop silence echoed in his wake, the absence of sound somehow louder than the commotion that had come before it. 'I can see there are still some lessons to be learned,' his father said, then looked over at Mr Quint. 'I think my son needs to learn about respect, and that feminine displays of emotion never end well for anyone. You have my permission to use reasonable force, if you deem it necessary.'

Mr Quint nodded, and I could have sworn I saw the slightest flicker of a smile twitch at his lips. His eyes looked as if a fire had been lit behind them. Mr Kellman's words had also caused a reaction in Mrs Kellman, who glanced sharply at her husband. For a moment I thought she was going to object, but she just lowered her gaze back to the floor and bent down to retrieve an exercise book that had landed by one of the reading chairs.

'I think it's time we were going,' Mr Kellman said. 'Thank you for your hospitality, Mrs Medlock.'

I saw them out of the house, leaving Mr Quint alone in the library. Once I had closed the front door, I returned to straighten things up. The tutor was sitting in a chair, a smug expression on his face. I ignored him completely and went to open a window to let some fresh air into the room. Silly, I know, but I felt it would help disperse the bad feeling. In doing so, I heard the crunch of gravel as the Kellmans walked across the drive to their car. Their words carried clearly on the breeze.

'She doesn't *seem* insane, does she? Mrs Medlock, that is.'

I froze, certain I must have misheard Mrs Kellman's words. Then her husband spoke.

'Well, she didn't say she was insane, did she. Just liable to a nervous breakdown, or perhaps some sort of early dementia.'

'Yes, that was it,' his wife replied. 'Lady Ashton wants to know how the party goes. I think it's some sort of test. To see if the woman is still capable.'

A thud sounded, followed by another. They'd got into their car, and seconds later the engine started and they drove away.

Stunned and embarrassed, I turned to look at Mr Quint. He

was still sitting in his chair, his eyes trained on mine and his eyebrows raised.

'I ... I don't ...' I grasped at the words, feeling I should respond, fill the terrible stillness now left in the room, mitigate his awful presence in some way.

'That was interesting,' he said, almost pleasantly, as if we had just sat through a film or a play and were about to exchange our views on it.

I decided it was best if I didn't say any more. I walked towards the door, not looking back, although I did pause when he spoke again.

'Please retrieve Ernest from wherever he may be hiding, Mrs Medlock. It's clear his father is keen for his education to step up a level. I have some important things to teach him. And I think we should begin immediately.'

Chapter 28

A Very Special Guest

Mrs Medlock, April 1979

Shortly before the party – less than a week before the day itself – Mrs Kellman telephoned for an update on the arrangements. She wished for reassurance that I was following her instructions to the letter. I promised her I was, and that the caterers had been arranged and the house would be cleaned thoroughly the day before the party.

'That all sounds very satisfactory, Mrs Medlock,' she said. 'I shall pass on to Lady Ashton how competent you seem to be with all this. There was just one other thing I wanted to make you aware of.'

I tightened my grip on the receiver, a bad feeling about her words already starting to rise within me. 'Oh yes,' I said. 'What might that be?'

The line crackled and snapped for an instant, then Mrs Kellman's words came through quite crisp and clear. 'A very special guest. A late addition to our number. Of course, her schedule's very busy, as you can imagine, but . . . ' The line started to crackle once more. 'Such an honour . . . Hello . . . Mrs Medlock, can you hear me?'

I noticed that she sounded irritated, as if the poor connection was somehow my fault. 'Yes, I can hear you,' I said. 'May I ask who the special guest is?'

Although the crackling continued, I could hear the name well enough, and my eyes widened. 'Well, I'm sure we'll make her feel most welcome,' I said. I was used to the occasional famous face attending dinners and parties here. If I ever chose to write my memoirs or publish my diaries, I could tell more than a few tales. Like the time Sean Connery spilled a glass of wine in the library, or when Lord Snowdon mistook me for a party guest rather than staff. But their visits had always been very much managed by Lord and Lady Ashton. In this instance, I had been made to feel like both organiser and, in some strange way, host. And I didn't like it.

I decided to warn Bessie about who was coming. 'Wow,' she said, her mouth falling open. 'Well I never. They say she's going to be the next prime minister. Imagine that – a woman prime minister. Makes me wonder how she'd find the time, with a husband and kids.'

I had no interest in having a conversation about women's liberation with Bessie, so I fell silent and let her ramble on while I prepared lunch for the children. In the run-up to the party, I had frequently emphasised how important it was that they stay out of sight on the night, with the exception of Ernest. He was, according to his parents, to be allowed to mingle, briefly, providing he was smartly dressed and remained polite. He would retire to his bedroom at nine o'clock. Master Rupert and Mary had been visibly appalled to find that they would miss out on the excitements, but I told them that life was full of hardship and they should just get used to it.

On the night of the party, I took a moment away from the hustle and bustle of the caterers getting organised ahead of the guests' arrival. Stepping out onto the porch, I felt a change in the air for the first time that spring. Summer was coming, and with it a sense of change, of times shifting. I didn't know whether they were good or bad, but I somehow knew our lives in that house were about to take a new turn. I've said it before, and I'll say it again: I don't hold with any psychic, ghostly, superstitious nonsense. But I do believe in trusting one's instincts, and that was how I felt that night as the cool but pleasant breeze made my anonymous and unremarkable black dress sway a little. I watched the trees move back and forth slowly, listening to the swish and rustle they made, and thought about how different everything already was since I'd walked down there in the snow with little Mary back at the start of the year, or when I'd sat in the shade with Master Rupert just a matter of weeks ago. Then my gaze drifted to the woodland at the far end, towards the hidden garden, where Mr Oakwood would be having his dinner right now. I had a sudden urge to walk away from my responsibilities, go down the little path, through the big wooden door and into his arms. But then Mrs Kellman called my name from the French windows, and my fantasy was interrupted. I returned to the house, pretending not to hear my own heart beating.

The party showed all the signs of going well until the commotion happened – an eye-wateringly embarrassing moment that at the time I thought would haunt me to the grave. Of course, so much happened subsequently – so many actually terrible things – that such a moment of social discomfort ended up paling into insignificance.

I had already been uneasy and tense due to a conversation I'd been having with a man named Michael Allerton, a friend of both the Kellmans and Lord and Lady Ashton. He and his wife, Cassandra, had been to Marwood Manor many times before and

I'd always found him a rather unnerving presence; he had dark, piercing eyes that seemed to follow you around the room, even when they were focused on someone else. On this occasion, his wife was engaged in an animated discussion with Sir Geoffrey Howe and an Irish radio presenter whose name escaped me, while Mr Allerton stalked around having short conversations with people while giving the impression of a hyena on the Serengeti stalking its prey. I thought I would be beyond his notice, but all of a sudden, as I was counting the remaining drinks on trays to see if a new batch had to be brought up, he was beside me. 'I hope this little occasion hasn't put you to too much bother, Mrs Medlock, when your master and mistress are away.' Although the terms 'master' and 'mistress' weren't exactly strangers to my working life, having spent over twenty years in service, I still didn't much like the way he made me sound like a character in *Upstairs, Downstairs*.

'It's no bother,' I said, giving him a half-smile. I got the feeling he was examining me like a human X-ray, and I suddenly felt as if I'd been caught without the proper amount of clothes on.

'It must be difficult for you, cooped up here all alone for months on end while the master of the house networks his way around Manhattan society.' He said this as if he had insider knowledge into what Lord Ashton was doing in America, which I suppose he probably did. I'd once heard my 'master' and 'mistress' having a conversation about him when they thought I couldn't hear. Lord Ashton had described him as 'the type of man who knows everything about everyone'.

I decided to ignore his comment about my employer's activities in the States and just said, 'I am more than used to it, Mr Allerton. And I have the children for company, of course.'

Then he said something that sent a rush of electricity down my spine. 'Oh, I didn't know you had children.' There was a strange, false note of interest in his voice. 'How old are they?'

I couldn't stop my head snapping round to look at him. I shouldn't have acted so alarmed, so obviously affected by his words, but it happened automatically. It was that feeling you get when you suddenly submerge yourself in cold water, and it was all I could do not to gasp. 'I ... I don't have any children. I was referring to the children in my care.'

He looked at me, unblinking but slightly smiling, for a good few seconds, then said, 'Ah, I do apologise, I misunderstood. You were speaking of the three young people in your charge. That orphan, a distant relation to Lord Ashton, the Kellman teenager and, of course, little Rupert Ashton, who the world hasn't seen for many a year.'

I felt like he was injecting his words with more meaning than was actually being articulated, and it disconcerted me. 'You seem to be well informed,' I said quietly. I found I now could not meet his gaze and instead looked in front of me, surveying the guests laughing and chatting and drinking, as if we were members of an audience at the theatre watching a play with a very large cast.

'I make it my business to be well informed,' he said. 'About my friends. And their staff.'

I was about to tell him I wasn't sure of his meaning, but then the calamity happened, and everything around us went to pieces, as I rushed to help the victim of said calamity, whose smart suit had been covered in alcoholic liquid, and apprehend the child responsible: Mary.

Chapter 29

An Ancient Creature

Mary, April 1979

I watched from my window as the guests arrived, in the same way I'd watched people leave on Christmas Eve. It reminded me of the Twelfth Night party, when I'd been caught out of bed. If my mum was still alive, she'd have probably told me I should have learned my lesson after that, but I wasn't very good at learning lessons.

Earlier, Rupert and I had sat on his bed as Ernest wandered around the room, making it obvious that the only reason he was there was to show off the fact that he was dressed in a 'black tie' outfit and allowed to attend the party. He was so smug about it, saying stuff like 'It's such a shame Princess Margaret was unable to attend, I would have liked to meet her again', and in the end I just turned away and started talking over him to Rupert about his drawing of a dragonfly. This made Ernest stop being so silly, and he ended up coming to sit with us, although he looked a bit awkward perched there on the bed in his smart clothes, which were obviously stiff and uncomfortable.

After a while, he got up and straightened his bow tie. 'I should be off downstairs now to greet the guests.' He made it sound like this was his house and his party, rather than him just being allowed down there for a couple of hours so his parents could act like they were a happy family. That was what I heard Bessie and Mr Quint saying when Mrs Medlock told them to help get the boy dressed and ready. Bessie had been spending a lot of time with Mr Quint. He ignored everyone completely most of the time, but when she was around he suddenly got all talkative with her, and she got all giggly.

I knew it was bad of me really, but I was cross about how smug Ernest had been about the party and I wanted me and Rupert to have some fun, so we hatched a plan. Well, *I* came up with the plan, and he went along with it. We were going to sneak out of the house while Mrs Medlock and Bessie were busy with the guests and run down to the hidden garden and plant all the new plants Mr Oakwood had waiting on his little metal trolley thing. It would be like fairies or goblins had planted them in the night, or magical spirits had helped bring the garden back to life.

Rupert, of course, saw problems with this plan. 'Wouldn't they know it was us?' he said, looking worried, 'And it's getting quite dark now. What if we can't find our way back?'

'Of course we'll find our way back,' I said. 'I've been down there in the pitch-black darkness and snow and could still see stuff. And if they suspect us, we can just deny it. They can't prove anything.'

Eventually he agreed, but only after I told him he was probably right to stay tucked up in bed as the walk down might be too much for him and wear him out. I thought that would work, and it made him immediately launch up and start getting dressed into proper clothes, while I went to my room to get my cardigan.

Sneaking out of the house later was easy: we just went down the servants' staircases and kept to the darker, emptier corridors. There were times when I expected the shadows that arched across the walls or fell from curtains around windows to suddenly come to life and snatch us away, but nothing like that happened. We arrived downstairs in one piece, undiscovered, and began the more treacherous part of the journey: making a bolt for the door and getting across the lawn without being spotted. I chose a back door I hadn't been through before, and we were very lucky it wasn't locked. There were a few seconds when I thought two men smoking thick cigars and laughing would see us, but they were too busy talking about something to do with 'Iran' and 'the Shah', two words I hadn't heard before.

We kept to the trees at the side instead of walking straight across the lawn, running from trunk to trunk, pressing ourselves against the gnarled wood. It was rather fun and we ended up laughing more than once, enjoying the feeling of being slightly afraid without things being too frightening. When we got to the hidden garden, though, it did feel more serious. The noise of laughter and chatter had died away and we were alone, finding our way through the maze-like pathways, trying to remember where Mr Oakwood had left his trolley of new plants. In the end, we found it next to one of the untidy, dying flower beds that needed clearing out.

I told Rupert it would be best to leave the clearing of the dead flowers to Mr Oakwood and just plant around them – a plan that worked until we ran out of clear earth and kept scratching our hands on the dead, rough stuff. Rupert had pulled up his sleeves and draped his coat over the trolley, but the mud had already found its way onto his shirt. I had bits of dirt speckling my cardigan, and I wondered whether I'd been a bit silly thinking we could easily lie about having come here if asked later on.

'I think maybe we should go now and come back tomorrow,' he said. 'Mr Oakwood might find us – he can't be asleep yet, it's not that late—'

He stopped talking when a noise cut through the surrounding silence – the sound of something being dragged across the ground, not too far away. Even in the darkness, I could see Rupert's pale face turn to me in horror.

'Do you think it's *her*?' he said in barely a whisper.

'Who?' I whispered back, wondering if he meant Mrs Medlock.

'Her ... her spirit ...' He seemed horrified, but I must have still looked puzzled, because eventually he said, 'The first Lady Ashton. The spectre you saw. What if she really did curse this place—'

He was cut short by another sound, although this time it was quite different: the noise of water splashing, then a high-pitched screech, then more water. I'd had enough of staying still and being scared. Ignoring Rupert's pleas to stay where I was and not leave his side, I got up and very, very slowly crept along the damp earth to peer through the hedge in front of us.

It wasn't a ghost – it was Mr Oakwood. He was standing next to a large metal pump, filling a bucket with water. Then he set it down and started to unbutton his shirt. Once he had taken off all his clothes, he began to pour the water over himself. A warm glow seemed to light him up, and I realised he'd left the door of his cabin open so that he could see in the dark.

I became so transfixed I barely noticed Rupert approaching me. 'I got scared,' he whispered. I didn't reply. I just kept watching Mr Oakwood as he rubbed soap over his tall, strong body. Next to me, Rupert gasped when he saw what I was looking at.

'Keep quiet,' I hissed in his ear, taking hold of his shoulder and pulling him back slightly, to make sure his face wasn't poking through the hole in the hedge too obviously.

I liked being close to Rupert like this, the smell of his newly washed hair filling my nose, mingled with the laundry scent of his shirt. I'd always found boys at school irritating, and wouldn't have ever thought I'd want to sit close to one like this, my arm on his shoulder, his hand in mine. After a while, I realised I was staring less at the figure of Mr Oakwood, and more at Rupert. At his face, his eyes glinting in the darkness like small pinpricks of fire. He seemed incapable of looking away from the naked man in front of him, as if it was something astonishing, something slightly scary but at the same time wonderful, rather than just a man having a wash in a makeshift shower. It was the same way I sometimes saw him looking at Ernest, like the older boy was some rare animal he desperately wanted to touch but was afraid might bite him.

What happened next turned out to be a serious moment. A moment that would change everything. At first I thought I'd cut myself on a twig, and cried out as I pulled my hand from the ground. But it wasn't a twig. As I shifted and felt around, I could tell it was something a lot harder. Brittle. Very different in the way it felt against my skin.

Mr Oakwood had towelled himself off and disappeared by the time I made my discovery. With the door to his cabin closed, we had almost no light at all, the moon above us giving only a dull grey-blue tinge to everything. In the gloom, I showed Rupert what was in my hand, asking him what he thought it was.

'Is it a bird's claw?' he asked, moving his head so close, his nose almost touched my fingers.

'I . . . I don't know. It looks like . . . a hand,' I said, then felt a sudden need to drop it, to get it away from me, off my skin and back into the earth where it had come from.

'Don't lose it,' Rupert said, and ferreted around in front of us to retrieve it once more. 'It's like a tiny arm, with a very small hand. Do you think we've found the bones of an ancient creature? Or something dull, like a rat or a fox?'

'I don't know,' I said. With every minute I felt colder and more worried, and I had a desperate need to leave the garden and go back to the house, where we'd be inside, warm and safe. But Rupert seemed too interested to leave. He scraped at the ground around us, feeling in the earth with his hands, plunging them deeper. At first I thought he wasn't going to find anything, but then he looked up at me and pulled something out. We both stared at it for a long, long time – first as we tried to work out what it was, then in stunned realisation once we had worked it out. Then we stared at each other.

We didn't talk about our discovery on the walk back up to the house. Rupert tried, but I didn't want to. He muttered a few things about Viking settlers or ancient burial grounds or Victorian graves, or perhaps an animal that had got into the garden and died there. I wasn't really listening. I just knew somehow that this wasn't any of those things, but something more important – important to us, important to the people in this house. And we should probably be very careful about mentioning it to anyone.

'Where have you two been?' said a voice from the darkness as we were walking among the trees at the edge of the main lawn. At first I thought it was Mrs Medlock come to tell us off, but the voice was lower and posher. Ernest came into view a few seconds later, still dressed in his smart clothes.

'We went to the garden,' Rupert said, before I could answer, making it sound like an achievement he was proud of. As though he expected Ernest to be impressed with him. I turned round and frowned, and he looked surprised. 'What?' he asked, sounding offended, then muttered more quietly something about how he hadn't realised it was a secret.

I could see Ernest was cross now and his tone got more scathing, 'Don't you think it's a bit childish to be sneaking off like that?'

'We *are* children,' I said defiantly.

He opened his mouth to reply, then something seemed to catch his attention, because he took a step forward and said, 'What's that you've got there?'

I looked over and saw what was in Rupert's hands. I'd told him to keep it in his coat pocket, to keep it safe, but here he was holding it out in front of him like a trophy. 'Put it away,' I hissed.

He ignored me, and even seemed pleased that he had Ernest's attention. The older boy reached out and took the little thing out of Rupert's hands, holding it up in front of his face to examine it more closely. Then he said, his voice less haughty than before, 'Where . . . where did you find this?'

'That's for us to know and you to perhaps *never* find out,' I said, folding my arms, still cross with him for telling us off like little children, as if he was the adult, and with Rupert for sharing our discovery.

'It was in the hidden garden. In the ground, in the hedge near the water pump.'

Again I shot a look of daggers at Rupert, but he lifted his chin in defiance, pleased with himself that he had news to share that interested Ernest. Those thoughts I'd had when sitting close to him in the garden came back to me. How jealous I was that he seemed to look at others in a way he never looked at me. *Jealousy never pays* was one of the phrases my mum always used to say whenever I wished I had a bike like a girl in my class or new shoes or a better school bag. But I'd never thought I'd feel jealousy about another person like this.

I was dragged out of my thoughts when Ernest did something very surprising. Instead of staying to discuss our strange find, he suddenly put it in his inside jacket pocket, then turned on his heel and walked quickly away from us towards the house.

'Hey!' I yelled out to him, all thoughts of being caught by Mrs Medlock now gone.

'Give it back!' Rupert shouted, looking shocked at Ernest's betrayal.

We ran towards him, reaching him before he could get to the patio outside the French windows. The two of us grabbed him at the same time and caught him off balance, so that he fell sideways onto the grass. Both of us got on top of him as he struggled, Rupert holding him down while I tried to get into his jacket pocket.

'I say, what's going on here?' One of the older men who had been smoking outside earlier had come over, and I could see other guests walking towards us too. The few seconds it took me to realise we were creating a fuss everyone could see and hear was enough for Ernest to wriggle free and sprint away from us, onto the patio and into the house.

'Get after him!' I yelled at Rupert. He didn't need my encouragement. He was already on the way, moving swiftly through the guests and into the house.

I lost them both almost immediately. I ran through the library into the hallway, then into another room where loads of people were standing round talking to each other, with young men offering trays of drinks and others collecting empty glasses. I paused at the doorway, looking around, then spotted Rupert darting across the other side of the room and through another door, apparently following Ernest. I ran to catch up with him, throwing myself across the room, unaware that a woman had stepped into my path, and one of the boys carrying trays had appeared from my other side. I hurtled into them both, crashing into the woman's waist while causing the boy with the drinks to trip. The glasses and liquid seemed to float in the air for a moment as I tumbled to the ground, followed by splashes and crashes around me and a gasp of surprise from the woman, who even in her shock reached down to catch me.

'Goodness me, it's a child!' she exclaimed, managing to take hold of one of my arms. She kneeled down to my level, while one of the men she had been talking to also crouched down and asked her if she was OK, apparently uninterested in me or the drinks boy struggling to get to his feet amid the broken glass.

The woman kept her eyes on me as she raised a hand to the man and shook it slightly, as if to say 'don't worry about it'. 'Now tell me, child, is anything broken? Can you stand?' She had a deep, loud voice, and I could imagine she'd be quite good at getting cross. She didn't seem annoyed with me, though – in fact, her strong tone made me feel calm, as if the situation was under control, or at least soon would be. Then I noticed that the spilled drinks had splashed her nice blue suit jacket, and worried that she'd become upset when she realised.

'Oh my goodness,' said another woman from behind me. I looked round and recognised her as Ernest's mother, Mrs Kellman. She didn't seem worried about me – instead she looked furious, her eyes wide, her mouth half open. 'Mrs Medlock, can you not control this child? Look what she's done!'

'I think she was following the other boys,' the lady in the blue suit said. 'Were you all playing a game?'

'They most certainly should not have been,' Mrs Medlock said. She'd appeared at my side as if from nowhere. I'd hoped I could escape before she realised what had happened, while also sort of hoping she'd appear and put an end to all this. At least being sent to my room and told I was naughty wasn't a new, strange experience. It was normality in this house.

The kind, deep-voiced lady tried to smooth things over, saying things like 'children will be children' and 'a bit of rough and tumble is good for the soul'. I could tell by the way Mrs Medlock pursed her lips, though, that she didn't agree and was thoroughly horrified. Once she'd managed to leave as politely as possible, leading me past the mostly smiling guests, she began whispering things at me as she hustled me upstairs. 'Never been so embarrassed,' she hissed, and then something about 'showing us all up in front of the guest of honour'. I didn't know what she meant by guest of honour. Now that I'd recovered from the surprise of my fall, I didn't really care much that the lady's suit was ruined. I was too busy thinking about Rupert and Ernest. And what we had found in the garden.

Chapter 30

The Small Hand

Mrs Medlock, April 1979

My goodness, that evening was awful. The combination of Michael Allerton's strange hints and unnerving questions, followed by those bloody children running riot and Mary crashing into the one guest everyone wanted to impress, then later, what happened in the bathroom... well, I'll come to that. But it's the worst of them all.

Once I had extricated Mary from the scene of broken glass and bemused politicians, I more or less threw her into her room, telling her she'd be lucky to get any supper for a week and how I had a mind to put her to work trying to get the mud and grass stains out of her clothes. She protested, of course, moaning that it wasn't just her, and how she was chasing after Rupert, who was chasing after Ernest, who had stolen...

'Yes?' I asked, the door poised, ready to shut it and leave. 'Ernest stole what?'

'He... Nothing.'

I eyed her suspiciously for a moment and could see her closing up, regretting whatever it was she'd started to say. I decided I couldn't be bothered to press her, and instead shut the door and marched off to find the boys. Ernest was nearest, so I flung the door to his room open. He was seated on his bed, scowling.

'Look at the state of you,' I remarked, staring at the streaks of mud, grass and bits of leaf that clung to his skin, hair and the once-clean, smart clothes. 'A bath, now, before you touch anything else.'

'I don't want a bath. I want to go back downstairs and—'

'You will *not* be going back downstairs, I'll tell you that,' I said, walking forward and taking hold of his arm. He made a show of trying to get away from me, but in the end he didn't put up much of a fight. He seemed to know a losing battle when he saw one. He muttered darkly about something that sounded like 'my parents' and I laughed bitterly, telling him his parents were no doubt ashamed at the spectacle he, Rupert and Mary had subjected them to. I delivered him to the bathroom he normally used, on the floor above, set the taps running, and told him to get washed and I'd be back with his pyjamas and a towel. He began to say again how he wished to re-join the party and not go to bed, but I closed the door on his complaints and continued upstairs.

Master Rupert, meanwhile, had decided to try another tack to avoid a scolding: he was curled up in his bed with the curtains closed and the light off, pretending to be asleep. I considered dragging him out by his feet and telling him to have a bath too, but upon closer inspection of his face, he didn't seem as dirty as Ernest. I decided not to wake him and just snatched up the clothes he'd left scattered on the floor with a view to dumping the lot in the laundry room for tomorrow.

On my way back down the servants' stairs, I ran into Bessie. 'I heard there was a fuss of some kind. The waiter boys were asking about clearing up some spilled drinks.'

'Yes, there was a fuss – and where were you, may I ask?' I didn't try to hide my anger or exhaustion, although even in my foul mood, I still noticed the pause before Bessie answered, as if she was choosing what to tell me.

'I had to pop outside. Someone needed . . . a drink.'

It sounded so vague, I knew it must be a lie, but I couldn't face interrogating her at this point. 'Mary will need a bath run for her. Best use the bathroom on the upper west side – Ernest is currently in the one below.'

Bessie frowned. 'Why do they need baths?'

I moved towards her on the stairs, trying to get past. 'They've been fighting in the garden or rolling around on the grass – God alone knows. Now let me through.'

I felt a twinge of regret about snapping at her as I went through the servants' corridor and onto one of the main landings. She did work hard, but I was annoyed at her absence earlier and the fact that she'd tried to mislead me as to where she'd been. I had a horrible feeling Mr Quint might have something to do with it. Perhaps the two of them had been enjoying some time together down in the greenhouses.

I took a clean towel from one of the airing cupboards, then went into Ernest's room – which was a state as usual, with shirts and pens and school books scattered around – and located some pyjamas. When I re-entered the bathroom, I was pleased to see he had done as he was told and got into his bath, although he yelled out in protest when I marched in without knocking.

'I say, a bit of privacy would be nice!'

I ignored him and laid the towel over the side of the bathtub. I then brandished the pyjamas at him and said shortly, 'Put these on, then bed. No more excitement. No more dashing around. Understand?'

He frowned, but nodded. His blond hair was darker when it was wet, and I could see a clump of dirt and a blade of grass stuck in his fringe. I had half a mind to tell him to be more thorough and hold his head down for him, but I suspected that would lead to further objections.

'I don't even wear pyjamas any more.' He tutted and rolled his eyes, as if this was a development I should have known about and he was frustrated at me for not keeping up. For a reason I couldn't fathom, I was suddenly pulled back to that strange morning when I'd entered his room and found him asleep with the scent of tobacco in the air.

'*Hello?*' Ernest said belligerently.

'I heard what you said, but the pyjamas are here regardless.'

He shook his head. 'Mr Quint says men of the world sleep in nightshirts or nothing at all. Pyjamas are for little kids and doddery old men.'

I couldn't help but frown, and took a step closer to the boy. He was watching me, his face defiant. 'That's a bit of an odd thing for a tutor to say,' I said, choosing my words carefully. 'Why did it even come up?'

Ernest shrugged. 'He's been teaching me how to be a proper man. How to be a grown-up. I'm tired of being treated like a child. I'll be fourteen soon.'

'Exactly. Which makes you still a child.' I folded my arms, as if to show him how immovable this fact was. But he was undeterred, and as he spoke, I started to get the feeling he enjoyed unnerving me.

'Mr Quint says women are there for two things only: the pleasure of men, and to continue the male line.'

I kept my arms folded, but started to clench my fingers together, feeling more uneasy with each sentence that came out of his mouth. 'I don't know what Mr Quint thinks he's doing, filling a boy with such horrible attitudes. The world has changed in the way it regards women. Even a woman in service such as myself.'

'Well, he's made me think about things. Because if women are here for pleasure and reproduction, what is the point of *you?*'

I must have looked shocked, because I saw a smile flicker at the sides of his mouth. 'I don't know what you mean,' I said, about to turn on my heel and leave, but there was something hypnotic about the conversation and the strangeness of him sitting there in the bath. Although I was standing over him, it felt as though he was towering above me.

'I mean, you're not continuing the male line by producing babies, are you? You're what, forty? The ship's almost sailed where that's concerned. So that means your only other worth is as an object of pleasure for men. And again, you seem to be failing at that. To be honest, your looks are fading. Mr Quint said that. He said he thinks you might have been quite beautiful when you were young, but middle age has crept up on you like a thief in the night and stolen your looks. So I don't suppose many men would want to be pleasured by you now, even if you wanted to.'

I know it wasn't right. But I couldn't help it. I lashed out. Before I'd properly registered what I was doing, I'd bent down and seized the boy and given him a powerful slap across the cheek. The rush of adrenaline that came after made me gasp, my heart beating fast, his face a picture of shock. I reeled back, instantly appalled and yet victorious in wiping that self-satisfied, sneering look off his features and interrupting the terrible things he'd been saying.

He staggered up and clutched at the towel at the side of the bath. 'You ... you ... you shouldn't have done that ... you ... you ... '

He apparently couldn't think of a word terrible enough, and continued to stutter. Even amid the water that had splashed around us during my attack on him, I could see his eyes were filling with tears.

I wasn't interested in any more discussion. I turned away, almost tripping over his clothes, which he'd left in a pile by the bath. As I bent down to pick them up, that was when I felt it. A hard jab in the hand as my palm connected with something that was much tougher and sharper than cotton. For a second, I thought he'd secreted a knife in his jacket or trousers – to do what with I had no idea – and as I rummaged, I started to worry that he was actually deranged and planned to murder us in our beds. But it wasn't a knife. It was something far more terrible.

'What ... what is this?' I held up the object in my hand so he could see. 'Where ... How ... ?'

'Put that down, it's mine,' he said moodily.

'Where did you get it?' I said, almost breathless. I would have screamed the words if I could, but with every syllable I feared that I would faint.

Ernest was silent for a few seconds as he rubbed the towel over his hair. Then he said, 'It's something Rupert and Mary found down in the hidden garden. They must have dug up some dead creature or something.'

The room was spinning, and I dropped what I was holding so it fell to the ground, as my hands became incapable of holding on to anything at all.

Only small, horrendous bursts of memory of the hours that followed stayed with me. I must have exited the bathroom in some way and made my way down the stairs, although I'm astonished I had the ability to do so. I do remember crawling at one point, but I must have been on the ground floor by then, because guests started to crowd around me, trying to help me up. One woman shouted, 'I think she's fainted.' Another said, 'Is she hyperventilating? Should we call an ambulance?' At last, a voice I recognised sounded in my ear. 'Mrs Medlock, what's wrong?' It was Bessie. I gave her the one instruction I could think of – the only thing that I knew would stop me from falling for ever into the depths of my own oblivion: 'Get Mr Oakwood. Now.'

*

I was taken to one of the largely unused reading rooms down the corridor away from the main party areas. Bessie had disappeared off to get Mr Oakwood, while a kindly lady I vaguely recognised from cinema posters helped me stand and, with the help of a younger gentleman, guided me away from the staring guests. Mrs Kellman also put in an appearance, marching into the room and demanded to know why I had been crawling along the floor and wailing like a madwoman. I told her to fuck off. I hardly ever used coarse language like that, but in that instance I felt she was well and truly asking for it. Of course, it didn't help matters. I think she would have started shrieking if she hadn't been worried her guests would hear, but she made dark threats in a low, quiet tone about personally ensuring I would be dismissed by the Ashtons as soon as they returned home to England. I didn't respond, and she stalked off, lips pursed. I had no words left in me – or rather, the ones I did have needed to be saved for when Mr Oakwood arrived. I needed him so strongly, it almost hurt.

And he came. Although it felt like three lifetimes had passed since I'd been seated in the dimly lit little room away from the guests, I got the feeling that he had arrived with remarkable speed, because all of a sudden I was in his arms and sobbing desperately, deeply, violently, like nothing would ever console me. I heard him ask someone to step out and close the door. I did not know who – a guest, perhaps, or Bessie, or the mortified Mrs Kellman. Whoever it was did as they were asked and left me to cry into that iron-strong chest in private. For those outside, the show was over. But for Mr Oakwood and me, it was only just beginning.

'They've found them ... they ... they found them.' He knew what I meant, even before I clarified. I could feel it in his body. But still I went on, desperate to get the words out, as if leaving them unsaid would poison me. 'The children have been to the garden ... They've dug them up ... A hand. They brought back a little hand.'

Chapter 31

Recollections

Natalie

Mrs Medlock is clearly distressed. Part of me feels terribly out of my depth, unable to cope with everything she's told me and the emotional impact it's having on her. I don't know whether to go and get help somewhere, or stay with her – but I don't even know if there's anyone on hand to assist.

'This house,' she's saying now, muttering almost, rubbing her hands together as if she's cold. 'This big old house. It's so cavernous, so many rooms empty, so many others packed full of ... of ... baggage. It's a prison. It will always be a prison for me. But I can't leave. I belong here. I belong here. I ... '

Once again, I get the feeling she's only just remembering that I'm here, and her attention swings back round to me. 'You ... I'm so sorry, you poor girl, I can't imagine you'll ever want employment here if this is the sort of welcome you get. I do apologise. What Lord Ashton would say if he could see me like this, I shudder to think. I don't believe I can continue talking about this any further.' She stands, but I stay sitting. 'Come along, I'll give you a tour and show you where you'll be working. Unless ... unless I have put you off.' She sits down again, now looking concerned. 'I have, haven't I?'

'No,' I say, keen to reassure her. 'I'm staying, I promise. I just ... Well, could you finish telling me about ... about what was found in the garden?'

She sways in her chair and takes a deep breath, but doesn't say anything. I get the feeling her mind has gone elsewhere again.

'Please, Mrs Medlock. I really want to know.'

Her eyes flick straight back to mine and she speaks in a quiet, slightly rasping voice. 'You'll wish you never asked.'

Chapter 32

Dreams into Nightmares

Mrs Medlock, April 1979

Late evening turned into night. Night bled into dawn. And still I sat there. Mr Oakwood stayed with me, telling anyone who knocked to go away. I briefly wondered if Mr and Mrs Kellman were so appalled they would leave that night, rendering Bessie's preparations for the guest bedrooms pointless. Someone did try to speak to us through the door, but I didn't catch what they were saying and Mr Oakwood was adamant with them that I wasn't to be disturbed. He was like a guard dog, keeping the evil outside at bay. There was enough evil inside my head to contend with. Eventually, when I heard the clocks chime six in the morning and the sky began to brighten, he moved from his chair next to me and said, 'I'm going to have to go down to the garden. Now that it's light, we'll have a better idea about what we're dealing with.'

I nodded. I knew he was right. But the thought of him leaving filled me with a sense of loss so sharp, it was like I'd just been informed of his death. 'Come back,' I said.

'I will,' he promised. 'And you should go to bed and have some proper sleep. I can take you there first.'

I shook my head. The sooner he was gone, the sooner he would be back with me.

I let him go and walked slowly and timidly through the empty house, its corridors and stairwells still dark, yet to be touched by the rising red sun.

I think I managed to sleep for perhaps an hour, perhaps a little more. My thoughts drifted towards memories, memories turned into dreams, dreams morphed into nightmares. The feeling of my body losing something. The pain, the agony, then the relief when it was over. Hearing the baby's cries. It was like I was there again, with the first being born – I was there, so real, so vivid, and then I wasn't. The memory was swimming away from me. And the nightmare of the present returned, hitting me with all the force of an assailant attacking a screaming victim.

'I'm back,' said the voice that woke me. I opened my eyes to find Mr Oakwood standing there, dressed still in his normal gardening shirt and brown trousers, only now with the sleeves rolled up and traces of mud on his arms. 'I came as quick as I could. You're right. They did find them. The earth has been overturned. If they didn't dig them up, it's possible animals did and the kids just stumbled upon the bones. But I need your permission to do what I need to do. I didn't want to make the choice for you.'

I blinked at him, my vision still blurred with sleep and tears. 'What choice?'

'Of where to rebury them. We'd be wise to find a different site, in case the children took it into their minds to go back to the spot and look about once more.'

I was out of my bed in an instant and pointing my finger straight at him. 'They will never ... *never* go back to that garden, do you understand me? Never so long as I live in this house will those cursed brats go near that place again.' It was only after I'd finished that I realised I'd been shouting. Mr Oakwood's silence didn't help. He stood looking at me, although his eyes held pity rather than reproach. When he did speak, he did so in his usual calm, measured tone.

'I think you should talk to them. Make up some story about a family dog being buried there long ago. Something innocuous that will satisfy their little minds until they can move on to the next thing of interest.'

I sat on the corner of the bed and put my head in my hands. 'There won't be a next thing of interest, because they won't be leaving their rooms. I knew something like this would happen. Something awful. Every part of me was screaming against all these changes, this terrible anarchy that has been allowed to spread through the house.' I was sobbing again, the words tumbling from me as if I were running down a steep hill and struggling to keep balance.

'I think you should take some time to calm yourself, then we can talk to the children together.'

I knew Ernest would be the difficult one, so I left him till last. Mary was already awake and having breakfast with Bessie in the kitchen. I was tempted to tell her to go straight back to her room in light of the commotion she'd caused the night before. But instead, with the guidance of Mr Oakwood, I decided that playing the situation down would paper over our predicament more effectively. 'I need a word with you, Mary,' I said, standing over her as she sipped at a spoonful of porridge.

'She's very sorry,' Bessie cut in, unhelpfully. 'She's been telling me how bad she feels for what happened with the drinks tray and spilling it all down Mrs—'

I held up a hand. 'Thank you, Bessie, I'm sure Mary can speak for herself.' Although I had no wish to allow the girl to do so. I had to talk, because if I stopped I wasn't sure if I'd ever get through this. Trying to act natural and forget the weirdness of the situation, I pulled out two chairs from the table so Mr Oakwood and I could sit down.

'Is this about what we found in the garden?' She'd hit the nail on the head with such jolting accuracy, I was afraid I'd visibly flinched. She didn't show any signs of noticing, however. She just carried on eating her porridge, and I exchanged a look with Mr Oakwood.

'Yes, it is. I just wanted to check you weren't upset . . .' I paused, trying to find my footing on this new, caring tone I was adopting. 'I understand you found the bones of a dead dog that used to belong to a gardener here at Marwood, before Mr Oakwood came to work on the property. The man had the dog buried there, and it's quite possible some animals discovered the bones and you and Master Rupert found some of the . . . um . . . pieces.'

'And Ernest stole what we found,' she said, her brow knitted, her eyes on her bowl. She seemed less disturbed by the ordeal and more irritated by the older boy's actions.

'Yes, well, I've had words with him,' I said, my thoughts flying to an image of Ernest's shocked face as I whacked him the night before. 'And the dog will be reburied later today, so—'

'Can I come to the burial?' Mary asked, looking up, her eyes alive with excitement.

'Absolutely not,' I said, appalled. 'You're in enough trouble as it is. If you set one foot outside today, I swear to God, missy, you'll be lucky I don't lock you in your room and throw away the key.'

I stood up to leave at that point – I thought it would be best, before I started crying again. Images of dirt and stones and little bones all mingling together came into my head. And then a thought struck me. He still had it. That boy still had it . . . or it had been left on the bathroom floor.

I felt myself sway, and Mr Oakwood reached out to me. I vaguely pushed his hand away and shook my head. I needed to go and talk to Ernest. But before I could do that, another obstacle presented itself in the doorway.

'Are you sure it was a dog, Mrs Medlock?' Master Rupert stared at me, a frown creasing his forehead.

'Yes,' I said simply. He wasn't getting any discussion out of me. Not today. 'And you should be in your room, in bed, resting. I cannot believe you went gallivanting off into the night yesterday. If your parents knew ... ' I had no idea how to finish that sentence. Because there was now a mounting list of things that would trouble Lord and Lady Ashton if they knew them. Like the sight of me crawling across the floor shrieking and sobbing while some of the country's most eminent politicians, businessmen and celebrities watched on, baffled by the spectacle.

'My parents don't care about me,' Master Rupert said. He spoke in the manner of someone expecting to be challenged in some way. I didn't have the time or the strength. I pushed past him, snapping at Bessie as I went to 'Get him back to his room, *now*.'

I marched up the main stairs, barely conscious of Mr Oakwood following me. 'Where are we going?' he asked as we climbed. I didn't say anything, not until I got to Ernest's bedroom. I flung the door open, expecting the boy to be asleep. But instead he was sitting cross-legged on the bed, reading a book, fully dressed with his hair tidy and combed. The quiet, alert look about him startled me and made me pause, giving him time to look up. And then smile.

'Visitors? So early in the morning?' Not for the first time, his posh drawl reminded me of someone in a play, speaking lines he'd rehearsed or borrowed rather than put together himself.

'Yes,' I said, 'and we are here to retrieve something. Something important.'

I felt Mr Oakwood put a hand on my arm, perhaps to stop me getting worked up, but I stepped away from him.

'And what might that be, I wonder?' Ernest said, a smile playing around his lips.

I took a breath. 'I understand you took an ... an item from Master Rupert—'

The boy cut across me, 'Do you know, Mrs Medlock, you calling him Master Rupert sounds a bit condescending. I think he would soon grow up and become more of a man if you stopped babying him.'

Patience has never been a virtue of mine, and God help me, my fuse snapped once again, because within a second I was grabbing his jumper in my fist and pressing my face close to his. 'Where is it?' I hissed. But the boy just continued to smile.

'I don't know what you're talking about, Mrs Medlock.'

Chapter 33

What We Found

Mary, April 1979

That night I dreamed I was buried with bones all around me. Bones that made small snapping and clicking sounds, as if they were alive inside, alive in a secret way that only people who lay with them for a long time would ever find out. In my dream, I had been buried there for being bad. For disturbing them. My punishment was to lie with them and feel them clicking and tapping and scraping and getting closer, touching me, claw-like hands holding me down until I started to bruise and bleed and scream.

My own shouting woke me up. I was worried it would cause Mrs Medlock or Bessie to run into my room and tell me off for waking up the whole house so early, but nobody came. I got out of bed and looked out of the window. It was a misty morning, the sun barely alive, the day cold and new. I decided I wanted to talk to Rupert straight away about what had happened the night before, and I dashed through the house in my pyjamas, running up to his bedroom, pleased with every corridor I turned down that I wasn't faced with someone telling me off or trying to stop me.

Rupert wasn't happy to be woken. I raced into his room and jumped onto his bed, throwing off his quilt, hoping it would get him to talk quicker. 'Wake up,' I hissed in his ear, tapping his cheeks with my hand. He stretched his arms and legs deliberately, like someone doing a slow-motion run, then opened his eyes. 'What are you doing here this early? What time is it?'

'I think we should go and find it.'

'Find what?' he murmured, sounding irritated, closing his eyes again and settling his head down as if about to go back to sleep.

'Wake up!' I said loudly. This got him properly annoyed. He pulled himself up on his elbows and looked at me, his face cross.

'Give me my quilt, it's cold,' he said.

'No. Get it yourself. We're going to find Ernest and get him to give us back what we found. And then we're going to *look at it*.' I said this last bit with as much excitement as I could, because I was certain that by looking at our discovery, we'd somehow be able to tell its story and find out its secrets. As if it would whisper it to us like the bones in my dream.

Somewhere far down below, in one of the lower floors of the house, I heard a door close. Then a distant whirring sound started up.

'Bessie's probably awake,' Rupert said, yawning. 'Or it's Ernest's tutor, having his morning shower.'

I stood up. 'Then it's the best time to go and find Ernest, before his tutor makes him start his lessons.' I was annoyed he wasn't jumping into action, keen to solve this mystery.

'It's Sunday. He doesn't have lessons on a Sunday.' Rupert sounded bored and grumpy and lay back down again as if about to sleep once more.

'Why are you being so moody?' I asked.

He didn't answer for a bit, then he just said, 'Go off and find Ernest. It's clear you want to spend time with him rather than me.'

I stared at him. 'What? Don't be stupid. I came to find you first, not him.' He didn't reply, so I carried on. 'You're the one who wanted to show him what we found! You're the one who spoiled it all by getting him to be part of it. It's your fault Ernest took it and ran off. I think you're just cross with yourself for being so stupid in the first place.'

Again Rupert said nothing, but instead rolled over onto his other side so that I couldn't see his face any more. I waited, hoping he would eventually give in and talk, but he stayed quiet so I gave up. Muttering 'stupid' out loud one more time, because it made me feel better, I left him alone on his bed to go back to sleep and went to look for Ernest.

My plan to find him before I was discovered didn't work. Bessie caught me on the way downstairs and took me off to the kitchen, telling me I was to have breakfast at the table for once where she could keep an eye on me.

During breakfast, Mrs Medlock and Mr Oakwood came to talk to me about the night before. I thought about their explanation as I ate my porridge. I was pleased that the bones weren't human, which meant my horrible dream was just a horrible dream. But I also felt a bit disappointed. It was like I had been told I was suddenly not going to a party that I had been invited to. It was as if our mysterious discovery was something a bit dull. Although I couldn't help thinking: if our discovery was dull, why was Mrs Medlock so upset? Why did she look like she'd been crying all night?

Rupert must have got out of bed soon after I'd left, as he came down to the kitchen and listened to what was being said. I saw him standing in the corridor while Mrs Medlock was speaking. She was already in a bad mood because I'd just asked if I could go to the reburial of the dog's bones, and she carried on being stroppy when talking to Rupert in the doorway. Eventually she just pushed passed him, telling Bessie to take him back to his room.

I was also escorted to my room, but eventually I found a quiet moment to sneak out. I was still annoyed with Rupert and how he'd been with me that morning, so I decided to go and find Ernest instead. He wasn't in his room, or the library, and I couldn't see Mr Quint anywhere either. In the end, I found him sitting on the front steps to the house, scratching at the stone with a stick, looking as moody as Rupert had been.

'What's wrong?' I asked, sitting down next to him.

He let his breath out, puffing his cheeks as he did. 'Everything,' he said.

'Is this about the bone we found? Has Mrs Medlock told you off? Can I have it back?'

He threw me a disgusted look. 'This isn't about some stupid thing you found in your precious little garden with your sad little boyfriend.'

I was hurt by his words, but decided to carry on, 'That's good, because Mrs Medlock says it was the bones of a dog we found. Mr Oakwood is going to rebury it later today.' He said nothing to this, so I tried again. 'Why are you angry?'

More scratching of the stick on the stone. Then he said, 'My parents. They left in the night without telling me. I woke up and they'd gone. They barely spoke to me and then they left without even saying ...'

'Goodbye,' I said, finishing the sentence for him. I wasn't sure what to say, but then something came into my head that I thought might help. 'My parents didn't say goodbye to me either. I think it's because they didn't want it to be goodbye. I think they hoped they would get better. But I think they did know it was goodbye. And said it without even saying it. They meant it, but just didn't say the words. Perhaps your parents didn't need to say goodbye because they knew you knew they would say it anyway. Does that make sense?'

A few seconds went past, then he said, 'No,' flatly, and got up.

'Where are you going?' I called after him.

'To talk to Mr Quint,' he said.

Chapter 34

Everything's Going to Change

Mrs Medlock, April 1979

I should have controlled my temper. And I shouldn't have treated a child that way, not even an arrogant wretch like Ernest. Knowing what we know now, I suppose he was a sort of victim himself. But at the time, I just felt pure rage. Mr Oakwood stopped me before I could do anything too damaging, removing my hand from the boy and muttering in my ear to leave and let him deal with this. I didn't listen. I just carried on shouting at Ernest as he sat there grinning, pleased as Punch that he was getting such an entertaining reaction from me. In the end, Mr Oakwood had to lead me away. I was furious, of course, as I just wanted to slap the boy silly until that smug smile vanished for ever.

'Listen,' Mr Oakwood said to me once we'd reached the privacy of the stairwell of the servants' corridor. 'Flying into a rage isn't going to help matters. He's clearly a crafty little prick, but you don't want to give him the satisfaction. The whole point of us telling little Mary and Master Rupert that it was a dog they discovered was to try to put the subject to bed. You acting like this is only going to make it clear that the whole thing is a lot more significant and a lot more interesting than they guessed in the first place.'

I knew he was right, but I was still enraged. Seeing me trembling, he suggested I try to get some rest and allow him to sort out the reburial down in the garden, then he'd wash and change and come back up to see me. A strong tug made me desperate to go with him, the sense that I should be there to oversee what he did almost overpowering my exhaustion and anxiety. Almost. But not quite. So I gave in to sleep – a deeper, more powerful sleep than I'd known in some time. He left me to rest and went down to the garden to do what needed to be done. I didn't dream.

I didn't wake for hours, and when I did, I could tell by the light that the day had slipped from morning to late afternoon. The clock by the side of the bed told me it was nearly 4 p.m., and a tray sat a small distance away from it containing a plate of cheese and pickle sandwiches and a glass of orange juice. I ate greedily, suddenly ravenous, grateful to whoever had provided me with immediate sustenance. Once I'd finished, I got up, changed and went downstairs.

I was about to cross the hallway and set off down to the garden when the telephone rang. I hovered for a moment, wondering if Bessie would race to answer it, but no footsteps sounded, so I went to take the call.

'Oh good, it's you,' said the person at the other end. I could tell straight away from the irritating, slightly high-pitched upper-class voice who it was.

'Yes, it's me, Lady Ashton,' I said, wishing I'd just let the phone ring out. Suddenly I knew what was coming, and I really wasn't prepared for it.

'Well, I'm glad I caught you before you went off to some sort of institution.'

A few beats of silence passed as I digested this. 'Er ... institution?'

'Yes,' she said, her tone fake sweet. 'I presumed after your display yesterday evening in front of some of the most important people in the country that you must have been taken off to a safe establishment where they can monitor your breakdown and keep you away from sharp implements. For your own safety, of course. I must say, ever since taking the call from Mrs Kellman this morning, I've been very worried about you. I presume you have somewhere to recover? It's probably best, actually, if you *don't* return. A scandal like this is best just swept aside for good, rather than be allowed to linger. And you do linger, Mrs Medlock. You've lingered at Marwood Manor for far too long.'

I could feel my pulse racing, the temporary sense of peace I'd gained after my deep sleep vanishing with horrible speed. But then something remarkable happened, something that happens so rarely as to be unparalleled when one experiences it: I knew exactly what to say. The words came to me, and I spoke with clarity and precision, as if I'd been rehearsing this moment for years.

'Lady Ashton,' I said, trying to mirror her tone, 'I have no plans to check myself into any institution, because I am not insane or in need of recuperation. I had a small upset last night. I regret it spilled out into a public arena and apologise for causing you embarrassment. May I ask if you've spoken to Lord Ashton about this?'

Silence for almost ten seconds. Then: 'He has been informed.' The honey-sweet tone had gone.

'And your suggestion that I go away and never return – have you run that past him? Is he of the same opinion?'

Further silence. When she didn't reply, I pressed on. 'I would hazard a guess he hasn't suggested – nor would he condone – any such plan.'

'He will,' she said, speaking at last. 'I'll tell him we have no choice.' She was almost spitting her words out now, and they arrived in my ear like tight little crackles, travelling down the international phone line all the way from her comfortable New York home. I could imagine her now, sitting on a sofa, clutching whatever expensive throw she'd recently purchased.

'Well, in the unlikely event that he is of a similar opinion, I would ask you to do me a favour,' I said, continuing my calm approach. 'Could you please remind him of these three things. First, I was in the house on the eighteenth of December 1971 when he and two other men welcomed the Member of Parliament John Lloyd-Hughes into the library at Marwood Manor. They talked to him for a while and then led him out of the front door and into a car. As you may recall, his body was discovered hanging from a tree in the New Forest the following morning. Secondly, he will remember the files in the top drawer of his desk in a folder marked Clover Shore Construction. I'm sure he's moved them now, but they made for very interesting reading a few years ago – something I'm sure both the police and the Inland Revenue would find utterly riveting. And lastly,' I took a deep breath, having to steel myself to say this part, but carried on quickly before she could interject, 'please could you just say out loud to him the date the second of October 1959. He'll know exactly what that means. I think you'll find that once you've ... jogged his memory, your husband won't support any steps to remove me from Marwood Manor.'

I put the phone down, savouring the rush of adrenaline. I'm not a weak, timid person, but it took a lot of nerve to say all those things to Lady Ashton. Things I'd kept buried and secret for so long. Things that caused me pain to say. Especially when I knew they would do some damage if she decided to mention them to her husband. But part of me suspected she wouldn't be in a hurry to do so. She turned a blind eye to things. She knew his history wasn't all that rosy. Raising the spectre of the past has consequences, and Lady Ashton wasn't one for consequences if they got in the way of a cocktail party at the Savoy or a dress fitting in Chelsea.

My feeling of achievement soon dissipated, however, as I crossed the lawn and headed towards the garden. Of course, I could have just waited for Mr Oakwood to return to the house, but I was ... there's no other way to explain it ... *pulled* there. It was a physical urge I couldn't deny, no matter how much I tried to put off the need to go, to convince myself I should stay in the house. By the time I was walking through the wooden door and towards the centre of the enclosed space, I was struggling to stop trembling.

Oddly, though, when Mr Oakwood called out to me and I went to stand next to him as he showed me the little grave he'd dug, my shaking stopped. A stillness came over me as he gently and carefully pushed the earth back into the ground on top of a little bundle, assuring me there was nothing in sight that would upset me. He was right, there wasn't. And although I was silent and calm, my heart still broke with the sadness, the pain, the sense of loss and the memory of how it felt twenty years ago when I lost my three little babies. My tears weren't the hysterical shrieks all the guests heard as I scrabbled around the floor the night before. They were probably barely noticeable, but they were there, cutting pathways down my cheeks, until eventually my eyes clouded so completely I had to close them.

I felt Mr Oakwood's hand on mine first, before I saw him. He'd moved around to my side while I had my eyes shut and he encouraged me to lean on him. 'I know it must hurt,' he said, so gently it was almost a whisper, 'but it's done now. It's easy for me to say the past is the past – easy compared to what you've been through. But it's the truth now. They're back in the ground, as if this last day and night never happened.'

I was about to say something about the children – about how we mustn't let them dig for flowers or even play in the garden at all. How we must lock them up, keep them away from this place, because all that this garden was good for was sadness and hopelessness, and I didn't want them mixed up in that. While I'm very sure Mr Oakwood knew my thoughts on all that, I didn't get a chance to speak them out loud. Because we were interrupted by voices.

'I'm not sure where they found them, I wasn't with them, remember? But I'm sure we'd find the turned-up earth or something.'

That was Ernest's voice. And he was speaking to someone. I couldn't for the life of me think who. His parents? I felt a sudden flash of panic spark through me as I remembered Mrs Kellman's mortified face the night before. But they'd gone home, I'd been told that much. So really there were only two realistic candidates. Bessie, or . . .

'Well, well, well, this looks like an interesting gathering.'

Mr Quint said these words while drawing himself up like a hunter who'd just caught his prey. Not for the first time, I was struck by how cruel and unpleasant his handsome features made him look when he smirked like that. I opened my mouth to speak, but he continued talking as he walked purposefully towards us. 'May I see what you two have been doing so secretly down here?'

'You may not,' Mr Oakwood said. 'And I'd like to point out that this garden is out of bounds.'

'Out of bounds?' Mr Quint repeated, as if he'd never heard anything so ridiculous in his life. 'Why, the children have been playing in here for a good number of weeks now. If it's fine for *them* to run free, I don't see why I should be kept out.'

Mr Oakwood's hand started to tighten on me, perhaps to hold me back, but I pushed him off. 'You are a tutor, Mr Quint. Your place is in the library, and when you're not in there, you're to stay in your room.'

He laughed at me with a mixture of hilarity and astonishment, as if a cat had just started playing the piano in front of him. 'You really are right in what you say about her,' he said, looking over at Ernest. The boy smirked back. There was an excited look on his face, like he was waiting for something.

'Go back to the house,' Mr Oakwood said, a hard warning note to his voice that would have caused most normal people to tread carefully. But Mr Quint wasn't normal. We'd soon be finding out how *ab*normal he was.

'Ah, you see, I think we've reached the end of you two acting like you're somehow above me in this fantasy hierarchy you've made up for yourselves. We'll go through that a bit more later on, but first ... ' The tutor reached into his trouser pocket and brought out what looked like a sock. It was deep burgundy, with a crest on the side denoting whatever London clothes company it had come from. I recognised it as one of Ernest's. Mr Quint unravelled it, turning it upside down with his palm underneath, and something fell out into his open hand.

I felt sick. I wanted to turn to Mr Oakwood, beg him to sort this out. But all I could do was stare at the piece of bone in Mr Quint's hand, with the smug, satisfied faces of both tutor and student framed in my peripheral vision.

'This,' said Mr Quint, 'is the hand and part of an arm of a child. Perhaps even a baby. It's missing a finger, which I presume fell off when it was disturbed. Ernest and I have had a very educational lesson about human bones. It was good of him to bring me such an unusual real-life example. But you see, I think you both know about this. From what Ernest has told me, the discovery of this little thing has caused quite a stir among the two of you.'

Some seconds of silence passed between us, until I asked the question he was surely waiting for. 'What do you want?'

'Well, I would say money,' he said, the slow drawl to his voice making it clear he was enjoying holding court and having us at his mercy. 'But to be honest, money bores me rotten. It really does. There *are* things I want, however. Things I'm going to insist happen if we're going to hush all this up. Why don't you both accompany me up to the house? I'm going to lay out the new regime for how the place is run. To put it simply: everything's going to change.'

Chapter 35

Their Little Bones

Mrs Medlock, April 1979

Things really did change. I have to make it clear that, like I said at the start of all this, my memory is not what it was, and although a lot of what happened during that spring is seared into my mind, the next stage is a bit foggy. I don't think it's the passing of time that's done it, I think it's the experiences themselves. Or experience. Because it does feel like one thing. One nightmare. A long, winding nightmare that feels both infinite and fleeting at the same time. It's disorienting, that's the word for it. Not just scary, even though it was, and upsetting, which it also was, but it made everything feel mixed up and surreal. We were trapped in a horror story and couldn't find our way out. Of course, there *was* a way out. Eventually. But it came at a terrible, terrible price. We'll get to that in due course. In short, this isn't a tale for the squeamish, the prudish, or those who are easily shocked. I used to be all those things, so to live through something that ticked every box ended up taking its toll on me in many respects.

I suppose, in a way, we were a country in miniature – a country under revolution, where one regime was toppled and replaced with another, more extreme order with sinister intentions. It steadily became clear to us what type of a man Mr Quint was. There had been clues, of course – clues that I kicked myself later for not following up on or properly investigating. First was the fact that he was sexually promiscuous. I know the modern way is to turn a blind eye to that, or even celebrate it, but his behaviour was beyond the pale. He had brought those two young women back to his room on that previous occasion, and had also started a relationship with Bessie.

The second clue, and perhaps more disturbingly, was whatever had gone on involving Ernest during that night of the tutor's liaison with the two women. Ernest was so young – barely even fourteen – and the line between boyhood and manhood should not be crossed. I had a suspicion it had been, but apart from discussing my concerns with Mr Oakwood, I had done nothing to protect the boy. Of course, evidence-wise, I had very little to back me up, only suspicion. Maybe the tobacco scent had floated in from Mr Quint's room during the night when the boy had opened his door to visit the bathroom. Perhaps he had stolen some cigarettes and tried them out himself illicitly. Not ideal, of course, and not something to be encouraged, but hardly a scandal. But there was something about that night that just made me ... well ... uneasy. I still blame myself for not acting on my suspicions sooner. So much might have been avoided. And a life might have been saved.

The afternoon when Mr Quint led us to the library gave me the feeling of being pushed off a cliff. I think it was the mounting sense of horror and realisation. Realisation that I was cornered. He made it quite clear that all his wishes had to be obeyed, or he would call the police and tell them that the body of a baby had been discovered secretly buried in the garden of Marwood Manor. He hadn't worked out the full truth. Hadn't realised it was more than one at that point. That came later.

Mr Oakwood, Bessie, Ernest and myself sat in the library, getting mud from the garden (or in Bessie's case, flour from the kitchen) on the carpet and chairs while he explained that in order for him to stay silent, he had specific demands. We had to allow him to bring in any visitors he wanted at any time to the house. We had to assure anyone who called on the telephone, such as Lord or Lady Ashton or Ernest's parents, that everything was normal. He had been assured that the Ashtons wouldn't be returning before the end of May, and any attempts to expedite their return would result in a call to the police. If they suddenly decided to come home early, this too would trigger a call to the police, so it was within our interests to try and put them off if we became aware of such plans. Any attempts to contact the Kellmans would, of course, have the same outcome. Among his other demands was the instruction that Ernest was to have the run of the house and do exactly what he wanted at any time, and not be ordered about by anyone other than him. The two other children were to be kept under control, mostly to their rooms, and not allowed to disrupt any 'proceedings'.

'*What* proceedings?' I asked. 'What on earth—'

He raised a hand to cut me off. A pale, carefully manicured hand, I noticed. The polar opposite to Mr Oakwood's rough, well-used ones, tanned from years of outdoor work.

'That will become clear over the next few days.'

Chapter 36

Strange Arrangements

Mrs Medlock, April 1979

Everything did become clear. And we just sat back and let it happen. Mr Oakwood pressed me to rebel, to phone Lord Ashton and tell him something strange was going on with the tutor the Kellmans had engaged. Get him to throw the vile young man out of the house for good. But I couldn't. He knew I couldn't. And so he accepted that we just had to wait it out and hope at some point the Ashtons would come home and put an end to it all – just not so early that Mr Quint would follow through on his threats.

Very soon after his little speech, Mr Quint did something I found so upsetting I could barely bring myself to think about it. He went back down to the garden to rummage around in the newly dug graves. It actually made me vomit when I discovered he'd done that, when he came back and told me what he'd found. 'Well, well, Mrs Medlock,' he'd said, brushing soil from his hands, 'there are more secrets buried there than I first presumed. Very interesting.' He smirked as he said it, then went to clean himself up. 'Oh, and by the way, I've taken the evidence for safe keeping. You'll never find them. Just thought I'd mention it, in case you planned your own little hurried excavation.'

That was when I'd been sick. I raced to the kitchen and threw up in the sink. I couldn't bear the thought that he'd touched the little bones. Gathered the pieces together. And hidden them away so we couldn't relocate them in secret.

The first person to arrive was a young man called Gary. I opened the door to him. He was a tall chap, pleasant-looking in a forgettable sort of way, and despite his height his face still had the smoothness of youth. I guessed he was around nineteen or twenty. He was wearing a coat, jumper and jeans, all of which were a tad scruffy and could have done with replacing, although his aftershave – a strong, evident scent that filled the room – was woody and fresh, the sort of thing I'd imagine an older, more professional man would wear. 'I . . . er . . . can I help you?' I asked as he strode in, looking around, apparently impressed by the house.

He stopped with a jolt. 'Sorry, I didn't mean to barge in – as you can tell, I'm a bit new to all this.'

None of this made any sense to me, so I just nodded, waiting for further explanation. I presumed, of course, that the visitor was something to do with Mr Quint, but I hadn't yet worked out what. If I had known, I'd have told this rather innocent-looking boy to run as far away from the house as his long legs could carry him.

'So do you . . . Are you a member, or do you run the house?' I saw his eyes scan my clothes, probably guessing I didn't own the place.

'I'm the housekeeper, Mrs Medlock,' I replied.

'Gary,' he said, offering his hand to shake. 'Sorry, I should have introduced myself at the door before I came in.' He had a slight West Country edge to his voice and seemed a touch breathless. I was about to ask where he had come from and why he was here when the creak of the stairs behind me made me turn around.

'Ah, our first arrival. Lovely to see you – Gary, isn't it?' Mr Quint approached with the confidence of a man at home in his own castle. Anyone would think he'd lived here all his life. He reached out and took the young man's hand, ignoring me completely. 'Where was it we last spoke? Don't tell me ... At the meeting at Dolphin Square? Or was it the one on Wynford Road?'

'Wynford Road,' Gary said, nodding. 'I'm honoured you remembered me and asked me to join.'

Mr Quint was looking at the young man in a way that made me think of a spider observing a fly. His intensity was disturbing, and perhaps Gary felt it too, as he awkwardly started gabbling about his bags. He had indeed been carrying quite a lot – a full suitcase that looked like it would burst at any moment, and something bulky but soft-looking wrapped in plastic. He'd left them both by the door as he'd walked in, and Mr Quint nodded at me, and then at the objects, his meaning obvious.

I sighed and picked them up. 'Which room?' I asked, hating myself for obeying his orders.

'Oh, Gary will be sleeping in the library with the other men.' He walked purposefully towards the doorway leading into the library, adding with a flick of his hand, 'The women will be in the drawing room. Or perhaps that connecting smaller library. There will be fewer of them, but still a good number.'

I followed, struggling with the suitcase and the plastic-wrapped thing, which by the look of some material poking out the end was either a thick quilt or a sleeping bag.

'I decided it would be beneficial if we all slept in the same room, rather than each having our own space as if we were in a hotel. That's much too dull, and would lead us to think rather selfishly. Privacy is the enemy. We need to connect, understand, inspire . . . '

He was talking nonsense, I thought, as I settled Gary's belongings on one of the armchairs. I watched with dread-filled fascination as Mr Quint and Gary started rearranging the furniture, shifting sofas to the sides and moving desks. Then the young man unwrapped his sleeping bag, settling it in a corner of the room. As they chatted away to each other, I tried to piece together the things I heard, but it was difficult. Very few specifics were mentioned, but I gathered they'd encountered each other at a meeting in London and were part of some sort of club, with members mostly based in the south-east, though Gary was from Bristol. What all of this meant, I didn't know. It would have been nice to be prepared for the things I would end up seeing, but all of it was so odd and puzzling I ended up walking out, muttering that I needed to oversee the dinner.

In the kitchen, I told Bessie about the new arrival. She'd had a worried, strained look on her face for two days, ever since Mr Quint had taken over the running of the house. I'd tried to get her to talk about it, but she'd either evaded my questions or changed the subject. She seemed to think denial was the best way to go. Perhaps she was hurt he hadn't involved her in his plans, or maybe he was being cool with her now he was in the midst of executing whatever strange arrangements were going on in the library.

The children, however, were harder to handle. 'Who was at the door?' Rupert asked as I ran his bath for him later that evening.

'Nothing to do with you,' I said, feeling the temperature of the water. I left the room while he bathed and went to tell Mary that it was time to start getting ready for bed. She had her head buried in a book, which turned out to be an obscure illustrated history of Victorian fashion.

'What's going on?' she asked. She'd picked up on the change of atmosphere in the house, and had no doubt spotted me and Bessie acting oddly.

'Nothing,' I said, trying not to snap, 'There are some people coming, that's all.'

I saw her frowning at this. 'Another party?'

'Sort of,' I said, shortly. I drew the curtains and cleared away some books and clothes while she put her pyjamas on and went to do her teeth.

Once both children were settled in bed, I hesitated outside Ernest's room. I hadn't paid attention to his sleeping habits over the past two nights – not since his allegiance to Mr Quint had been made so clear. But as I got to his door, I noticed it wasn't properly closed and the room was in darkness. Taking care not to creak the hinges, I edged it open very slowly to take a look. There wasn't much to see – the room was empty. Too empty. It wasn't only Ernest who was absent from it; his quilt and pillow had vanished as well. It took me a few moments for everything to slot into place, then I realised what must be going on.

I strode with determination down the main staircase and towards the library. The door was open, and Ernest, already in his pyjamas, was laying out his duvet to the right of where Gary had settled. Mr Quint was making himself a bed too, presumably from bedclothes taken from his own room.

'Why is Ernest here?' I asked the room at large. Gary looked up straight away – he'd been partly hidden by a sofa, but now I saw he'd changed into a black top and some grey pyjama bottoms. Mr Quint was in his underwear and a white T-shirt. It's important, all this, because disorientating as things were, there was still some essence of normality. Nothing *too* extreme had occurred. Yet. At this point it was just two men and a teenage boy camping out in the library. Rather odd, certainly. But nothing illegal or obscene. They even had mugs of cocoa or tea (I presumed Bessie had been instructed to bring them), and the reading lamps on the desks and tables had been turned on; to be honest, it all looked very cosy. But I knew there was something strange afoot; I was suspicious of any plans of Mr Quint's by default.

None of the three answered my question straight away. Ernest pretended I hadn't spoken, Gary clearly heard me but didn't seem to think it was his place to answer, and Mr Quint seemed to take great pleasure in making me wait as he straightened his pillow on the floor, next to one of the cabinets housing rare copies of *Grimms' Fairy Tales* and *The Arabian Nights*. Eventually he straightened up. 'Mrs Medlock, it's time we said goodnight.' He gave me his best aren't-I-so-handsome smile – the one that always made me want to slap him – and waited for me to leave. I did no such thing.

'Why is the boy here?' I asked again. Behind me I heard Ernest sigh, as if I were a slow child in class who was holding up the rest from going off to their lunch break.

'Ernest is a member,' Mr Quint said simply.

I looked over at Ernest, who was now lying back on his makeshift bed, his hands behind his head, staring up at the ceiling, apparently as relaxed as someone on a beach. 'A member of what?'

This question resulted in a scoffing sound from Mr Quint and a short laugh from the Gary fellow on the floor. I realised it was unlikely I was going to get a proper answer, so I decided to stop with the questions and make something clear. 'Look, I don't know what sort of strange *club* you've started for yourself here—'

'Started?' Mr Quint said, raising his eyebrows. 'Nothing's *started* here, Mrs Medlock. We were already in being. Have been for a long time: seekers of truth, seekers of our true selves, seekers of the dark core of the universe hidden behind the trivial performance of everyday life. And I'm no founder or architect of all this. I can't take any credit for our assembly. But I told you the first time we met that I was good at seizing opportunities when they arose. Well, I've seized an opportunity here. And I plan to make the best of it. If others choose to follow me as a reward for my ingenuity and initiative, who am I to argue?'

I stared back at him. Unable to think of any direct response to all this, I chose to bring the subject back to the main cause of concern: the child. 'Some weeks ago,' I said, trying to give my voice a boost of authority, 'I noticed the scent of smoke in Ernest's room. Either cigarettes or something else. I don't know if he was the one smoking – perhaps someone had given him material with which to do so – but I want to make it quite plain: it is to never happen again while you are under this roof.' Although I directed my words to the room as a whole, I finished by resting my gaze squarely on Mr Quint, trying not to blink.

The young man took a few steps so that he was right in front of me. I could smell his aftershave – something more aggressive and masculine than the one I'd noticed on Gary earlier. His eyes were moving in a roving, circling movement, giving the impression he was taking me in, assessing me. The smirk that spread across his face suggested he remained unimpressed with what he saw. 'From now on, I advise you to choose your words very carefully, Mrs Medlock,' he said. 'Because if you don't, I'm going to get creative about your role in this house. You, and Bessie, and that monosyllabic cunt down in his weird little hut. You'll all be dancing to my tune so enthusiastically, you'll wear yourselves out.' We looked each other in the eye, mutual hatred throbbing in the air between us. Then he turned away and went to sit cross-legged on his bed. 'By the way, can you send Bessie in? We need some more refreshment.' His tone had ceased to be low and threatening and gone back to dismissive, almost bored. He tilted his head towards the door, making it clear I was to leave.

'I can get you refresh—'

'I said Bessie,' he said, a harder note returning to his words.

I didn't stay to argue. I walked out of the room, not looking at the other two, and went back to the kitchen to find Bessie. I wondered whether I should give her Mr Quint's instructions or shield her as best I could from whatever strange games he was playing. I didn't want to send her into that room.

The whole situation with Mr Quint had created a strange atmosphere between me and the maid. We'd never been chatty or exactly friends – we just had a comfortable way of working together, with her occasionally talking away without expecting me to reply, or me giving her stern reprimands if she got something wrong. But now we seemed to have drifted into an uncomfortable silence – a symptom of how quickly things had changed over the past few days. To be honest, just my breakdown at the party might have been enough to make things awkward between us, but the developments with Mr Quint had added a level of tension to the air. That and the fact that the girl clearly had her suspicions about what he had discovered down in the garden. I was certain that whatever explanation she had cooked up in her brain, it was bound to be incorrect. If I'd been certain I could have got through the story without crying, I would have tried to give her a very basic retelling of what had happened here all those years ago. A retelling that wouldn't incriminate me or the man I loved. But I knew that was an impossibility. It could give way to more questions than answers. So at that point, I was set on choosing the easier path. Silence and secrets.

I did eventually give Bessie the instruction from Mr Quint, telling her to take in whatever drinks or food they wanted, then leave. I would go up to the library with her, wait outside, then meet her when she came back out. I didn't know if I was going to keep up this protective stance during the weeks ahead, or if it was just tonight, while I was feeling particularly unsettled. I just wanted to be sure nothing terrible was going to happen.

Whatever I intended, the plan didn't work. As soon as we reached the hallway, I heard scampering footsteps above, and caught sight of a flash of light-coloured material. A dressing gown. 'Bloody Mary,' I said, running to catch her, any thoughts of staying with Bessie driven from my mind. I saw the little girl disappearing up the stairs towards the second floor, and followed, cursing as I went. Of all the evenings to misbehave, why did she have to choose this one? When I got to her room, I found her under her blankets, pretending to be asleep. I could tell she'd only just managed to fall into the covers by the way her dressing gown was half sprawled over the edge of her bed, where she must have flung it.

'Mary, I beg you,' I said to the girl, her eyes still closed, 'stay in your room. It's very, very important you stay in your room.' I got no response from her. Whereas before I would have shaken her until she admitted her wrongdoing, on that night I couldn't face any kind of opposition from her.

As I left the bedroom, I pulled out my large bundle of keys from my front pocket. It was a pointless thing to do – I knew the chance of me having a key for this inconsequential bedroom was remote – but I still glanced through them in hope. There was a large writing desk in one of the spare rooms on the third floor that had a drawer full of keys along with various other bits and bobs. I'd always meant to spend a quiet rainy day trying them all out on the various doors and getting them sorted, but after twenty years that rainy day had never arrived, and I reproached myself strongly for putting the task off.

The drama of the evening hadn't finished; indeed, it had only just got started. From my viewpoint on the landing, I saw Bessie walking quickly in the direction of the kitchen. I hastened to follow her, wondering what could have happened in the short time it had taken me to check on Mary. I found her clattering about with some pans in the kitchen, trying to be busy while at the same time dabbing at her eyes.

'What's wrong?' I asked as I walked in. 'What did they say to you?'

'Nothing,' she said with a sniff.

'Well it's obviously not nothing,' I said, walking round so that I was standing beside her as she lifted two saucepans into the sink and turned on the tap. 'Tell me.'

A few more sniffs followed, then she said, 'He's changed. It's ... it's like he's someone else.'

I digested this. The awful man had clearly tricked Bessie into thinking he was some sort of hot ticket – perhaps even a way out of her life of low pay and limited expectations. I'd been wise to him from the moment he set foot here. Not that I'd ever dreamed things would spiral this far out of control; it was more that I just knew he was a man you couldn't trust – that behind his handsome, smiling face, a beast snarled back.

'Come on, leave that and sit down,' I said, as patiently as I could, steering Bessie away from the sink and into a chair. The water continued to gush away behind us, but I let it run. Its noise gave the room a sense of activity, a safety blanket protecting us from our predicament.

'What happened in the library just now?' I asked quietly.

The poor girl dabbed at her eyes, then straightened up. 'Mr Quint ... he wanted to ... wanted to ... '

She didn't need to finish the sentence. I felt a chill run down my arms, and my back went tense. 'You mean ... in the library?'

She nodded, 'It's hard ... I can't say too much. I don't want to lose my job ... '

'You're not going to use your job,' I said firmly. 'Just tell me everything.'

Chapter 37

Regrets

Mrs Medlock, April 1979

Bessie gave me a fuller story than I'd expected. She detailed the affair she'd been having with Mr Quint – well, I suppose affair is the wrong word, since neither of them was married. Liaison, perhaps? Regardless, it had all started very early on; his first night in the house. I'm not going to lie about how shocked I was when I heard this. But it was one of just many shocking things that had happened – or would happen – in this house, and in the grand scheme of things it pales into insignificance. I still raised an eyebrow when she told me, though.

'He was just so charming and ... what's the word ... touchy-feely ... tactile, that's it. Not, like, naughty gropey, just laying a hand on my arm or my shoulder when I brought him food in his room and stuff like that. The first evening he was here, he asked me to show him around, and I thought, well, there's no harm in it. We went for a look around the outside of the house, and there was a full moon and we stopped to look at it. I was cold and he offered to wrap his jacket round me. He said when the moon was full like that, one should make love beneath it. I was shocked, but he was serious. Then I told him that ... that ... well ... that I'd never done it before. And he said there was nothing to it, and then he was kissing me and I was kissing him, and he led me over to the trees and we kissed again, and then he was pulling down his trousers and pulling up my skirt and ... we did it up against one of the old oaks. He didn't force me or anything, I wanted to do it. It was just so exciting. All of it. It was like I was in a film. Not just boring old me with my boring life, same thing every day. He made me interesting that night, or made me feel like I *could* be interesting ... like someone men would want.'

I rubbed at my eyes, more to allow me to avert my gaze than because I especially needed to. 'You could have been seen,' I said, and I couldn't help the note of reproach that crept into my voice.

'I know,' she said quickly. 'I'm sorry, I'm really sorry, I was just caught up in the moment, you know?'

I knew. Of course I knew what she meant. But I wasn't about to tell her that, or share my own experiences of being caught up in the moment. And anyway, I was growing increasingly impatient to get to the heart of what had happened in the library tonight that had upset her. 'I'd suspected things had been ... going on,' I said. 'Mr Oakwood spotted you.'

A look of horror filled her face and she raised a hand to her mouth, clearly appalled.

'Calm down,' I said quickly. 'He's not one to judge. But if you were having an ongoing ... thing with Mr Quint, I imagine this very odd situation we're now in is rather ... difficult?'

She looked like she was going to properly cry now. 'Yes. He's been so lovely. *Was* so lovely. Things started to go wrong when he brought those two women home from town. He did it to punish me. Because I said I wouldn't lie to you and pretend I was going to visit my old foster parents in Taunton. He wanted me to go away with him to Paris for a weekend. And I couldn't do that, leave the country without telling you – I don't even know where my passport is. I think I've lost it, or it's out of date. I've never been abroad, you see. So when I said I couldn't, he went off in a right huff, and then ...'

I nodded. 'I see. Well, I should have thrown him out when that all happened. It's one of several major regrets that I didn't.'

Bessie rummaged for a tissue and blew her nose loudly, then wiped again at her eyes and carried on. 'After that, I didn't want to see him any more. But I couldn't resist. He was so charming; he said he was sorry and wanted it to be just us from then on. I don't want to go into detail, but it became a routine. After he'd finished teaching Ernest for the day, I'd go into the library and ... well ... we'd do stuff right there at the desk where he taught his lessons. So anyway, tonight, when I went in with the refreshments, he patted the seat at the desk and said, "Come on then ... assume the position," and the other two, that new bloke and Ernest, they laughed ... They all laughed, and they seemed to know what he was talking about, so he must have told them.'

Her tears flowed freely and she struggled to stop herself sobbing. 'Why is he doing this? What was it he found in the garden that means we can't just phone Lord and Lady Ashton and tell them to make him leave?'

Part of me had expected Bessie to ask me this. And all of me had hoped she wouldn't.

Chapter 38

Mrs Medlock's Diary

September 1958–February 1959

5 September 1958

We made love down in the garden this afternoon. Although the season is on the turn and the leaves have already started to fall, the sun was warm, as it had been back in July. He was less awkward this time. Less bothered about me, in some ways, but I liked that. It felt like he was more interested in his own pleasure, whereas before I got the sense he was partly embarrassed for a member of his staff to see him in such an intimate way. It was nice to feel him let go. That harsh, stiff frame finally relaxing and falling into me, moving on top of me. And even though I'm sure it was only his pleasure he had in mind in that moment, he was very much pleasuring me in a constellation of different ways: both in my body and in my mind, and with thoughts of what could happen as a result - all of this swirling around in my head. I was becoming part of him, and he part of me.

If only my parents could see me now, I thought, when we were done and he was pulling up his trousers. Fornicating with the young son of the manor house. The future lord of the manor. They would be appalled, of course, and shocked. But there was something delicious in the thought of that: of them being shocked that I should ever do something so reckless. They'd always implied I was boring and plain, too bookish and obsessed with hard work. I was a puzzle to them, although not quite interesting enough to be a concern. Well, what I did today was interesting. Nobody could deny that.

6 September 1958

Honoria wanted to have tea on the thin gallery balcony in the library today. I thought it an odd place, but she often likes to squeeze herself into tight, unusual spaces to do ordinary things, like reading in the pantry, much to the chagrin of Mrs Grose, who says a cook should be free to make food for a household without finding members of the family crouching in cupboards or devouring Dickens up against the jams and preserves. I told her that Honoria never read Dickens; she read modern novels about interesting young women, or fairy stories for children. That earned me a light clip round the ear.

We had a wonderful afternoon sharing tea on the balcony, sitting cross-legged on the floor on a blanket, occasionally peering through the wooden railings to the room below, as if we were royalty surveying our kingdom. When she asked me what it had been like with her husband, it didn't feel strange and I didn't mind answering. I said it had been fine, and she laughed and said, 'Gosh, I hope he improves as time goes on. Fine isn't what he should be aiming for!' But I told her that if it got the job done, I would be content. And she said she would be too. We are united in our desire, our desperate need for a child to be born at Marwood.

7 September 1958

We did it again today, in almost the same place as before, although this time up against one of the strong oak trees. He grows more and more enthusiastic with each session. More confident in his technique. Louder with his grunts and moans and expressions of pleasure. When I first started here last year, when I was nineteen and he twenty-two, I always thought his silent, stern demeanour was built from life experience, wealth, privilege and the natural authority that went with being male. But when we had sex the first time, all of that became fractured in my head. He was an awkward boy, not a bold, serious man. Now, though, after we've done it a number of times, my old impression of him is starting to return. He's found a way to retain his hard-backed authority while still allowing me to see his most vulnerable parts and feel him close to me in his most primal, passionate moments. He is an enigma: one I feel both intrigued and confused by.

After we'd finished today, he pulled up his trousers as usual, dusted off his shirt and left me there in the garden while he made his way back through the trees and plants, presumably to go up to the house. I didn't get the sense he did this out of coldness or cruelty. More that he considered our transaction complete and didn't have enough space in his attention to be polite or even consider me at all. The strangest thing about it was that I didn't mind, nor did

I consider it rude. Hours on, writing this now, I still don't. I believe I am slightly hypnotised by him. By everything about him. Is it possible to be obsessed with a man without loving him? Because if I had to choose that word – love – it would more readily describe my feelings for Honoria. A sisterly love. Something deep and familiar, something so firm, so strong that it defies the need to be pinned down and explained. But I do not love her husband. I'm just bewitched by him.

 The day was not done after our time in the garden. Once he'd dressed himself and wandered off, a strange situation occurred between myself and Gabriel Oakwood. I'm finding it difficult to even write it down, although I suspect I shall go madder still if I don't. I'm still feeling very unsettled by it, but also excited. Yes, excited. Gabriel had been watching us. I suspected he might. I'd even said it was a risk, before we'd begun doing what we were doing, but apparently it wasn't much of a concern. He was just the gardener's boy. He was nothing, in the eyes of the young future lord of the manor – the man who believed everyone was there to serve his way of life rather than be autonomous in their own. Why would such a boy have thoughts and beliefs and ideas and desires? His own aspirations, fantasies and secrets?

 'You're risking your position,' he said as he came into view, once he was sure I was alone. He emerged from behind one of the other trees, a little way down the pathway. He went on to tell me that I would be sent away without a reference as soon as the Honourable Thomas Ashton grew bored. He'd heard of such a thing happening at the large house in the village he grew up in in Yorkshire. (I think he feels a certain closeness to me because of that – that we were both born and bred in the same county, even though

I grew up a good forty miles away from his village.) I told him to mind his own business and that he shouldn't watch women from behind trees, as it was undignified. He said he could say the same about having it off in the garden with my employer.

I marched over to him, ready to give him a good smack. Then something odd happened. I looked at his shirt, scuffed and torn from hacking about with bits of trees and brambles. His tanned skin, already looking tough and worn on his arms and hands, even though his face still seemed smooth with youth. It was like a sudden noise filled my ears and a bright light shone in my eyes. I knew what it was. It was desire. I wanted this lad, in the same way Thomas had wanted me, moments ago, there to satisfy some need, both practical and physical. Now, I wanted to be the one in control.

Do you want to do it with me? I asked him. He opened his mouth and his gaze locked on to me. It was the only sign that my words had surprised him. But suddenly there was hunger in his eyes. Or perhaps it had always been there, it was just I'd never noticed it before. Gosh, what a look he gave me then. I don't know him well, but he's always been a very polite and respectful boy. Deferential to the head gardener, the gruff Mr Weatherstaff, who these days spends more and more time at home, nursing his worn-out limbs. Courteous to the other members of staff at the manor, including myself. But at that moment, I got the sense he was tempted to throw off all sense of decorum, all notion of good behaviour. I offered him the apple, and he willingly took it.

The sex wasn't all that different to that with Thomas, although it was over quicker. Gabriel had a more endearing sense of inexperience, but he became confident enough as he got into his stride and eventually moaned and thrusted and grunted in much the same way. Perhaps all males are the same in that respect, when they're in the throes of lust. The main difference was that afterwards, when he got up to pull on his clothes, he didn't walk off and leave me there, discarded in the grass. He lay back down and stayed with me, and we watched the leaves fall and the sun shine through the branches, listening to the rustle and swish of the plants. It was very beautiful. All of a sudden, I wished Thomas didn't feature in my life at all, and that Gabriel and I had stumbled across each other in a field one day and done this intimate deed without having any prior knowledge about each other. I wished we were a thousand miles away from Marwood and could just walk off into the sunset – perhaps together, perhaps alone. Or perhaps just fade away.

None of that can happen, of course. We can't fade away. There is work to be done. And I've made a promise to Honoria. A promise that binds us together. For ever.

January 1959

I can see the despair in Thomas's eyes each time I tell him it hasn't worked. Each time I shake my head. Sometimes I tell Honoria first, and we cry together. Other times he catches me in the corridor, just after I've spotted the blood. It's as if he knows it's failed before I confirm it. I feel sorry for him whenever it happens.

I think each time he imagines what it will be like to lose everything. Today – during the whole Christmas season, in fact – I've been obsessing over the thought of having to leave Marwood. The thought of Thomas and Honoria being evicted. The place being stripped and renovated and turned into some ghastly hotel. Because that is what Thomas's distant cousin, Richard Mason, will do if he inherits. I remember Honoria's wide eyes as she told me about it – how if Thomas fails to produce a child, preferably a son, before his father dies, he will be disinherited and the whole estate will go to Mr Mason, who lives an idle life filled with drink and debauchery in Vienna. Lord Ashton is – rather bafflingly – fond of Mr Mason, and as he already has a son (having impregnated a Polish opera singer, apparently), the succession is guaranteed. I've never met the Mason man, but he sounds awful.

How could a father be so cruel to his son? I gathered from Honoria's explanation that there was some sort of row – a suggestion by Thomas that he would deliberately not have children. So his father inserted a nasty and rather archaic clause into his will decreeing that he would be disinherited if he didn't, and as a final added pressure, he had a limited time to do so. Such strange games these people play with the lives of their loved ones. It makes me rage into my pillow at night to think about it.

But leaving all this aside, I'm trying to carry on, for Honoria's sake, with everything that we've been doing. So today, at the couple's Twelfth Night celebrations, I invented a reason to steal Thomas away from his guests and took him into an old broom cupboard. It was quick, hurried, and we both enjoyed it.

Later, when all the guests had either gone up to their rooms or departed in their expensive cars, I crept out of the house and walked in the dark down the lawn to the garden. Gabriel has recently taken up permanent residence in the gardener's cabin, now that old Mr Weatherstaff has finally thrown in the towel. And it's this cabin I visit whenever I can, tapping on the door to see if he's awake. Getting into bed with him and feeling his arms wrap around me. Then, once it's done, tiptoeing back to the house at dawn, hoping nobody suspects a thing.

25 February 1959

I've been in a dream state all day. The Ashtons had guests over for dinner and I was kept busy all day. But at night, once the house had officially been put to bed for the evening, I crept up the servants' staircase to Honoria's bedroom. I've just come from there now, and had to write this all down – I'm so beside myself with joy.

'It's worked,' I told her, rushing up to her bed, where she was stretched out on her front reading a novel. 'I've been waiting and waiting, but my monthlies haven't come. I'm pregnant.'

The joy in her face was almost too painful to witness. Then it clouded over. 'We have to make sure,' she said. So I am to see a ladies' physician tomorrow morning. It all has to happen in secret. Thomas will arrange it. I'm not sure where they'll take me, but I presume it will be in London. Then, if the doctor agrees with my guess, the Ashtons can start planning the next stage of all this: how they're going to create a fictional pregnancy for Honoria without their plan being discovered. Regardless, Honoria will have her baby – it will be both of ours, a shared angel we can nurture, with me always here at Marwood to watch it grow with every advantage a child could wish for – and Thomas will have his heir and fulfil his father's requirements.

That is, if the baby is actually his, of course. I can't help thinking back to all the occasions over the course of this winter when I've gone down to the hidden garden to spend a snatched hour in Gabriel's arms beside the fire in his cabin. But really, when it comes down to it, I'm not sure it even matters. They won't be able to tell either way.

Chapter 39

The Names of Women

Mrs Medlock, April 1979

I sat in my seat, thinking back to the events of twenty years ago. Those entries I wrote in my journals, detailing my innermost feelings, my most secret thoughts. I could very easily get up and fetch them from my room and thud them down on the table in front of Bessie; they would explain everything. But I couldn't tell her the full story. That would have been an impossibility. To be honest, it's a marvel that I'd go on to be able to speak about it in the future – I'd never have believed such a thing if someone had told me then. I used to be quite cynical about the idea that time heals wounds, but it is true what they say. I just wouldn't advise telling someone in pain that. It's like telling a drowning man that oxygen still exists somewhere in the world and expecting him to feel grateful for the knowledge.

When I told her selected portions of my story, I could see Bessie struggling to compute the information. And wondering how she could go forward in her employment at Marwood Manor knowing what she now knew. About me. And about Lord Ashton.

'We began our . . . our relationship two years into my working here. I'd started as a maid at eighteen, so I was twenty when we first ... well, when we first got up to what you've been getting up to out there.' I nodded to the outside world beyond our gloomy kitchen surroundings. Bessie looked awkward but didn't say anything, so I continued.

'Of course, things like this do happen from time to time. Lord Ashton isn't the first man to sleep with a maid, the first employer to have his head turned by a young woman who worked for him. I flatter myself that I wasn't bad-looking back then. And he was the first man I made love to. And if two adults ... copulate ... enough without taking proper precautions, there are ... consequences.'

I saw Bessie's eyes widen. She was working it out. Filling in the gaps, connecting together the bits she already knew or suspected.

'I ... I gave birth to triplets ... ' I said the words quietly, afraid they wouldn't come out of my mouth at all, and when they did, a lone tear fell down the side of my face. I took a deep breath and forced myself to carry on. 'None of them survived the night. A terrible night, it was. A huge storm outside, thunder, lightning. Sitting there, sheets covered in blood, I felt like I'd been thrown into hell. The babies ceased to cry one by one. Until at last there was silence.' I rummaged in my pocket for a tissue, mirroring Bessie's pattern earlier of talking, then dabbing away the tears that followed, then trying to talk some more.

'Of course, there would have been a huge scandal. Aside from the doctor and midwife who attended – and were no doubt paid handsomely for their silence – nobody was to know. It's a secret I've kept for twenty years. Knowing that down in the garden, hidden away, were the bodies of my three children. My three little darlings. It was helpful that the garden also became something of a monument to the first Lady Ashton after her death. It became a place of grief that nobody went to, aside from Mr Oakwood, who was tasked by Lord Ashton to always keep it maintained but not *enthusiastically* so. That was how he put it. The idea of people enjoying the place was out of the question. That is why I've been so disturbed about the idea of letting Rupert, Mary and Ernest play in the garden while Lord Ashton is away. It's like them stepping back into my past. And I was right to be worried. They did find something down there. They uncovered my secret. And they've set in motion a series of events, and goodness knows where they'll take us. But I suspect it isn't going to be good.'

For a moment, I thought Bessie was going to start crying again too, but instead she asked a question. 'Is that why you haven't disobeyed Mr Quint and phoned the police? Or Lord Ashton?'

I nodded. 'No one can know,' I said. 'No one.'

I expected her to argue. To offer up reasons why my position was flawed, selfish, even dangerous. I knew all these things. But I also knew something she didn't. That I wasn't just trying to conceal a scandal and protect Lord Ashton's name. I was trying to cover up a murder. But of course, I didn't tell her that.

After we finished talking, I faced another test of my nerve. Or rather, my conscience. I walked past the library, just to get a sense of what was going on in there. I smelled the fire before I got close to the door. Then heard the crackle. Without knocking, I opened the door and looked inside. The three of them were standing around the fire in the grate at the far side of the room, and seemed to be each taking it in turn to burn pieces of paper they were clutching. In itself, it seemed rather harmless and peaceful, but it wasn't, of course. It was horrible. I only found out how horrible when Mr Quint, spotting me at the door, told me to come inside. I was hesitant at first, but then my curiosity got the better of me. I was still worried about young Ernest's safety, being in the company of the other two in the same room all night. I half expected to see the boy already smoking or glugging back vodka, but thankfully that wasn't yet on the cards.

'What are you burning?' I asked as I got nearer, looking at the paper in their hands.

'The names of women,' Mr Quint said, quite casually, again sounding a little bored.

'What women?' I said, imagining for a moment all the pieces of paper having my name scrawled on them.

'Women who have been, shall we say, missed opportunities.'

I didn't understand what he meant by this, and I was gripped by my familiar need to be out of the room and away from him. Not waiting for him to explain further, I left. If I felt bad abandoning young Ernest to whatever awaited him, it was lessened by the sight of his smug face, accompanied by the sound of an obnoxious, sneering laugh as I exited.

Chapter 40

Shimmering Souls

Mrs Medlock, April 1979

They all arrived the next day: around fifteen men and ten women. A minibus brought them up the drive to the main steps of the house. They seemed like a cheerful bunch, smiling and laughing, reminding me of the university students I'd sometimes see on my rare trips into the centre of town. There was nothing unusual about their clothing, most of them dressed in jeans and jumpers, quite a few of the girls in skirts or casual dresses. I struggled to spot a unifying feature, something that clearly said what sort of people they were.

I watched from the first-floor landing gallery as they wandered into the entrance hall. Mr Quint welcomed them in, Gary and Ernest standing either side of him, and proceeded to tell them that the men would arrange their sleeping bags in the main library and the women would walk through into the connecting North Library and set up their sleeping quarters in there. I noticed that two of the young men were carrying what looked like crates of fruit. They put them down on the floor and Mr Quint stepped towards them, peered down and then suddenly looked up at me as if he'd known I'd been spying on them the whole time. He clicked his fingers and pointed at the crates. 'Come down and sort these out. Put the food on trays or platters and bring them into the library.' He then walked off, leaving the words of his imperious command echoing in the entrance hall.

Bessie and I made no comment as we divided up the food in the crates, discovering that they held fresh bread and cured meats as well as fruit. I just told her what needed to be done and she got to work and did it. We only spoke when Mr Oakwood arrived at the kitchen door to see how things were – he'd spotted the arrival of the minibus and was curious about the new guests.

'They look like students – not that different to the ones we usually get in Oxford,' I said to him as I arranged a selection of apples, pears and mangoes on a tray, trying to sound as if I were remarking about something perfectly ordinary. I'd decided this was the best way to cope with our strange circumstances: just act like everything was going to plan, even when it was in danger of falling apart. It reminded me of that night during the missile crisis when everyone thought the world was going to end – trying to act normally while being horribly aware that something was very wrong.

Mr Oakwood offered to take the trays in to them, but I told him to stay put – Mr Quint might not react well to another man in the house; someone less easy to intimidate than myself and Bessie. If it came to a fight, Mr Oakwood had a good deal more muscular power than we did, although I suspected Mr Quint was relying on my influence over him, hoping I could convince him not to take matters into his own hands. It's odd, looking back, to think how insignificant Mr Quint probably thought he was – no doubt just 'the gardener' or another servant, there to do his bidding. If only he'd known the full extent of Mr Oakwood's involvement in this sad, twisted tale: his hold over us would have increased tenfold.

When Bessie and I carried the trays to the library, we found the young men filling up the floor space, either sitting cross-legged on their sleeping bags or lounging around on them. Most had taken off their shoes, although there was one man in the corner, leaning lazily up against the wall, still wearing tan leather boots and apparently unaware he was scuffing the antique Iranian carpet each time he jiggled his leg.

Mr Quint ordered me to put the tray I was carrying down on the coffee table in the centre of the room, and the young men eagerly gathered round and started to help themselves to grapes and slices of bread. None of them said anything to me, although they were chatting away to each other. There was a strange combination of pleasant normality, watching them munch cheerily through handfuls of fruit, and disconcerting oddness – like I'd fallen into one of Lewis Carroll's children's stories and the world had turned upside down. In an attempt to remind Mr Quint that this wasn't actually his house and that normal life must resume at some point, I mentioned how perturbed Lady Ashton would be if anything was spilled on the carpets. 'Well, she's not here is she,' he shrugged, 'and what she doesn't know won't bother her.'

'But she will be back, Mr Quint. And so will Lord Ashton. Then all of this,' I waved a hand at the guests, the plates of fruit, the sleeping bags, 'will be over.'

He smirked at me. 'You're not very good at living in the present, are you, Mrs Medlock. Always having to disrupt the here and now with worries regarding what's to come. Or things from the past, I dare say.' One of his eyebrows arched, and I knew what he was referencing. I chose not to pursue the conversation any further. Not for the first time, I didn't trust myself to keep my composure.

Bessie and I took another bizarre step through the looking glass when we went into the North Library to find the group of young women all sitting quietly, not looking at each other. Some had taken books from the shelves and were reading; others were brushing their hair. Like the boys, they'd laid out sleeping bags around the room and were sitting on top of them. A few looked up as Bessie set down the tray on one of the step stools at the end of the room, and a girl to my left muttered, 'Thank you,' but other than that, there was total silence. Bessie and I exchanged a quick glance, then left the room, picking our way back through the men in the main library and out down the hallway.

'Perhaps it's some sort of club,' Bessie said, and I could sense she was doing her best to sound matter-of-fact and normal, even though she was probably just as uneasy as me, 'Like ... I don't know ... stamp collectors or something.'

I let out a bleak laugh that sounded more like a cough. 'I don't know what they're here for, but I'd bet the whole contents of this house it isn't stamp collecting.'

I was right, of course. I wish I wasn't, but it was starting to feel inevitable that we would, as time went on, be plunged further down the rabbit hole.

As the days passed, and April turned into May, nothing too alarming happened. In fact, our new guests were more of an inconvenience than anything. Bessie and I spent most of our time keeping Mary and Rupert away from them, and evading their questions.

'But why can't I go and speak to them, they're in my house?' Rupert demanded when I escorted him from having his bath only to find two young men waiting outside the bathroom door holding towels, one in just boxer shorts and the other in tracksuit bottoms and no top. I steered Rupert past quickly, hissing to him,

'They're not to be spoken to, end of story.' When the visitors had first arrived, I'd told both him and Mary that their visit was something educational to do with Ernest. They were experts brought in to help with his studies. I suspected neither child believed this to be the whole story, especially since these 'experts' were camped out in sleeping bags in the library and regularly wandered around the house in their pyjamas.

I was rather shocked to see one of the young women lying on her sleeping bag completely topless, her blonde hair spilling over her naked breasts like one of those models you occasionally saw in magazines – not that I regularly read such publications. And even though there were multiple bathrooms throughout the house, they all seemed to gravitate towards the same handful in groups of three or four. They'd go up and shower or bathe together at the same time, laughing and chatting away. At first, I was worried there was something ... well ... *sexual* about all this, particularly as Ernest seemed to be very much in the thick of it all, but I was wrong – they stayed separated by gender and it seemed to be more about camaraderie than anything obscene or distasteful. That would come later.

At times, I listened at the library door, in an attempt to get some essence of what their day-long meetings and discussions were about, but I could only pick up a few sentences, and even those didn't make much sense. Something about giving up their bodies to 'wandering spirits' and searching for the 'shimmering souls' rather than the ones that would 'poison them from within'. It made me wonder whether Mr Quint was actually a religious zealot or some theological or spiritual extremist. I'd heard about such people from the newspaper, although they tended to be mostly based in the United States. Of course, nowadays it would probably be obvious to anyone what they were. They were a cult. But I should make it clear once again how sheltered we were, myself, Bessie and Mr Oakwood. We hadn't seen much of the world – hadn't seen any of it, other than Marwood and the surrounding countryside. All of this was so new to us, it defied logic – indeed, attempts to define it felt like trying to catch hold of smoke between one's fingers.

We get now to the part where things did start to become ... how shall I put it ... more concerning. I'd been down to see Mr Oakwood at his cabin. I had been quietly terrified that Mr Quint would lead his group of guests down to the hidden garden, but mercifully he hadn't done so. I'd been playing down the oddness of what was happening each time I spoke to Mr Oakwood, partly to stop him worrying, partly to ensure he didn't make himself too present at the house. I'd decided that if we all kept our distance, our guests would do what they needed to do and then hopefully leave. All attempts to downplay the group's activities went out of the window, however, when upon walking back up to the house, the two of us were confronted by a sight so startling I truly thought I was dreaming.

The men were standing on the lawn in a large circle, their arms stretched out so their fingertips were touching. As we got nearer, we saw that the centre of the circle was filled with women, lying on their backs, their arms also stretched out. All this alone would have been enough to unnerve us, but the truly horrifying thing was the discovery that the women were unclothed. The men were dressed in long, flowing white robes, with the exception of Mr Quint, who came into view as he walked around the outside of the circle, dressed in a long dark red robe that seemed to shimmer and glint as the late-afternoon sun caught it.

'What in God's name ...?' Mr Oakwood said next to me, sounding as stunned as I felt. 'This can't be right. What ... what are they doing?'

Of course, I didn't know, although educated guesses started

to fill my mind: some kind of religious service, perhaps? A ritual of some sort? The word conjured up other words even more disturbing, like 'offering' and 'sacrifice', things I really didn't want to think about while confronted with an already disturbing sight.

'I think...' I said, quietly, 'I think we should just leave them to get on with it.'

He turned to look at me. 'Say the word and we'll go. We'll just leave this place.'

This panicked me more than the sight of the naked women on the lawn. 'We can't. How can you suggest such a thing? You *know* why we have to stay. You know we can't just... just... abandon this place. And what about the children? What about—'

With a jolt I remembered Ernest, and I looked back over at the circle, which had started to rotate, the men stepping to the side, their faces fixed upon the women in the centre. Sure enough, I saw one of their number was a touch shorter than the others. 'That's it – we're taking him back up to the house,' I said to Mr Oakwood, and I marched across the lawn towards the strange gathering.

We'd been very much in view up until that point, although nobody in the circle had paid us any attention. When we got close, however, Mr Quint stood quite still watching us approach.

'Ernest is coming back up to the house,' I said, as firmly as I could manage, making it clear it wasn't a question. Mr Quint reached round and tapped one of the men on the shoulder, and the circle came to a sudden stop. I looked down and saw that the women on the floor had started to move their arms and hands so they were mingling with each other, and on their toned, slim stomachs were symbols. I think I could make out a moon, and some stars, and perhaps a cross – not a Christian cross, more a letter 'X'. I couldn't work out what they'd used, paint or lipstick perhaps, although it didn't smudge as their hands started to caress each other's bodies, floating and merging over their torsos and their breasts and through the long waves of their hair.

'Perhaps you want to join them, Mrs Medlock?' Mr Quint said. My attention snapped back to him. He was studying my face with apparent amusement, a crooked smirk playing around his lips.

'I'm here to take Ernest inside. This is wholly inappropriate for a boy his age.' As I spoke, Mr Oakwood took off his jacket and offered it to Ernest. The boy didn't break from the circle, but he turned his head to look at Mr Quint, as if asking for permission. Mr Quint paused for a second, then nodded. Without speaking, Ernest took the coat and wrapped it round himself over the thin robe. Although the evening was mild, it looked as if he had become suddenly cold.

'Come, lad, let's go inside,' Mr Oakwood said to the boy, nudging his shoulder. The two of them started to walk towards the house. I was about to follow when Mr Quint spoke.

'You're trying my patience, Mrs Medlock. I've allowed this interruption so as to preserve the delicate equilibrium of our practice here tonight. Next time I won't be so agreeable. Do I make myself clear?'

I hated him so much at that moment, standing there in that weird red robe, looking like some strange wizard from a fantasy novel, and still having the temerity to threaten me, to speak to me as if he were my master or employer. I didn't reply to his question. I just turned my back on the lot of them and hurried to catch up with Mr Oakwood and Ernest.

Chapter 41

Scary Things That Happen at Night

Mary, May 1979

I'd been trying to work out what was going on in the house, but couldn't seem to get anyone to tell me or even properly talk to me. Rupert returned to his stroppy, bossy ways, like when I first found him. Ernest didn't spend time with us any more and preferred to go around with Mr Quint and his weird visitors, wearing odd clothes and chanting in the library. They burned things – Rupert said they were 'incense' – that smelled spicy and strange. This, to him, was proof of something he had become very worried about: that Mr Quint was a witch and he and the other people were here to conjure dark forces that would bring forth spirits – not just the first Lady Ashton, but other spirits, other things living in the house. And they wouldn't be nice. He was sure of that. They would wish us harm. I asked him if a man could be a witch, and he told me writings on the subject weren't clear but he might perhaps be a 'warlock', which was a sort of man witch. 'That isn't any better, though,' he'd said, shaking his head at me, looking afraid. 'In old English, some say "warlock" translates as "deceiver". It could even be argued a warlock is always linked to the devil. So either way, he's not good. He's a bad man.'

If ever I asked Bessie or Mrs Medlock what was going on, they either didn't answer and wandered away looking worried, or just said, 'Never you mind,' or something like that. But I did mind. And eventually Rupert and I came up with a plan.

'I think we should write a letter,' I said to him one evening, while he turned the pages of an art book full of pictures of paintings in a sulky way.

He looked up. 'Who to?' he said, frowning.

'Your dad. Your mum. They would want to know.'

He stared at me for a bit, thinking, then said, 'I don't think they would like it.'

'I know,' I said, nodding. 'And they might come home and things could go back to how they were. They could kick out all of Mr Quint's strange visitors. Maybe kick *him* out. And they'd be so pleased that you're better now. They'll want to do nice things with you – we could go out on trips. You could show them how you can be out in the sunshine and nothing can hurt you.'

Rupert looked about him, suddenly seeming worried, and shifted his legs on the bed. 'I think ... I think perhaps it wouldn't be a good idea. What if I got ... what if I got *feverish*? What if I began to burn? I could still die, you know. Maybe the effects of all this exertion are ... delayed.'

'You are not feverish,' I told him, a bit puzzled at all this, 'and you look healthier. I heard Mrs Medlock and Bessie say so. I don't think you need to talk about dying. Your father will be happy to hear you've got better.'

'I don't want you to tell him!' Rupert said fiercely. 'It will only disappoint him if I get worse again – and I may get worse right now ... this very night, even. I might have a raging temperature. In fact, I feel as if one might be building.' He raised his hands to his head, and then to his eyes, as if blocking out the light. When he lowered them, I saw that there were tears on his hands and cheeks. 'I won't have letters written to my father. Please, Mary. My mother will just get upset, and my father will get cross and send for a doctor. Oh gosh, I feel hot already.' He began to flap his pyjama shirt to let air to his skin, 'Do you think it's the burning? Has it started?' He hurriedly tugged up the material to look at his arms and stomach. There were no marks.

'There's nothing wrong with you. We've been telling you this for ages now.'

Rupert seemed to be trying not to cry, but some more tears escaped. 'I hate being written and talked about as much as I hate being stared at. Even if I said I was better, they wouldn't listen. Nobody would listen. No doctor would come and prove them wrong. And if they did ask a doctor to look at me, they'd just tell him I was lying. They'd choose one who would just nod and agree that I'm weak and must be kept safe.'

'Stop crying, right now. Come on, please, Rupert. We'll write a letter and just tell them about Mr Quint. Is that all right? We'll leave you out of it.'

After a lot of deep breaths, he straightened up and nodded.

We walked to the post office in the village early the next morning. Nobody spotted us leaving, although we did have a close escape when Bessie turned the corner of a corridor carrying a washing basket and we had to go very still and press ourselves against the wall. I thought it would be a short walk, but it took ages to get to the end of the driveway, and even after that it still took a very long time, though it was in a straight line.

It was very strange to be out of Marwood, and I quite liked spotting the little cottages, or a tractor, then maybe a car would pass us. But mostly it was quiet – even when we got to the village, which looked quite a lot like the village I grew up in, with a tiny shop, a butcher's, a post office and a church. We went straight into the post office, which was just opening up, and the woman seemed very surprised when we went to the counter and asked her to post a letter to the United States of America. Rupert knew they were staying in their Long Island house, and after some tense moments looking – with me keeping watch outside – we'd found the address on a piece of paper in Lord Ashton's study, along with some banknotes in a drawer.

Even though the woman seemed confused by the whole thing, she still sorted out the posting costs and took the money from Rupert. I felt guilty in that moment, when he turned to smile at me and I saw the woman walk away behind the desk with the envelope in her hands. Rupert and I had written the letter together the night before, but once I'd got back to my room, I'd carefully slid it out of the envelope and rewritten it, this time adding a bit about him being much better. I thought if his parents read that, they'd have to come back – they'd want to see him for themselves. And then they could get rid of Mr Quint, throw out the guests and we could start to go back to how it used to be.

Chapter 42

Nobody Can Help Me

Mrs Medlock, May 1979

I think for many people, finding Ernest taking part in that strange ritual would have been the final straw. But for us, it was just the beginning. That evening, we put him to bed with no complaint – the boy was unusually amenable, even when I told him he wasn't to mix with the guests ever again, no matter what Mr Quint said. He just nodded and went to sleep, considerably earlier than his usual bedtime. Perhaps he just wanted rid of us. He didn't obey my instructions, of course, and before long – a couple of nights later – I found him crouched on the floor in the library with the other men as they made little objects out of a box of hay or straw that had appeared from nowhere. Later that evening, they burned their creations outside on the patio while Mr Quint said strange words in another language. I watched as they added the straw figurines – yes, I could see that they were made up to look like people – to a tin bucket and poured paraffin or some other chemical onto them.

'Are they having a bonfire?' said a little voice behind me. I looked round to see Mary standing there, watching me as I gazed through the French windows out into the garden.

'No,' I said. 'Back to bed.' I marched her upstairs to her room, using the servants' staircase. On my way back down, using the main stairs this time, I noticed a figure dart across the main hallway. As I reached the ground floor, I saw it was one of the young women. She was dressed in just a bra and slip and I noticed she had little flowers – daisies, I think – threaded into the fabric, although I tried to keep my eyes away from the abundance of flesh on show. I got the feeling she'd been peering into rooms – the lounge, the rarely used dining room – as if looking for something. Or somewhere to escape to.

'Can I ... er ... help at all?' I asked, unsure if I should be speaking to her.

The woman, who had frozen completely still when she'd seen me, now raised a hand to brush her hair out of her eyes. I saw that she was trembling. 'I ... don't know. I don't think anyone can.'

I took a step nearer. That was when I saw the fear in her eyes. Pure, undiluted and terrifying to behold. A single tear fell and made its way down her smooth young face.

'You must be cold, dressed like that,' I said. 'Perhaps you could put on some more clothes, then we could have a chat?' I wasn't sure if this was a kind or unwise thing to do, but I just couldn't bear to see the girl so upset like this.

'No ... nobody can help me. I ... have the bad one, you see.'

I frowned. 'The bad one?'

'Inside of me.' She tapped her head with one hand, while the other snaked down to her stomach.

I didn't like the sound of this. 'I'm sure there's nothing bad about you. What's your name?'

She shook her head. 'He told us ... he said the women ... We're not supposed to have names ... not the names we were born with, anyway.'

'What name were you born with? Come on now, you can tell me.'

Another tear fell and she took a deep, rattling breath, as if stealing herself to do something that required a lot of bravery. 'Marjory. My name's Marjory.'

I took another step nearer so that I was close enough to lay a hand on her arm. She was cold to the touch and I felt her shiver as our skin connected.

'Please, don't be kind to me,' she said. 'I ... I don't deserve it.'

'Listen to me, Marjory. I don't like this. I don't like anything about what's going on here. And if you don't either, I think you should leave.'

She gasped and took a step back, 'No, no, I couldn't do that. I can't leave. I still have that bad one inside of me, don't you see. My soul doesn't shimmer in the light, it shines black instead. I came here to feel right, I left my family for their own safety.'

I felt a pang of sympathy for her. 'Do your parents know where you are?'

Her brow creased. 'Not my parents. My husband ... he knows, but I told him it was a retreat ... a retreat to make me feel better. We have a little girl. She's named Katherine, but we call her Kitty. Wonderful child, but ... I've been sad, very sad, since she was born. I just needed a rest. I came here to rest. They told me this would heal me ...'

The scrape of a door cut through the air, followed by the sound of people coming into the house from the garden. I didn't have time to move before everyone started filing in, filling the space around us. The men were clothed in dark brown cloaks, and Mr Quint was once again in his red attire. Like the distressed girl in front of me, the women were in their underwear. It all made me feel rather nauseous.

'I wondered where you'd got to,' Mr Quint said to Marjory. He wrapped an arm round her and began to lead her away. 'Thank you for rounding up our little stray, Mrs Medlock,' he called back to me. I didn't answer. I just stood there, helpless, as they all went into the library and Mr Quint closed the door behind them.

It all kicked off that night. It was Ernest who alerted me to it, although not intentionally. He'd gone back up to his room, apparently to get an extra blanket. 'Why do you need an extra blanket?' I asked, when I saw what he was doing. 'Why don't you just sleep in this bed in your room – perhaps you could even go back home to London with your parents and—'

'Just get out of my way,' he said harshly. I stepped back to let him pass me on the landing. It was as he walked down the main stairway that I heard the noises. The moaning. The sounds of ecstasy. I was instantly pulled back to that night Mr Quint had brought home those two young women. I walked quickly so that I caught up with Ernest just before he reached for the library door handle.

'Don't go in there,' I said urgently. 'Ernest, please. Just go back upstairs.'

His lip curled in a sneer. 'I know what they're doing in there. I'm not as innocent as you think, Mrs Medlock.' He said my name as if it were preposterous, as if I were a joke, unworthy of his attention or respect. It's a marvel I didn't hit him again, but my protective instincts had been ignited and all I wanted was to stop him crossing that threshold and becoming caught up in something adult, obscene, sinister – perhaps even dangerous.

'I don't doubt it. But it isn't something you should be involved in.'

He gave me a hard shove. 'Too late,' he said, and disappeared inside before I could get even a glimpse of what was going on.

I stood in the hallway, perhaps more torn and conflicted than I had ever been in my life. I knew that moment was my test. When I started to hear more of what was happening – the moans and grunts and quick breaths, followed by what sounded sickeningly like applause and cheers – I ended up running down the hallway to the kitchen to use the telephone. I sat there holding on to the receiver, silent sobs making my body shake, trying to reconcile my dilemma. Find peace with my conscience. Only for it all to be in vain when I realised there was no dialling tone. He'd cut the phone lines, of course. Perhaps he knew I'd break at some point. Finally I had made the momentous decision I had been struggling with for so long, only to have it snatched away from me.

I'd never known fury like it. I pushed past Bessie, who was coming into the kitchen, and marched down the corridor.

Flinging open the library door, I saw that the room had been completely rearranged. Sleeping bags, tables and chairs had been piled against the back wall and the bookshelves. In the centre, on top of a blanket – the one Ernest had been carrying – a man and a woman were copulating. The woman was sitting astride him, with the man lying on his back. They were naked, while everyone else standing around them was wearing those horribly familiar cloaks. Without warning, the young man lifted the woman off him, pushed her over and began to thrust into her vigorously from behind, grunting loudly as she moaned. I was both sickened and mesmerised by this, especially when I realised it was that innocent-looking, affable young man who had arrived before the others – Gary, I think his name was.

For a moment, I forgot the reason I was there – to save Ernest from witnessing this spectacle – but before I could do anything, Gary gave an almighty moan and the whole room erupted into whoops and cheers and clapping, like they were a crowd at a sporting event. 'A thousand congratulations to you,' Mr Quint said, detaching himself from the group and helping the exhausted-looking young man up from the floor. 'From this moment on, your birth name of Gary shall fall away. You are, from today, Argento.'

'Ar-gen-to,' the crowd recited in unison, then they all bowed to him. Gary – or Argento – looked both pleased and embarrassed as he ducked out of the circle and walked over to the side of the room, where he began to pull on a cloak draped over a sofa. I saw his eyes flick to me, then back to the floor. Perhaps they'd all been told to ignore me, pretend I didn't exist, to resist engaging with the difficult servant woman. Well, I was about to give them an engagement they'd remember.

'This must end. Now. All of you need to leave.' I said the words loudly, almost shouting, causing some of their number to instinctively turn round.

'Mrs Medlock,' Mr Quint said, as the group parted to let him through to me, 'we've discussed this before, and I think I made myself clear. Our activities are not to be interrupted. If they are, there will be consequences. In fact, I think we could involve you in our activities in some way. And you wouldn't like that.' His smirk grew broad and cruel, and some of the young men laughed at his words.

'It would be neglectful of me to leave Ernest here in your company while this is going on,' I said, trying my best to look unfazed. 'He is ... he's ... ' I looked around, suddenly panicked, unable to see him anywhere.

'He's in the North Library. Waiting for his turn.' Mr Quint's grin grew broader still.

I felt sick. I pushed my way through and walked over to the archway connecting the main library with its smaller cousin. Inside, Ernest was sitting in a chair, now dressed in a long cloak that was too large for him. When he looked up, he seemed hopeful, excited even, until he saw it was me who had entered.

'Oh God, what now?' he said, sounding irritated. He raised his hand to his lips, and I realised what he was holding just as he took a puff on it.

'Put that out and get up,' I said, appalled.

'It's just a bit of Dutch courage, to help him relax,' Mr Quint said from behind me.

I turned to face him. 'I'm taking him away from here. We'll go into town and phone the police. He's not spending another minute in this house while you and your friends are—'

The slap sent me toppling to the ground. Mr Quint had delivered the blow with such aggressive force my vision disappeared for an instant, the wood-panelled walls and the low candlelight swimming and merging out of focus as I tried to work out how I'd ended up on the floor. Then the kick to my stomach made me curl up into a ball in pain.

'This is just a taster, Mrs Medlock. A sample of my displeasure. I won't let you ruin this for us. I won't let you—'

He let out a shriek as I grabbed his foot and sank my nails as hard as I could into his shin. He pulled himself free, causing him to topple back into the wall behind him. I could hear people talking, some of them shouting, perhaps offering to help, although whether their calls were for him or me I couldn't discern. 'Get away from me!' I yelled as he threw himself towards me again.

It all happened so quickly, I don't remember anything other than the impact. Because suddenly there was a heavy iron paperweight in my hand – a paperweight shaped like a globe that had been sitting benignly on a coffee table. In my panic I'd reached for it, and smashed it into Mr Quint's head as hard as I could. I only realised what I had done when he hit the ground.

While there is a lot about those few minutes that I struggle to remember, I'll never forget the sound he made. It started as a grunt, and tight breathing, followed by a high-pitched scream, like an animal writhing in pain, choking and spluttering. And then, most terrifying of all, silence. Stillness. Save for a slight twitching of his legs, hands and eyelids, and the slow advancement of his blood staining the rug.

I dropped to my knees. Around me there was chaos – people running in and out of the North Library, someone else shrieking, then a male voice saying, 'We need to go ... we can't be here ... we need to go.' I must have sat there for a while, because by the time my mind properly focused again, I was alone in the room, with Bessie standing just beyond the archway into the main library, staring at me with a look of horror on her face.

Chapter 43

What Happens Now

Mrs Medlock, May 1979

Everybody left that night. The visitors, that is. They fled into the darkness like vanishing spirits called by a higher power. For a moment, as Bessie helped me to my feet and led me through the empty library, I wondered if I'd just imagined the whole thing – if there'd never really been anyone here but us all this time. Then I saw the sleeping bags and discarded robes, and I knew it had all been true.

Bessie and I walked slowly to the kitchen, where I washed the specks of blood off my hands and splashed some cold water on my face. Then I slumped into one of the chairs at the table and said weakly, 'Please . . . fetch Mr Oakwood.'

The poor frightened girl did as she was told. Perhaps I should have considered her feelings more. The fact that her former lover had just been bludgeoned in the library by her – for want of a better word – superior must have shaken her up. But we'd all been shaken up for such a long time by that point, I didn't think much about how she must have felt. I just knew we needed someone to lift the body.

Mr Quint's weight didn't pose much of a challenge for Mr Oakwood, who was quite a bit taller and a great deal stronger. I accompanied him as we walked slowly towards the hidden garden. He put the body down for a quick rest at the large wooden door, then scooped it up again for the last stretch of the journey, into the twisted pathways of the garden. A garden that would soon be drawing nutrients from Mr Quint's flesh as he decomposed beneath it.

I sat silently on the hard ground as Mr Oakwood chose the spot and began to dig, and dig, and dig. I didn't offer to help, nor did he expect me to. I was beyond such a task and he was well aware of it. I don't know how long this task took him, but suddenly I realised the pile on the ground that used to be Mr Quint was unfurling slowly like a puppet being taken from its box, as Mr Oakwood dragged it towards its makeshift grave.

I wasn't cold as I sat there. The evening air was surprisingly warm and there was no breeze. I could have stayed there all night if I'd had to. But once the grave had been filled in, Mr Oakwood encouraged me to stand, and led me through the trees and bushes, back onto the path towards his cabin.

There I slept, his arms wrapped around me, his lean, muscular frame reassuringly solid and certain in a world so full of doubt and disruption. We barely spoke until morning, then I sat up and looked around to find him making tea on his little stove. It was like I'd travelled back in time to before all this happened, back when my most pressing concern was insubordinate children wanting to play outside.

I took a few moments to rub my eyes and take a few deep breaths, then I asked him what seemed a dauntingly momentous question. 'What happens now?'

His answer was typically calm and soothingly simple. 'Now, we go back to normal.'

Chapter 44

Recollections

Natalie

'But it didn't go back to normal?' I prompt. Mrs Medlock is staring wistfully off into the distance once again, and I lean in slightly to catch her attention, seeking out eye contact. She jolts when she sees me, as if she's forgotten I'm here at all.

'What's that, dear? Oh, no. No, it didn't.'

Silence again. I'm feeling a little awkward. While she's talking, it's easy to get wrapped up in her memories. But during her pauses, I suddenly realise how odd this situation is. I wish I felt at home enough to go into another room for a bit, or put the kettle on, but I don't like to break the spell if she wants to carry on. In the end, I decide to risk it. I stand up. 'Shall we have some more tea?' I ask.

She smiles. 'Of course. Apologies, you sit down and I'll make it.' She bustles off and fills the kettle, humming slightly under her breath as she does so. 'I'm worried I've been boring you to tears, my dear. We'll have some tea and then I'll show you around. I'll take you up to your room and you can get settled.'

I shift in my chair, knowing what I want to ask but not

wanting to sound too eager or insensitive. But I have to find out. 'That wasn't all that happened, though, was it, Mrs Medlock?'

I hear the thud of the kettle, the sound of water swashing around inside it. The steady drip, drip of the tap. Then, in the tense silence that follows, Mrs Medlock turns back to face me. 'I'll finish the story. I can see you want to know how it ends. But I'm worried. Worried you'll . . . '

'You're worried I'll leave? Like I said, I promise you I won't.'

'Or go to the police?'

I feel a jump within me, as if someone has just dropped a lump of ice down my back. 'I won't go to the police. Please carry on.'

A few seconds go past. Then she gives me a slow nod. 'I'll carry on. But I warn you, you're going to need a strong stomach. Some things . . . once witnessed . . . once spoken about . . . you can never be the same afterwards. At least, I've never been the same since it all happened.'

Chapter 45

The Boy's Meddling

Mrs Medlock, May 1979

Nothing about the days that followed was normal. The day after it all happened, Mr Oakwood and I burned our clothes from the night before in one of his little fires by his cabin. He then walked to the house to check how Bessie was and fetch me something to wear. He reported that the girl was subdued and pale, potentially in shock, but she had made the children breakfast and successfully persuaded them to stay in their rooms.

'We need to go and sort out the library,' I said, feeling suddenly panicked by all the things that had to be done. 'And Ernest . . . he saw everything. What if he goes to the police? And all the other people . . . any one of them could—'

'Words like "what if" and "could" are not useful here,' Mr Oakwood said quietly but firmly. 'We'll control what we can control. Everything else . . . well, what will be will be.'

I wished I could have his calm, methodical mindset at moments of intense stress. It took an immense amount of effort to go back up to the house with him and supervise the removal of the large rug in the North Library. 'It's probably worth thousands,' I said, as Mr Oakwood folded it. 'Lord Ashton will ask questions.'

'Tell him Mr Quint dropped a lit cigarette onto it and started a small fire, so we disposed of it,' Mr Oakwood said.

Once we had it rolled, we stared at the carpet for a while, deciding what to do. 'I fear it's too large to burn,' he said, 'We'd need a huge bonfire for that and I'd worry about it raising suspicion, if anyone came poking around.'

'What other choice do we have?' I asked.

'We hide it,' he said. And that was what we did. The carpet and the sleeping bags were taken by me and Mr Oakwood on several trips upstairs to the very top of the house. We stored most of the sleeping bags under one of the beds in a room that hadn't been used for years. Others, along with the carpet, we took to the room that preceded Rupert's bedroom, already so packed full of miscellany that it was close to impossible that anything would be spotted among all the old belongings. We wedged the cylindrical shape into a cobweb-filled corner, dislodging several spiders, and then blocked it in with old trunks and suitcases and draped an old curtain across it. After we'd finished, it looked as if it had been there for decades.

The most upsetting part of our reclamation of the house was the discovery of the little bones. The ones Mr Quint had taken from the ground and stolen away, an act that felt equivalent to him ripping out a part of my soul. He had been incorrect in his assertion that we'd never find them. Or perhaps he'd just been arrogant in presuming we wouldn't dare go looking through his things. But there they were, in one of the drawers in his bedroom. The drawer that housed his socks and underpants, something that felt like an added insult. They were wrapped up in an old supermarket shopping bag – another horrible detail that pained me greatly. The callousness, the disrespect was awful to comprehend. In the end, I had to ask Mr Oakwood to rebury them. He took the bag down to the garden and promised me they would be returned to the ground. Be at peace.

We'd been careful to enact many of our operations while Master Rupert was occupied – either having his bath or eating supper in the kitchen. Although this was managed successfully, the nagging problem of the children still hadn't been solved. Or rather, one of the children.

I discovered from Bessie that after the night of violence, Ernest had retreated to his bedroom, and there he had remained ever since, not talking and barely eating the breakfast or lunch she brought up to him. Things continued in that way, although occasionally I noticed some bread or cheese going missing, leading me to believe that the boy was stealing down to the kitchens at night. One day I found him coming out of the main bathroom on his floor clad in his dressing gown, his hair damp, suggesting he had taken a bath. I decided to see this as a good sign, that he was getting back into a normal routine, although I was naturally nervous about how this new normal would present itself – this boy had the power to undo us all.

Mr Oakwood and I spoke to him. There had already been some attempts to do so over the previous days, all of which had ended in him lying back down on his bed to go to sleep. But eventually he participated.

'There's something important you have to remember,' I said to him, kindly. 'Mr Quint was a bad man. A very, very bad man. And in self-defence, I had to use force to stop him hurting me. You'll remember how he was hitting me and kicking me?'

Ernest nodded.

'Well, he left me little choice but to do what I did. I'm sure you can understand that.'

He didn't nod this time, but narrowed his eyes. 'Then why not just call the police?'

This was probably the most difficult question he could have asked, and one I couldn't give him a straight answer to. But I could sketch out a general understanding to him and hope he would swallow it.

'Well, you see, we wouldn't want you and Master Rupert, and Lord and Lady Ashton, and potentially your parents, mixed up in all this, would we? What Mr Quint was doing was illegal. He brought drugs into the house. Gave *you* drugs. Made you take them. And tobacco, and perhaps alcohol. He had you take part in ... activities ... that aren't suitable for a boy your age.'

He opened his mouth to argue, but Mr Oakwood spoke for the first time before he could interrupt.

'I know you feel old in yourself, lad, and you may think yourself ready, but you'll soon realise that you weren't. There's time enough for all that. And in a more wholesome way than Mr Quint presented it to you.'

I nodded, pleased at how plainly he had spelled it out.

'I still don't understand why you don't go to the police,' Ernest said slowly. 'I mean, I don't *want* you to. I agree, it's much better if we don't. But I'm just interested, Mrs Medlock. I don't think you're telling me the full story. I think this has a lot more to do with what's buried in the garden than it does with protecting the family name, or your loyalty to Lord and Lady Ashton.'

I had to stop myself getting furious at this. Furious at the boy's meddling, furious at how intelligent he was, and how he could deliver such terrifying sentences as calmly as if he were discussing what we should have for tea.

'I'm glad we agree that this should be the end of it,' I replied eventually, after digesting what he'd said and everything I was feeling as a result. Something told me I was better off not pushing him too far on this. He'd probably already worked out that he now had the upper hand in the situation. I just had to hope he wasn't going to use it.

Chapter 46

Sail Home Now Please

Mrs Medlock, May 1979

The process of restoring the house to normal was a task both mentally therapeutic and physically tiring, so at night I slept soundly and dreamlessly. Bessie, whose state of mind had improved since Mr Quint had ... well ... left, threw herself into the tasks of sorting out the kitchen, the living room and dining areas, while I concentrated on the libraries and bedrooms, all the while keeping an eye on the children. Mr Oakwood visited every day and stayed for longer than he would in normal times, either sitting at the table and chatting to Bessie and me as we cooked, or putting himself to work lifting heavy items and even having a go at silver-polishing, though I think he regretted the latter undertaking. He was a man more at home with plants and shrubs than a set of glinting knives and forks.

Rupert and Mary had obviously noticed a change in the air, and seemed surprised when I told them they could play on the lawn for the first time in weeks, although I stressed that the hidden garden was out of bounds and behind a now permanently locked door. Even Ernest shuffled outside, leaving his room with a volume of Ancient Greek history under his arm, and sat on the patio, occasionally watching whatever game Mary and Rupert were playing, sometimes reading, and sometimes just staring off into the distance, apparently caught up in his own thoughts. I tried not to think about what those thoughts could be. I was just reassured that things so far remained uneventful and fairly calm.

The tranquillity didn't last. Late one evening, the telephone rang. I was startled by the sound, having not heard it since before everything involving Mr Quint had occurred. Mr Oakwood had fixed whatever the tutor had done to the wire, although as soon as I'd picked up the receiver, I wished he'd left it as it was. Lady Ashton's cool tones sounded in my ear, causing me to tense immediately.

'Mrs Medlock? Is that you?'

'Yes,' I said bluntly.

'Well, I am relieved. I didn't know what was going on.'

I frowned at this and told her I didn't quite follow.

'Oh, don't you? Perhaps you'll be kind enough to explain as to why the children – more specifically, Mary – are sending me letters about mad tutors and the house being invaded by strangers.'

It was as if she had shot me. 'She ... you ... what?' I spluttered. I was suddenly finding it hard to take in oxygen normally, and had to sit myself down on the little chair by the telephone table.

'She sent us a *letter*.' She emphasised the word, slowly and clearly.

My hands trembled as I gripped the receiver. 'And what did this letter contain?'

'Well, I can read it out to you. It wasn't actually sent to me, it was addressed to my husband, but he had been called into Manhattan on urgent business, so I opened it and thought I should telephone. Right, here we are.' I heard a rustling of paper. '"Please, Lord Ashton. There are things you should know. Ernest's tutor man has gone mad and has taken over. We think he is probably a witch. Mrs Medlock cries all the time I think she's worried as she seems more sad these days instead of her usual crossness. There are strangers everywhere and we don't think it's right, especially after what was found in the garden. We are sorry for the trouble but maybe you should sail home now please, thank you, Mary. P.S. Your son Rupert isn't sick any more. You'll be glad to know he has got better."'

She left a silence after this, allowing the waves of amazement to roll over me. After a while, she prompted sharply, 'Well? What do you make of it?'

I took a deep breath. 'I think ... I think Mary has quite the overactive imagination.'

Silence again. Then Lady Ashton said, slowly, 'So none of it is true? The Kellman boy's tutor hasn't gone mad and there aren't a load of strangers traipsing in and out of the house? Mary has just invented this?'

'So it would seem,' I said.

'I certainly hope she hasn't been interfering in the care of my child, Mrs Medlock, a duty I left to you. If I find out he has been exerting himself in any dangerous way, I will be furious.' I couldn't think of anything useful to say in response that wouldn't risk such fury, so I stayed silent. A few seconds passed, then she went on, 'And how on earth did she get to the post office? And pay the postage costs for sending a letter here, to the *United States*?'

'I ... ' I had no easy answer for this. It was a question I wanted to get to the bottom of, but Lady Ashton didn't give me the chance to say anything more.

'Regardless, we're coming home. I was going to return soon anyway to sort out arrangements for the men to start work on the swimming pool. I did mention that to you before I left, do you remember?'

She hadn't done any such thing, although I'd overheard her mention it to guests on a number of occasions, so I'd suspected it would happen before too long. Lady Ashton was used to getting what she wanted.

'I'd ideally like to have it all finished before summer is over,' she said, not waiting for me to confirm or deny her imagined conversation about it. 'Not much fun swimming in the autumn and winter. Of course, an indoor pool would be nice too, but it's probably a bit much to do all at once.' She sighed, and I heard some more rustling, then the scrape of what might be a chair along hard ground. 'Getting back to the main problem in hand,' she said, a note of frustration in her voice, as if I had been the one going on about swimming pools, 'I spoke to my husband earlier and he's as unsettled by all this as I am. We've let the Kellmans know that something odd has been going on, but they're in Morocco at present and can't get back for another week. Lord Ashton should arrive with you tomorrow. I'll be coming home on the *QE2*, so that will of course take longer.' There was a pause, followed by: 'Oh, by the way,' with her voice taking on a higher register, as though there was about to be a grand announcement, 'I'm pregnant.'

I felt the impact of the words as though they were bullets flying down the phone line. Keep calm, I told myself. Keep a clear head. But I couldn't help my overwhelming sense of panic and dread, the thought of the cries, the wails of a newborn baby echoing throughout the house once again. It had been extremely difficult when Master Rupert was a baby, but as the years had passed and it looked as if Lord and Lady Ashton wouldn't have another, I had been relieved. Very relieved.

Lady Ashton carried on talking, but I was barely listening.

'Early days, of course, but that will mean some changes going forward. I'll need a calm environment and I'm keen to avoid any stressful situations when I return.'

I remained silent for too long, and Lady Ashton's prompt of 'Hello? Are you there?' jolted me back to the present.

'Yes,' I said faintly.

'Well, sorry if I'm boring you,' she said, sounding annoyed now. 'I'll let you go, I imagine you have a lot of work to do. But be warned, Mrs Medlock: I am not satisfied with the responses you have given me today about what has been happening in the house during our absence. We're going to need answers when we arrive home. And then we'll have that much-needed discussion about your future at Marwood.'

The line went dead. I put the phone down, but stayed seated for a while, thinking. Remembering other times when the news of a pregnancy had been broken to me. Thinking back to Honoria. How different this house was when she was in charge. As the memories rolled through my head like waves on an unsettled sea, my eyes fell on the little box sitting beside the telephone. I knew immediately what it was. Honoria's mother-of-pearl letter opener. I vaguely remembered Bessie telling me she had put it here, ages ago, when Mr Quint first arrived, but amid the frustrations of Mary absconding on that day, I hadn't properly registered the details. How apt that it should be here now, I thought. A blade that had played an important part in one of the most devastating nights of my life. I opened the lid and looked at the implement. I didn't dare touch it, but closed the box and put it in my pocket, planning to put it away properly later.

Eventually I rose to my feet and walked along the hall, preparing to go down to the garden and tell Mr Oakwood everything Lady Ashton had said – or as much as I could face repeating. Warn him that the thing we'd feared – the return of the Ashtons – was imminent. As I walked through the kitchen, I heard a creak to my left and fancied I saw a slight movement out of the corner of my eye. However, when I turned around to look, there was nothing there. Just the pantry door swaying in the wind. I listened hard, but all was quiet. Even so, I suddenly felt an overwhelming urge to leave the house and get out into the open. So that was what I did, striding down the lawn towards the hidden garden to pour out my heart to the man I loved, hoping that once again we could come up with some sort of a plan.

Chapter 47

The Part of Ourselves We Hide

Mary, May 1979

As soon as Mrs Medlock had finished her phone call, I quietly moved from where I was standing out of sight in the corridor and walked as silently as I could up the stairs. Once I was on the floor above, I ran through the corridors and up the stairs to Rupert's bedroom.

'They're coming back!' I shouted as soon as I was through the door. 'Your parents, they're coming home.'

I was hoping Rupert would be pleased that our letter had worked, but he turned his head to face me looking gloomy. And he wasn't alone.

'Could you clear off, please,' Ernest said. 'We're engaging in grown-up conversation. Just for us two. Us men.' Both boys were sitting on the bed, looking at some items in front of them. As I stepped close, Ernest scooped them up.

I laughed. 'You're not men, you're boys. And what are you looking at?'

He sighed and dropped the things in his hand. One was a bottle of wine, I knew that right away. But the other two I wasn't sure about.

'Tell her about them,' Rupert said.

Another sigh from Ernest, then he said, in his usual bored voice, 'This is ceremonial wine. It's to be drunk from a goblet and passed around during chanting meditation hour and copulation rituals.' He nudged the wine with his hand, then moved on to the second thing – a small foil square, with something that looked like a ring inside. 'This stops conception. The conception of a child is only to happen at certain times, so this is to be used by the man to stop that happening.' He then pointed to the third item, which looked like a rolled-up piece of crumpled paper. 'This is cannabis. You light the end and smoke it like a cigarette and it makes you feel floaty but helps you get in touch with the shimmering being inside of you.'

I frowned. 'What's a shimmering being?'

Ernest rolled his eyes, as if he didn't feel he should have to explain this because everyone should already know. 'We all have one. It's the part of ourselves we hide from the real world. The part we want to let out. It sparkles because it's rarely shown the light. And when we let it free, we can indulge in the things we really want to do. Be the people we really want to be.'

I didn't understand and I didn't really care. 'Well, all that stuff doesn't matter anyway, does it, now Mr Quint and his weirdos have gone. The thing that matters is that Rupert's parents are coming home.' I looked over at Rupert, hoping he would at last be pleased about this. But he looked cross, and I became worried he would have one of his tantrums.

'Why did you have to go and send that letter?' he said, looking moodily at the bed rather than at me.

'*You* wanted to write it too.'

'No, you wanted to and I went along with it. And now they'll come back and I'll probably get a raging fever and have to stay inside for ever.'

I walked away from the bed, turning my back on them both. 'I'm sick of your raging fevers. You haven't had a temperature the whole time I've been here. You're being silly. I thought you wanted to be better and enjoy things, not be stuck inside.'

'I do, but my parents won't,' he said, 'and you bringing them back is going to make everything worse.'

I ignored him and left the room. He could tell Ernest about his raging fever, I thought. I was sick of it. I'd thought he was brave, I'd thought he was getting better. But now I realised he was a spoilt, silly posh boy with bad manners.

I sulked in my room until it got dark. I must have slept for a bit, because I started to have dreams where Rupert and Ernest were drinking that ceremonial wine and laughing while Lady Ashton held me down in a chair and forced me to take medicine, saying, 'My God, girl, what a raging fever you have!' as the boys laughed and pointed. But even this was in a sort of half-sleep, and eventually I got up and rubbed my eyes and decided to go and see Rupert again. Try to make him understand that it was a good thing his parents were coming. That although he was cross with how they were with him, he was lucky to still have parents at all.

I crept out of my room and walked quietly along the landing. As I did, something made me stop suddenly. I felt a prickling at the back of my head – that strange tingle you get when someone scares you, or when you just know something isn't quite right. A shape at the end of the corridor was moving slowly in the darkness. The only light was from the night sky outside from a window a long way off. In the gloom, I couldn't see if the thing at the end of the corridor was moving towards me or away from me. Then it stopped moving and just stood there. Silently. Very still.

I ran. Ran to the door on my right, down the servants' staircase and through onto the landing below. Ernest's room was just a few steps away from me. I thought I could shelter in there and tell him to go and sort out whatever it was I had seen. But I never got there. Because the door to the room Mr Quint had stayed in was open, and there was something inside.

Something on the bed.

Something terrible was on the bed.

I screamed.

Chapter 48

Dead By Dawn

Mrs Medlock, May 1979

When I returned from the garden, it was already dusk, and I went to my sitting room and had a slice of toast, thinking over what Mr Oakwood and I had discussed. I had chosen not to mention Lady Ashton's pregnancy – it was something I was going to have to come to terms with in my own time – and had kept the discussion to the more immediate problems at hand. We didn't have a plan except to play down everything Mary had said, suggesting Mr Quint was more unreliable than mad, and that he had just had some rowdy friends to visit before going on his way.

I had planned to go straight up and make sure that Bessie had fed the children and was aware of the 'party line', so to speak, but I was so worn out I ended up falling asleep for nearly an hour. By the time I woke, darkness had well and truly fallen and the house was silent around me. Too silent, I thought. Bessie should have been getting our supper ready, and I was confused to find the kitchen empty, with no pans simmering or any evidence of a meal in preparation. Wondering if she'd been delayed by some problem with the young ones upstairs, I diverted to my left along the near-pitch-black corridor to the servants' stairs. The lights were off, which was odd, since Bessie wasn't supposed to use the main staircase unless she was cleaning. This suggested she had gone upstairs when there was still enough light to see by.

I was halfway through my ascent to the first floor when I heard the scream, then the sound of someone running. A chill ran through me and I paused, allowing a thousand fears to crowd my head. Were the visitors back? Had they not all left? Or was there some fresh disturbance newly arrived to plague our days and nights? I tried to tell myself that Mary and Rupert were playing a game and had got carried away in their excitement. This thought was a comfort; I hoped I would just have to give them a tired reprimand and usher them back to their rooms.

It *was* Mary who had screamed. But the reason was so terrible – so horrific – that it would render me almost physically sick whenever I thought back to that moment of discovery. She was collapsed on the first-floor landing, her back against the wooden railings. She appeared to be pressing herself into them, and even though the wood was more than sturdy enough to take her weight, I felt a pang of panic and fear for the child. 'What's happened?' I said, rushing over. In the dim light, I could see the terror etched onto her stark-white face.

Breathing quickly, she raised a hand to point down the landing towards a door. A door that was open. A door that led to the room Mr Quint had once occupied. A light flickered within.

'What ... Who ... Mary, what's wrong?'

She continued to point, her breath still shallow and fast. She tried to speak, but only managed two words: 'In there ...'

The desire to flee was strong, but I mustered all my strength and bravery and stepped towards the doorway. The room was silent. Nothing moved. Nothing except the candle. The lit candle sitting on the bedside table on the other side of the room, its flickering yellow glow illuminating the bed and the wall above. The bed that wasn't empty.

When I heard the scream, I thought it was Mary again, but then realised it was me. I backed away, hands flying to my face, a rush of nausea and heat and ice-cold chill enveloping me all at once until I was completely paralysed with the disorienting mixture of those sensations. I was past full sentences, for if I had been able to speak, I would have shouted for help, or at least offered some instructions to the traumatised child sitting mere inches from this room of horrors. But I could not. I could only say one word, one word full of anguish and sadness and regret and sorrow. 'Bessie.'

She had been opened up. Even in the light of the single candle, I could see the damage that had been wrought upon her young body. Her corpse lay facing the ceiling, arms splayed as if she'd been writhing then had gone limp. Blood stained the white bedsheets around her and covered most of her bare torso. I could see the things hanging from the cavernous hole in her stomach and chest. The fragments. The parts jutting out at odd angles. The meaty way they flopped over the torn shreds of skin. And then I saw the writing on the wall above. Words that I realised instantly had been daubed using blood from her fatal wounds.

YOU WILL ALL BE DEAD BY DAWN.

Chapter 49

We Must Leave This House

Mrs Medlock, May 1979

'Should we call an ambulance?'

Mary asked the question from out on the landing, apparently having regained her ability to speak. The fact that her words had returned seemed to restore some of my own capabilities, and I replied, 'No. It's too late for that.'

'What ... what should we do?'

The child needed someone to take control. And I realised that if I pushed my emotions to one side and dealt with the crisis at hand, I could do it. I could be the adult this frightened girl needed. After all, it wasn't the first instance of bloodshed I had seen. I had to look at it as just another experience to endure. Then, once the situation had been made stable, I could start to process its impact.

'We need to leave,' I said, surprising myself with how robust and strong my words sounded. 'Where are the boys?' I walked out onto the landing, as if expecting them to be already there, waiting. Then a jolt of panic shot through me. 'Ernest ... oh my God ... ' The boy should have been in the room next door,

I realised then – the room next to where this appalling violence had occurred. He must have heard it ... or could he ... could he have ... The thought was so dreadful, I could hardly entertain it for a second. But it was a thought I had to consider.

Wasting no more time, I left Mary where she was and walked along the landing to the next room, flinging open the door without knocking. It was dark and empty, the bed made, with Ernest's belongings spread around the room untidily – although that was normal where he was concerned. I left the room and told Mary to follow. She got up without hesitation or complaint and together we set off up the main stairs and through the dark corridors. With each step I imagined a hand on my shoulder or the sudden pain of a blade or dull crush of something hitting me from behind. Something monstrous in the darkness, waiting to strike. But no such thing occurred, and we reached the winding staircase leading to Rupert's bedroom without incident.

To my immense relief, I found the two boys playing chess, cross-legged on the bed. Rupert was wearing his pyjamas and Ernest was in his thick, expensive-looking bathrobe, hair still damp, suggesting he had made a detour here after his evening bath. Or perhaps, I wondered, a feeling of dread increasing within me, he'd needed to wash himself. To eradicate the evidence of what had happened in that room below us. Did I need to protect myself in some way from this boy? Could he perhaps have a weapon secreted within the folds of his bathrobe? Was he at risk of lashing out and harming Rupert, sitting less than two feet away from him? I tried to tell myself that if Rupert was going to be harmed, it would have happened already.

The two of them stared at me as I stood mutely on the threshold. I made a quick decision. 'We're in the middle of an emergency. It's important we leave the house immediately. Boys, please come with me now.'

They stayed completely still. Eventually Ernest just said, 'Why?'

I examined his face, searching for some knowing glint, some barely concealed smirk, some sense that he was playing with me. Nothing was obvious. He seemed genuinely confused.

'I'll explain on the way.'

'Where are we to go?' Rupert asked.

I hesitated. 'To the garden. We're going to Mr Oakwood's cabin.'

The boys exchanged a look, then Rupert said, 'I thought we weren't allowed to go in the garden any more. You said—'

'I know what I said. Just do what you're told for once in your goddam life!' I was shouting now, on the verge of losing control, undoing my attempts to handle the situation calmly and efficiently. The two boys looked quite scared, and glanced at each other in alarm rather than confusion.

'I'm sorry,' I said, holding up trembling hands, 'I'm sorry, I shouldn't have shouted like that. There's been a serious incident. Something that means we need to get out of the house right now.'

'*Another* serious incident?' Ernest asked, frowning slightly. I knew what he was alluding to, and I didn't want to get into all that.

'Please, both of you, get off the bed right now and come with me.' I'd gone about this the wrong way, I thought as the boys stood up grudgingly, Rupert muttering something to Ernest. I should have just made it seem like a treat or a game rather than laying down the law so curtly. But I was never good with playfulness or levity. I'd never had the chance to interact with children in that way. And now they depended on me for guidance and safety, and I was tragically ill-equipped.

Rupert looked cross and almost on the verge of tears as he started folding away the chessboard.

'There's no time for that, we need to leave *now*.' I marched over and took him by the hand, but he pulled himself away.

'All right, all right, I'm coming,' he yelled at me, then pushed past.

'You too, Ernest,' I said, praying he wouldn't put up a fight. He didn't – he just frowned again at me distrustfully, then followed Rupert down the winding staircase.

I had hoped we would make it out of the house calmly and quietly, without incident, but as we turned to walk down a dark corridor that connected the north side of the house with the centre and the main landing galleries, Mary came to a sudden stop next to me.

'Come along,' I whispered, reaching out to grab the girl, but she stepped out of my reach and pointed to something with a shaking hand, just as she had minutes before outside that terrible room. I looked down the corridor, but couldn't see anything. Only darkness, dimly diluted by the night-time light from a window at the front of the house.

'What are you pointing at?' I asked her, unwilling to go any further until I had some more details. I glanced over at the two boys, who were waiting patiently, looking from Mary to the empty corridor in front of us, and back to the girl.

Slowly, in the quietest voice possible, she said, 'I thought I saw something move.'

A chill shivered its way down the back of my neck. I took a deep breath, then replied in a similarly quiet voice. 'What did you see?' I laid a hand on the little girl's shoulder, and this time she didn't resist. I could feel her trembling.

'I'm not sure,' she said, a tear falling down her face, her voice dissolving into a sob. 'I think it was someone standing there ... down at the end there ... '

I could literally hear my heart pounding within me.

'I could go and check,' Ernest said, in way too loud a voice. I shot him a furious look and raised a finger to my lips to signal quiet.

'I'm not scared,' he replied, although his eyes betrayed him. He *was* scared, and so was Rupert, who I saw had taken hold of the older boy's dressing gown sleeve and was holding it tight. To Ernest's credit, he hadn't shaken him off.

'What do we do now?' Rupert asked in a trembling voice. I knew then that I needed to try and keep hold of some authority – keep up the pretence of control I'd feigned earlier. I was about to suggest we avoid this corridor and the main stairwell and take the servants' staircase instead. Then something happened that convinced me this was the only possible course of action. The door to one of the rooms down the far end of the corridor, where Mary had been pointing, started to move. It swung open, slowly and almost silently, and the very faint sound of creaking met our ears. It wasn't possible to see who or what had caused the movement, how the door had moved in this way, but no matter the answer, it thoroughly disturbed me.

'We need to leave,' I said, not for the first time that night. 'We're ... we're going to take the back stairs ... the servants' staircase. Stay close to me.' My voice was barely a whisper, but the children heard and understood. Little Mary pushed herself close to me, and Ernest took Rupert's hand from his sleeve and held it tight. Then, as a pack, we turned, with me slightly in front, holding onto Mary, and I led the way in the opposite direction, towards the entrance to the servants' staircase, silently praying there wouldn't be anything waiting for us when we got there.

Chapter 50

The Nightmare Garden

Mrs Medlock, May 1979

We left the house successfully, although with every step I was convinced someone was going to stop us. I imagined terrible things happening to me and the children, over and over, my mind constantly spinning me back to the hellish scene in that bedroom. The blood. And the message on the wall. Could it possibly be true? Would we really all be dead by dawn? I was so caught up in the vortex of my own mind that I barely noticed the journey across the moonlit lawn, not thinking about how exposed we were until Ernest said quietly, 'Don't you think we should keep to the shadows?' From that point on, we did as he suggested, keeping away from the open section of grass until we reached the start of the woodland area and began our walk along the little pathway to the stone wall.

For one horrible second, I convinced myself I'd left my ring of keys inside the house, on the kitchen table or in my living room, but at last my fingers curled round them and I hurriedly let us in. Once inside the garden, I gave the children strict instructions not to wander off into the darkness. The winding pathways were difficult to navigate, and I thanked the heavens that the moon was bathing the whole place in a silvery glow, since I hadn't had the presence of mind to bring a torch. Time ceased operating properly – we seemed to have been moving through the bushes and trees for both hours upon hours and only mere seconds – but at last we came to the stone fountain. The water wasn't flowing, giving the clearing an eerily silent air. But there was light from the windows of Mr Oakwood's cabin, less than a hundred yards beyond, now finally in view.

'We're here,' Rupert said in a small, cracked voice, and the way he spoke suggested he hadn't expected us to make it.

Mr Oakwood must have heard us approach, for the door opened just as we reached it. 'What . . . what's happened?'

He saw in my face immediately that some calamity was upon us. And if the children had not been there, I might have broken down in the same way I had at the Kellmans' party, in front of all those guests. But there was something in my role as protector that made my legs support me and my mind just about stay under control. 'Bessie's . . . Bessie's dead,' I said, the words faint and fractured, my eyes meeting his, trying to communicate the horror of the revelation without spelling it out.

'When? How?' he said. I shook my head mutely, and he took charge. 'You three, come inside,' he said. They obeyed, walking into the hut in silence. Ernest marched over to the bed and sat down with a thud. Rupert followed and sat next to him. He tried to take the older boy's hand again, but this time Ernest withdrew it to his lap. Perhaps reaching our place of sanctuary had caused him to regain some of his natural arrogance and aloofness. I made sure Mary was settled in the chair by the fireplace, then Mr Oakwood and I stepped outside the cabin and I began to tell him what had happened.

'She's definitely dead?' he said. 'Not just . . . passed out?'

I had difficulty finding the words to explain how definitively she was beyond all hope of medical attention. 'She was ... brutalised,' I said. 'Her stomach ... it had been opened. I think parts of her had fallen out onto the bedding and the floor.' I felt myself growing nauseous as I said these words.

'But who ... ?'

'I think they've come back ... or one of them. One of the visitors. Or perhaps they never left. Someone must have stayed, that night when everyone fled ... someone who saw what we did ... what *I* did ... and is going to take revenge upon us.'

Mr Oakwood looked grave, but he took my hands in his and said, 'We're going to sort this. One way or another.'

'Like we sorted Mr Quint? How long do you think it's going to last? Can we really carry on pretending? That everything can go back to normal? Because nothing's ever been normal here, has it? We've both spent our adult lives staying silent, denying ourselves what we've always wanted because of all the mistakes, the lies ... *my* mistakes, my lies.'

He moved his hands up to my shoulders and gripped them firmly, 'You are *not* to blame. I said that to you at the time, and I say it to you now. You are not to blame.'

I felt the sob rise within me, the tears start to fall, 'But you are just one person. A thousand others might say different. God might say different.'

'God is an added complication that we don't need right now.'

'Unless this is God's purpose? Unless he has sent an avenging angel to put a stop to our wickedness?' I was talking in an irrational way, speaking the sort of language I usually wouldn't tolerate, but something had split within me, and some deep crack was now running through my mind, my body, my entire soul. I started to shake, but even that couldn't stop the words tumbling from me. 'Either that, or it's Mr Quint. He's returned in another form. He's walking among us, neither alive nor properly dead, and we are his purgatory playground and will have to suffer his spirit for eternity.' I was starting to talk in fast whispers through my tears, and I could see Mr Oakwood's fear for me grow with each terrible word. Then his expression changed to something else entirely.

'Oh ... oh Christ ... please don't let it be so.' And he let go of me and walked away into the darkness, leaving me there in front of his little home.

'Wait ... don't go ... ' I said, but my words were cut off as he called back, 'Just stay there!'

I didn't know whether to go into the cabin with the children or remain out in the cold night on my own. I was about to reach for the door and let myself in to the safety and warmth when a noise to my left alerted me to Mr Oakwood's return.

'Where did you—'

'Get inside now.' There was a terrible urgency to his words. An urgency mixed with something even more disquieting. Panic. And Mr Oakwood didn't panic unduly.

'Where did you go? What have you seen?'

He raised a hand to his brow, and I saw it shake as he did so. 'His grave is empty.'

Those four words had little immediate effect on me. I just stayed completely still, trying to make sense of them.

'Do you understand what I'm saying?' he said. 'Mr Quint's body has gone from the grave. There are marks in the earth around it. It wasn't deep. I think he must have ... crawled out.'

'But ... how?' Even as I spoke, I knew what it meant. And the terrible truth became clear.

'He wasn't dead when we buried him,' Mr Oakwood said. 'Mr Quint is still alive.'

Chapter 51

Bad Things

Mary, May 1979

The night we spent in the garden was probably the scariest of my life. All the way across the lawn and through the gate in the wall, I thought a hand was going to snatch me. I imagined a creature with claws tearing at me, clutching me, bringing me close to its teeth, ready to cut and chew, slice and crush. Or perhaps worse, the cold, dead hand of a ghostly apparition – the first Lady Ashton, finally ready to take us off to the spirit world, where further pain and torment would await us. But whether it was a monster or a ghost, the terror didn't truly come for us until we were finally in the cabin.

We sat together listening and waiting, every creak in the wooden walls, every scratch of a tree branch outside making me wonder if the cabin would be invaded and we'd all be left on this bed like the blood-covered mess in the room up in the house. I knew something terrible was out there, I could feel it, the terror shivering through my body like an illness I would never shake off.

'Where has Mr Oakwood gone?' I asked Mrs Medlock, my voice as small as a mouse, my hands trembling as I gripped the edge of Ernest's bathrobe.

'Shh!' She held up a hand, and I saw her edge a little closer towards the door.

'What?'

'I said shush!' she whispered.

'Be quiet,' Ernest hissed next to me.

Something seemed to have scared Mrs Medlock – even more than she was already. I watched her turn the side of her head towards the door, as though trying to hear something.

As she did this, I thought I heard something myself on the other side of the cabin wall. A slow scraping. Followed by a shuffle. Then nothing for a few seconds. Mrs Medlock looked at me. She'd heard it too.

Then something snapped. Maybe a twig. A twig that had been stepped on.

'Is that Mr Oakwood?' I whisper. 'Is that him outside?'

'I don't know,' Mrs Medlock said. Three terrible words that made me feel so much worse.

'Why did he leave us?' I whispered.

'To get something we can use to defend—'

She never finished her sentence. Because the door was ripped open. The monster had found us.

I thought I was scared before that moment, but when it happened, a rush of terror ran through my body like I'd been thrown into a frozen lake. This was the end. I knew it right away. He had come for us. *It* had come for us, moving like a violent gust of wind, or a sudden flash of lightning. In that moment, it wasn't a man who snatched Mrs Medlock from the cabin, but a creature – a creature with horns and hooves, a thing so terrible I desperately tried to push its image out of my head. And suddenly I was back, for a few seconds, sitting on Rupert's bed, looking at the book of paintings, paintings that made me feel strange about the world, like there was something very wrong buried inside it, inside all of us. In the end, we were all just like those cloaked women crawling on the ground in that picture Rupert had shown me. Crawling on the ground in front of the creature with horns.

'What should we do?' I asked the boys, after Mrs Medlock had been taken. Mr Oakwood hadn't returned – maybe he had been snatched too. Or worse. With all the bravery I could find in myself, I got up and walked as quietly as possible towards the door. I thought I could hear scuffling outside. The snapping of twigs, perhaps footsteps. And then something that made me run back to the bed. A cry. A woman's cry of terror. Or pain.

Back on the bed, I landed on top of the two boys, but they didn't complain. They pulled me close and we held onto each other. Tried to stay still. The cabin was spinning, rocking, like a ship on evil waves, waves that meant us harm, until eventually we would drown.

'What should we do?' I asked again, whispering the words into the mass of boys' hair and arms and ears that crowded around me. Whispered more quietly than I'd ever whispered anything before.

'I think we should stay,' said Rupert.

'I think we should go,' said Ernest.

Something broke between me and Rupert that night, when I chose Ernest's plan instead of his. I stood up and went with the older boy to the doorway and out into the night, leaving Rupert there all alone on the bed. I wanted him to come with us, but he was too terrified to move. I just knew I couldn't stay with him. That cabin might have been a place of safety, but it was also a trap, and we were the helpless animals waiting to be slaughtered. It was like the cellar where I had been made to hide while my parents died upstairs, coughing and moaning and crying out until eventually they didn't make any sound at all. It was a place where we would lose everything, and I wanted to live.

So I had to go. I had to leave him there.

*

Out in the darkness, I took Ernest's hand. He had chosen a direction decisively, but I worried he was wrong.

'I don't think we should go this way,' I whispered.

He carried on with his bold steps.

'Ernest, the path this way isn't right,' I said a little louder. 'It's too wide. We'll be seen.'

'Be quiet,' he said. He suddenly went still.

'We should go down the thin little paths,' I carried on.

His hand shot out, covering my mouth. 'I thought I heard something,' he whispered, almost mouthing the words, although it was so dark I could hardly see his lips move. After some seconds of listening, he said, 'OK,' and went to lead us forward.

As well as being afraid, I found it hard, as we pressed on, not to feel sad about what was happening. Sad that this garden was being made horrible, ugly, after we'd spent so long trying to make it a nice place, a place we could play in and feel safe in. And now we didn't feel safe at all. Now it was becoming spoiled. Spoiled in a way that could never be undone.

It wasn't long before things got even worse.

In the darkness, we heard a cracking, then a crashing. Ernest made a gasping sound and tried to pull me in a different direction. I couldn't get a proper grip on his fingers. I couldn't see where he was or work out which way I was being pulled. Then there was nothing. Maybe he'd run off and left me. Maybe he'd taken another winding path and lost me accidentally, thinking I was following. Either way, I couldn't see him anywhere. And then, as I realised with panic that I was suddenly alone, I felt a huge pain, like an explosion in my head. Then silence. Just a prickly, twinkling blackness.

Chapter 52

Something Extreme

Mrs Medlock, May 1979

My shock at the door flying open behind me barely had time to register before hands seized my shoulders and neck and dragged me outside. Fingers clutching tight, nails driving painfully into my skin, keeping hold of me. The moon must have gone behind the clouds, because everything was in darkness and I couldn't see a thing other than the light from the doorway, which added to my disorientation as the strong male arms gripping my upper body pulled me away from the relative safety of the cabin. Through my watering eyes I watched the door recede, my limbs heavy and the terror making movement impossible. A sense of hopelessness set in. There was nothing I could do. I had fought to survive, but I had lost. I was going to die.

I started to think of the children. Unprotected and frightened, huddling inside the cabin. Then I thought of what fate might await them if I was no longer on this earth to protect them. That was enough. Enough to send an unexpected swell of strength rushing through me. My mind was suddenly alert, focused, back in the present, and my muscles responded, control of my limbs returning to me. I began to claw at the arm holding me until whoever it was cried out in pain.

Of course, I knew who it was. I knew who had come back to find us.

'You have been a thorn in my side for too fucking long,' a voice full of snarling venom spat in my ear. 'Well tonight it's your turn to suffer – I'm going to make you fucking scream, just like that bitch did when I took out her insides.'

I was terrified. Terrified that he was going to kill me, that he was about to do the same to me as he had done to Bessie. When fear like that grips you, it can go two ways – immobility, or extreme energy. I was lucky. My energy returned and I suddenly became like a wild, desperate thing, flailing around and shrieking until I felt my nails dig so deep that the arm holding me tight became warm and soft and wet and had no choice but to let go.

'You fucking witch!' he shouted into the darkness as I fell with a thud onto the floor and began to crawl, sobbing as I did so, pushing myself deeper into the bushes, crunching through plants, snapping twigs, scraping my neck and face against branches and leaves. I felt cuts to my hands as I clutched around me, registering the pain but refusing to give it power, refusing to allow myself to be delayed or distracted. 'I will find you.' The words weren't shouted, just said loudly and clearly somewhere behind me, and they spurred me on until at last I had to stop to get my breath, my entire body tingling and shaking with a combination of fear and pain.

I crawled and stumbled and fell and tried again, desperate to put as much distance as I could between myself and my attacker. When my hands touched gravel, I knew I had reached one of the pathways, although my relief quickly gave way to outright horror when a hand shot out from the darkness and grabbed hold of mine. My scream caught in my throat, and in the moment of silence a voice said, 'Hush now, it's me, it's *me*.'

There was something wrong with Mr Oakwood's voice. I knew it as soon as I heard it, as soon as I realised who was speaking.

'Christ ... Christ ...' I started to say. As I turned my aching, grazed body around, the garden came into view, moonlight flooding the pathways and hedges, along with a scene that horrified me. A shape was writhing and moving on the floor. I could see flesh, and blood, and the agony in his face. For a second, I couldn't recognise the shape. Even though I had heard his voice, felt him close to me just seconds ago, I couldn't believe it was him. It was as though he had transformed into an unknown being – a creature that had crawled over to me, nestled at the edge of the bushes, hoping to find somewhere to rest, somewhere to die.

'Oh God,' I said in barely more than a broken gasp.

'I'm fine ...' he said, again in the strange voice. Too slow. Too laboured. 'Just need ... to stop ... the bleeding.' His shirt was ripped and some of it had come off completely, lying in tatters in the grit and gravel of the pathway. His right arm and shoulder were a mass of what looked like deep gashes, although he'd torn strips from his shirt and bound them tight around them.

'We need to get you help ... a hospital ...' I said, dropping down next to him and tentatively laying a hand on his shoulder. 'I should have called for help ages ago, before I came down here ... but I just wanted to get the children out of the house and ... The children ... oh God, the children ...'

I stared around me. In that moment, I couldn't work out how far I'd come through the garden, which bit of the pathway we were lying in. I strained to listen, but aside from the rustle of the trees and bushes, I couldn't make anything out. We were quite alone. For now, at least. I turned to him, unable to hide the terror shooting through me. 'They're still in the cabin. I didn't mean to leave them. He took me ... carried me out here. I couldn't stop him.'

'It isn't ... your fault ...' Mr Oakwood said, wincing and taking a deep breath. 'And now ... you need to ... go and get help.'

I knew he was right. We had to get away while we could. But I couldn't just leave him.

I was rigid with fear and regret and fury. 'We need to find the children. And get you off the pathway. If we can reach the cabin, perhaps we could barricade ourselves in—'

I jumped back then, as Mr Oakwood moved suddenly, flailing a little then rising to unsteady feet. 'Let's go,' he grunted. 'I don't know ... how long ... I'll be able to ... We need to move if we're going to ... We need ... to be quick ...'

I didn't argue. He chose the direction and I let him, allowing him to lean on me as we followed the path until we came out at the central area with the little fountain.

'We're nearly there,' I said, a glimmer of hope coming to me. I could see the cabin. The children were inside. I kept telling myself that. The children were inside. They'd be fine. Waiting for us.

'I can't ...' Mr Oakwood said, and with a whimper he collapsed onto the hard floor, leaning up against one of the curved stone benches.

I stole a look back over to the cabin. It wasn't far. I was tempted to risk calling out to the children. Or just try to drag him over there myself.

The sound of footsteps wiped all thoughts from my mind. I turned my head in the direction of the noise and almost screamed. A figure, shimmering in the moonlight, was approaching, the illumination giving the sight an impossible, other-worldly quality that made me think I was going mad. Then my eyes adjusted and I was able to make out what it was.

'Ernest,' I said weakly, reaching out a hand. 'Ernest, quickly, come over here.'

The boy didn't do as he was told. He just carried on moving

very slowly towards us, placing one foot in front of the other as though he'd only just learned to walk. He was still in his dressing gown, and he clutched it to him, perhaps out of a mixture of cold and fear. His slippers must have been discarded, and his feet were dirty with mud and some small bloody cuts. Although I was relieved to see him, his presence and unsettling demeanour only raised more questions.

'Where are Rupert and Mary?' I asked, my eyes pleading with him, hoping he'd say they were safe. Even if they'd all left the cabin, perhaps they had somehow got away, maybe back upstairs to their rooms. But he didn't say this. He just shook his head.

Mr Oakwood gave a groan. Ernest turned to look at him, his eyes widening as he took in the sight of him on the floor. 'Is he going to die?' he asked quietly.

The question sent another prickle of panic through me. 'No, he isn't. He just has a wound – quite a large one, but nothing we can't sort out.' I was coming to a decision, knowing what I had to do. Deep down, I'd always known.

'Come here, Ernest,' I said. 'We're going to create what's called a tourniquet with these remaining bits of his shirt. That's what—'

'I know what a tourniquet is,' he said, although without his normal belligerent confidence.

He came to a stop just before the gap in the stone benches opposite. My view of him was partially obscured by the fountain in the centre, and I shifted to the side to see him properly. 'Just come over here, Ernest,' I said, trying to inject a note of my usual commanding tone into my voice.

He shook his head.

A prickle of anger spiked across me. I understood he was probably afraid, realised he might have been traumatised somehow out in the garden, perhaps had endured something horrific at the hands of Mr Quint, but I couldn't waste time dealing with all that now.

I was about to march over to him and fetch him myself when I saw something move behind him. And then I realised why the boy was acting so strangely. I saw why he couldn't move.

'No ...' I said, stepping back.

'It's too late, Mrs Medlock,' Ernest whispered. I saw then that he was trembling.

'What ... is ... it?' said Mr Oakwood from the floor.

I couldn't speak. I felt frozen from within.

'He found us,' Ernest said, his voice quivering. I couldn't take my eyes off his throat. And the blade pressed against it. Whether it had been there the whole time, or had only just been placed there, I did not know. Perhaps it had been held to his back up until that moment, pushing the boy forward, step by terrible step. But whichever it was, the strangeness of Ernest's arrival now became apparent. He wasn't alone.

I watched as Mr Quint gave the boy a nudge in the back, causing him to take a few steps forward and bringing the man behind him into view.

'He's already killed Mary,' Ernest said.

I realised the large knife at the boy's throat wasn't the only thing Mr Quint was carrying. With his other arm he was gripping something slung over his shoulder. Mary's limp body. And then, to my horror, he grinned. His eyes were wild, his face marked with mud and blood, including a run of deep-looking scratch marks that I suspected I had inflicted during my attempts to flee. 'She didn't stand a chance,' he snarled. He dropped the little girl on the floor and she flopped down like a ragdoll.

I felt myself unfreeze. Courage and determination came to me once more. I stepped boldly towards Mary on the floor, but Mr Quint was too quick. He lunged at me, and for a moment I thought he would once again seize me, manhandle me as he'd done before, even try to murder me with that large knife, just as he'd butchered Bessie. But he kept the knife stretched towards Ernest and instead stamped on my left foot. Until that point, I'd have regarded such an action as trivial, perhaps even childish, but he used such ferocious force, and the pain was so extreme, it made me scream. I fell to the ground in an instant, clutching at my shoe, feeling as though the contents must now be bloody fragments of tendons, skin and bone.

'That's just a taste, Mrs Medlock,' he said, his voice loud, the inflection of his words alarmingly pitched, making him sound deranged. 'Stay where you are, you hear me? Or you'll end up like this little shrew here.' He gave Mary's body a kick. 'Or that whiny little boy in there,' he added, raising the knife to point in the direction of the cabin. 'God, the fuss he made when I laid into him. I had a bit of fun with him before I finally killed him.' His voice was getting louder, his tone jeering. 'Do you want me to tell you what I did to him?'

I realised I'd started to sob, the mixture of the pain and the terrible words becoming too much. 'Please stop,' I cried.

'Christ, why the fuck would anyone care about such a whining little rat? Well, I sure did make him whine. Gosh, the shrieking.' He let out a laugh. 'I'm surprised you didn't hear it. Maybe you did. I was good and thorough, Mrs Medlock, good and thorough. Took out his eyes first. Then cut off his little fingers, one by one. He couldn't see what I was doing by that point, of course, but by God did it sound like he felt it.'

I vomited onto the stone floor. Coughing and spluttering, the taste of bile and blood in my mouth.

'I really don't know why you've got yourself in such a state. Who gives a fuck what happens to them? They're nothing in the grand scheme of things. Nothing. I was going to bring his body up to the house – hang it from the chandelier as a present to his parents when they return. I opened up his stomach, you see, just before the end, so it would have made quite the display. But I couldn't carry him at the same time as this little cunt.' He gave Mary another kick. 'And Ernest here is proving a tricky boy.' I heard Mr Quint walking back over to Ernest. 'Sit here,' he instructed. I raised my head in time to see him putting his hand on the boy's shoulder, pushing him down onto the stone bench to his right.

'None of this ... had ... to happen,' Mr Oakwood said with what sounded like a great deal of effort.

'Ah, you're still with us,' said Mr Quint. 'The caveman speaks. The man of the woods awakens. Nice of you to contribute, old fellow. And you're quite right. None of it had to happen. If my followers and I had been left to carry on in peace, everything would have been very smooth and amicable. But you and Mrs cunting Medlock became irritants.'

I saw Mr Oakwood jerk a little, as if he was trying to stand up, but he gave up with a grunt as soon as he tried to use his injured arm. It looked as though he was close to blacking out. I wanted to go over to him, but the shooting pains in my foot made movement impossible.

'More than irritants,' Mr Quint went on. 'You also tried your hands at murder.' He let out a sudden crazed laugh, and scratched at his head with the handle of the large knife, the blade glinting in the moonlight. 'Which, obviously, you failed abysmally at. Although, to be honest, I should be thanking you. When I crawled out of that grave, spitting out earth and leaves and dragging myself into the dark night air, it was as if I was reborn. I'd held myself back in my previous life. I was too cautious and mild-mannered with my followers. I should have shown my commitment to them sooner.'

'Your followers showed no commitment to you,' I said, my voice shaking. 'They ran off into the night the moment things turned sour.'

Mr Quint considered this for a moment, his harsh chin jutting out, his head tilted. 'I wouldn't be so sure. But I do regret I didn't move things along sooner. I was afraid – yes, I admit that – of going too far too quickly. The main tenets of our belief are based on commitment and passion, do you understand me? Showing that we are not afraid to break boundaries, push against what society tells us is acceptable. Do things that people like you, frigid and dried up and repressed, find appalling simply because of how ignorant and naive you are. It's quite amusing, really, to think how shocked you were about me bringing two women to my room back when I started here. How trivial that seems now. Well, what I've done tonight isn't trivial, Mrs Medlock. And it's about to get a whole lot worse for you. Boundaries will certainly be pushed, I can tell you. I'll take you to breaking point.'

I clenched the edge of the bench behind me, hatred making my fingertips vibrate, my heart pound. 'It wasn't trivial for Ernest.'

I could just about make out the boy's face, saw him glance over at me. Mr Quint looked at him too. 'I think Ernest enjoyed his education,' he said with a smirk. 'And those women were only doing me a favour. They'd have done anything I wanted. They would even have paid you a visit, Mrs Medlock, if I'd asked them to. What would you have done, I wonder, if they'd arrived at your bedside, ready to touch you. Hold you. Make you writhe and moan, feel things you've never felt before. I have wondered what it must be like to be so tragically untouched, you have to fuck the reclusive gardener just to satisfy your human desires.' He kicked at Mr Oakwood's solid frame, even harder than the blows he'd aimed at Mary, causing him to let out a sound that broke my heart: a primal, anguished groan of pain and desperation.

'And while we're on the subject of our dear Mr Oakwood, you three' – he used the knife to point at myself, Mr Oakwood and Mary – 'almost ruined everything. So your punishment should be equal to the gravity of your crime. Let me put it this way – the carnage you discovered back in the house with sweet Bessie will seem like a mere starter compared to what's going to happen here. Remember my words. The writing on the wall? Do you understand?'

I didn't answer, although my brain was suddenly swimming with images. The blood, the gore, the words daubed above her. *You will all be dead by dawn.* After staring at me a little longer, Mr Quint transferred his gaze to Mr Oakwood on the floor.

'What happened to Bessie was quite enjoyable. You see, I had only just reconciled myself to living a truer, more free life. I'd been recuperating in the little woodshed on the edge of the garden, curled up in there. But I became concerned when I could hear Mr Oakwood working nearby. I didn't want him to open the woodshed door and get a nasty surprise, not before I'd regained some of my strength. So at night I made my way to the house cellar, away from all of you, until I knew I was ready to do what needed to be done.

'I'd like to say she didn't suffer, but, well, in all honesty she did. You never know how much one feels after being knocked out. Something fascinating, though: it wasn't when the knife slid into her that I felt closest to myself, closest to the shimmering light inside of me. According to the beliefs our group was founded on, it's often the fatal blow or cut that produces the most exquisite reaction within us, or when we submerge the dying soul in water and allow the light of the moon to bring their inner being to the surface. But it was different in this instance. It wasn't the first slice of the knife. I didn't have a river or lake to submerge her in. No – it was when I held her in my arms. Held her integral parts, her heart, her lungs, felt their warmth. *That* was when I felt the light inside of me grow. When I knew that what I was doing was pure, an act of true primitive importance.'

'You're insane,' I said simply, not bothering to keep the revulsion from my face.

'Do you really think so?' Mr Quint said, frowning, tilting his head as if I'd made an interesting point. 'I'd urge you not to be so closed-minded, Mrs Medlock. Not until you've had the chance to experience the same thing.'

He looked down once again at Mr Oakwood on the floor, still bent over in agony.

'I think we'll start with him. Ernest, what do you think we should do with him?'

In my peripheral vision, I saw the boy jolt. He didn't speak, just stared back at Mr Quint, waiting.

'I think,' Mr Quint said slowly, 'he should have the chance to experience something strong. Something ... extreme ... before he dies.'

'Please ...' I said, deciding it was worth one last attempt to save at least some of us. 'Please, just ... just stop and think. If you're going to kill him, you'll have to kill me. But there's no need to have Ernest here. There's no need to make him watch.'

'Oh, he's not going to *watch*, Mrs Medlock,' Mr Quint said, with a devastating smile. 'He's going to participate. He's going to very much participate. Ernest's going to experience the next part of his education, right here in the garden.'

'Please,' I gasped again. 'Just let him go. Let him get away from ... all this.' *Run off and get help*, I urged silently in my head, trying to meet Ernest's gaze. I knew it was pointless, though. No help was coming for us. We'd reached the end. The end of everything.

I turned my gaze back to Mr Quint and saw him watching me with a raised eyebrow and a slightly crooked mouth. Then he spoke just one, terrible word. 'No.'

That was when he plunged the knife into Mr Oakwood. Quick

and brutal. A flash of red. A desperate half-groan, half-howl – a sound so terrible I felt it leave its stain on me as it echoed through the clearing. Mr Oakwood rocked forward in his already slumped position, then went limp, falling over onto his side.

'We'll let him bleed there for a while. It should take him quite a long time to die. He must have lost a fair bit of blood when I tried to cut him up earlier. But with any luck, he'll be awake to enjoy some of the games we're going to play. And we're going to play *such* games.' He sent a horrible smirk over to where Ernest was sitting. 'Every boy should learn how to use a knife properly,' he said, lowering his voice and speaking with a sense of hushed excitement. 'It's an important part of becoming a man. Come here, Ernest.'

To my dismay, Ernest obeyed. He got up off his bench, and walked solemnly, as if in a trance, over to his tutor, who held out the bloodied weapon. The boy took it, holding it with his right hand and running his left down the blade. Some of the blood came off on his fingers, but he showed neither fear nor disgust. His expression was blank.

'I know, dear boy. I know,' Mr Quint said, laying a hand on Ernest's shoulder. 'You can feel it, can't you. That true part inside of you starting to stir. The piece of your very identity, ready to wake once again.' He looked at me, and there was true, undiluted malice in his eyes. 'You will find beauty in what's about to happen, Mrs Medlock. I promise you. Your immediate reaction may be to reject it. But I think it's time we—'

He stopped mid-flow, his terrible sentence hanging unfinished in the air, his gaze fixed to his left. To the place on the floor where Mary's body lay. Stirring. Mary's body was stirring.

I saw the surprise in Mr Quint's face. Then Mary turned over and sat up, blinking. Evidently confused and, judging by her expression, in pain. But alive.

And at the same moment as Mary's Lazarus-like return, I discovered something upon my person. Something I had entirely forgotten about. In my discomfort and pain, I had leaned to my side, using the base of the fountain to prop myself up as Mr Quint continued his unhinged monologue, and that was when I felt it. A thin, solid object. I pulled it out from the folds of my dress, realising what it was as my hand closed around it.

I knew in an instant what I needed to do.

And I knew I had to act immediately. I had to be fast, push down my astonishment and relief at seeing Mary move. It was as if in that moment I was able to split myself in two. While one half marvelled at how such a small creature could sustain such violence and still raise herself, the other part of me was taking control of my limbs, giving me strength I didn't know still resided in my bruised body.

Now, I told myself. *It needs to be now.*

I managed to leave the pain in my foot on the floor where I had been crouching, for by the time I was upright, I felt nothing. I was made of night air and moonlight and a strong resolve. A resolve to fight back. To protect. To avenge.

Mr Quint's head was craned towards Mary on the floor, exposing the expanse of his neck. I launched myself at him, drawing back the knife with a primal howl: part anger, part rage. As I moved, everything slowed. He began to turn towards me, his expression shocked. For what felt like an age, but could only have been a second, our eyes locked. It was as if, within that second, he saw me properly for the first time. At last, a degree of understanding, mingled with fear. I plunged the little blade of the letter opener into the space just under his jaw. And with a quick, tugging movement, which took all the strength I had, I brought it down and across, tearing as hard as I could, ignoring the spray and spatter that coated my face as I did so.

Mr Quint clutched at his streaming neck, the dark liquid pouring over his hands, down his shirt, onto the floor. His eyes were wide and astonished and, for the first time that night, scared. He was afraid.

Mary, still sitting on the floor, seemed unaware of the crimson stream splashing onto her, covering her hair, her dressing gown and pyjamas. It was a surprise to see that such a thin, pale man could have so much blood in him. None of us did anything to help him. I probably should have tried to remove Mary, take her away from the horrific spectacle, but movement had left me once more and all I could do was watch as Mr Quint struggled and writhed and twitched and gargled. It was an incredible sight. Impressive – awesome, even. I know that sounds like a strange thing, after all I had witnessed across that terrible night. But there was something mesmeric in the sheer awfulness of it. Maybe, just maybe, that was what Mr Quint had meant when he said I would see the beauty in what was about to happen, in spite of my attempts to reject it.

The gargling became a bubbling, wheezing sound. Then there was just the noise of the dying man's weird little kicks, his shoes scuffing the edge of the stone bench where Ernest sat, as still as a statue, watching his tutor's hands jutting out like the claws of a stretching dog that had woken up from a very long sleep. Animal, that was what he was. An animal.

We carried Mr Oakwood. I'm astonished we managed it as far as we did. I was dimly aware of the pain in my foot, but I was fairly sure it wasn't broken, and my mind seemed capable of putting aside the discomfort in order to focus on the task at hand. I'd used the belt of Ernest's bathrobe as tourniquets. The boy allowed me to take it without protest, all the while staring at Mr Quint's body on the floor. I used some of the shreds of Mr Oakwood's shirt to bind his other wounds. I made the decision to bring him up to the house, unsure if it was wise. I just knew I couldn't bear to take him into the darkness of the cabin. I was certain he would die in there, that place of death. And the sight of the mangled corpse of Master Rupert would have finished me off completely.

'Shouldn't we leave him?' Ernest asked when I told him we needed to carry him.

'We should get him to the house ... into the warm ... then an ambulance can get to him.' I spoke in small snippets, preserving my energy by limiting my words. I had no idea if we'd achieve my plan, but I knew I'd have to try.

'If Mr Oakwood's going to die,' Mary said in a tiny voice, wiping her blood-soaked hair out of her eyes, 'wouldn't it be nicer for him to die here in the garden with the plants and flowers he liked so much?'

I couldn't answer that. It made logical sense, but it was a possibility I couldn't face. Leaving him there was choosing death. I needed us to choose life. And that meant carrying him.

Of course, the plan was a foolish one. I wasn't in my right mind at that point. I saw that in retrospect. I don't think anyone who had gone through what I had could have retained a sense of order and calm and chosen the right thing under those circumstances. We did manage to get him out of the garden, carrying and half dragging him along the paths, through the door in the stone wall, but came to a stop halfway up the lawn.

Ernest was flagging with the effort. My foot had started to throb with pain. And little Mary, who had only been holding one of Mr Oakwood's arms in a token gesture of help, said in that small voice, 'I'm very tired, Mrs Medlock.'

'I am too,' said Ernest.

'Let's pause here,' I replied, breathless and exhausted.

So we paused.

I didn't know if he was still breathing. I was scared to check.

I looked at the night sky. The swaying trees. The hulking mass of the house still quite a way in front of us. The moonlight had gone, and although it was still dark, there was a lightening on the horizon that signalled dawn wasn't far away. But that wasn't the only light. Something else was out there, more pronounced and definite. Shining in the darkness.

'What's that?' Ernest said, spotting it too.

'I ... don't know ...' I replied. But it didn't take me long to guess as the light came into view again. Moving, making steady progress across our field of view, heading along the driveway.

It was a car. Winding its way towards the house. We stayed completely still, frozen, watching as it came nearer. The sight made me feel both fearful and hopeful in equal measure. Then, with a stretch still to go before reaching the house, it stopped, and a figure – tall and slim, clearly masculine – got out.

Although irrational and absurd, I had a sudden fleeting fear that it was Mr Quint, that somehow he had cheated death for a second time and returned to wreak brutal vengeance upon us. But then it became obvious to me who this must be. And moments later, as he became visible in the ever-lightening grey of the dawn, it was confirmed.

'What in God's name is happening here, Mrs Medlock?' Lord Ashton asked.

He helped us take Mr Oakwood up to the house. After realising how acute the situation had become, he moved with efficient determination. I told him that Mr Oakwood had been attacked by Mr Quint, who was now dead, his body down by the fountain in the garden. Lord Ashton just nodded, then made it clear to me that further explanations could wait until we had sought medical attention. We laid Mr Oakwood down on one of the sofas in the library, with Lord Ashton instructing me to light the fire to give him instant warmth. Then he attempted to make a phone call in the hallway, but found there to be no connection, so returned to his vehicle to use the car phone.

While he did this, I watched Mr Oakwood's chest rise and fall. Very slowly, but still moving, still breathing. I turned my attention to Mary, who had nestled herself in one of the single-seater chairs, already leaving brown-red patches of blood on the upholstery. 'We may need to get you to hospital,' I told her, lifting her pyjama top and looking at the bruises already starting to bloom where she'd been kicked. 'To check everything's all right inside.'

She just nodded in a docile way. 'I think I want to sleep,' she said. I didn't know if this was a good idea or if I was risking her never waking up. I decided it would be too cruel to say no. So I said it was fine to close her eyes, and she drifted off in the chair, while I patted her arm and Ernest sat watching us from a spot over by the window.

I don't know how much time passed, but the result of Lord Ashton's phone call from the car felt almost instantaneous. A man with grey hair and a faint moustache who told me he was a doctor asked me to step back from Mr Oakwood. Then, along with another younger man, he carried him into the dining room next door, and I watched from the hallway as they doused the area around him in liquid. For one awful moment, I thought it was petroleum and they were about to set him alight. But then they brought out instruments and materials and I realised they were going to help him. The younger man noticed me watching, and without saying anything closed the dining room door.

Lord Ashton drew me back into the library. 'Mrs Medlock, I know you've been through an ordeal, but I need you to tell me: where is my son? He's not in his room.'

And I'd thought it was over.

I'm surprised you didn't hear his screams.

For a moment, the room spun around me. I put out a hand and rested it on Lord Ashton's chest to steady myself. Feeling him there, beneath the material, was strange and unsettling. A reminder that behind his controlled exterior was a human being with a beating heart and veins and bones. I hadn't touched him for over twenty years. But I pushed aside those thoughts. Because once again, he was going to need me to be strong. 'He left Rupert in the cabin. I'm so sorry.'

We walked down there together, in the still, misty morning air. As we left, four men, all dressed in suits but wearing white plastic gloves, entered the house.

'What are they doing?' I asked.

'Tidying up,' he said simply.

He didn't speak again as we walked towards the trees, alongside the stone wall and through the big oak door. I didn't speak either. I had no words, and I knew I would need them when we found the body. And he would need me, in his own quiet way.

When the cabin came into view, my legs started to shake. A building I had once viewed as a place of comfort, a place of passion, a place of love had become the monster in a horror story. As we walked towards the door, it was as if I could hear the screams that Mr Quint had spoken about. Taunted us with. Telling us how he had broken the little boy's body. How Rupert had died out here in the dark, alone and in pain and scared. The terror he had endured, for it all to end here, in a small cabin in a garden drenched in grief.

We opened the door.

We saw him on the bed.

Lord Ashton walked slowly inside.

I couldn't follow.

Chapter 53

The Boy in the Garden

Mrs Medlock, May 1979

'You came back.'

Those were the three words Rupert managed to utter before he started crying. He was huddled on Mr Oakwood's bed, his face red with tears, the sheet pulled up close to him. He'd pressed himself into the corner, a frightened little bundle, not knowing who was approaching the cabin.

The relief was extraordinary. But after it had lessened, enough for me to force myself to step inside and help Lord Ashton coax his son off the bed, my mind started to crowd with thoughts once more. Thoughts about how Mr Quint had lied. How he had either decided not to kill the boy – a moment of mercy amid the carnage of the night – or had simply spared him out of necessity. Let him live in order to corner the rest of us before we made it back to the house. I would never know.

Unlike the other two children, Master Rupert never saw a single drop of blood over that twenty-four-hour period. From the cabin doorway, Mr Quint's body was mostly hidden by the fountain in the centre of the circle, but I wrapped one of Mr

Oakwood's cardigans over the boy's face as he was carried out, just to be sure.

'What about ...' I started to ask Lord Ashton, but trailed off, unable to bring myself to say the word 'the body'.

'It will be sorted,' he said. When we returned to the house, I saw a collection of the gloved men making their way down the lawn in the direction of the garden, two of them carrying something long and thin between them, possibly a roll of something. They looked like a firm of decorators. I knew what they must be doing. I understood why it would be necessary. The library door and that of the room where Mr Oakwood had been taken were both closed, although I could still hear voices inside. The same was true of the bedroom on the first floor where Bessie's life had come to an end.

I found Mary and Ernest together in the boy's bedroom. They had been left unattended while the unknown, unspeaking men moved about the house. If I'd had the presence of mind, I'd have made sure they stayed clear of the first floor while the work was done in the room next to them. But there were so many things they should have been spared. To list them all would take a lifetime.

I was pleased to see Mary awake, and decided I should free her from her bloodstained clothes and wash her hair. We did this in our usual bathroom. I had instructed Ernest to run himself a bath on the floor above while I tended to Mary. I wanted them both to be clean, for all evidence of the night to be washed away from both body and mind. But while the former was possible, I knew the latter was not.

Mary sat in silence as her hair gave up its red-tinged mixture of blood and dirt and leaves and twigs. She said nothing while I combed and scrubbed and rinsed. She only spoke when I'd got her dry and into some clean pyjamas and told her we were going to have a day of rest and go to our beds and sleep. 'I slept, but then

I was woken,' she said. 'Ernest took me upstairs. He's been nice to me.' I told her I was pleased to hear this. 'I thought you said I needed to go to hospital?' she added.

I said that perhaps she might and that I would ask one of the doctors downstairs tending to Mr Oakwood to come and look at her bruises. They could make a decision. I had made enough that day and I wasn't sure I trusted myself to make any more. 'It will all be better when you wake up,' I said.

She stared at me for a bit, unblinking through partly closed eyes, as though sleep was just seconds away. Then she said, 'Is Rupert . . . ?'

'He's fine,' I said. 'He's safe.'

Ernest was silent when I went to check on him. He had just got out of his bath and was towelling himself dry. I left a pile of clothes to the left of the bathtub and went to leave, then said, 'I think it's best if you sleep in a different room on a different floor.'

He just nodded.

I drifted downstairs as if my legs were being steered by someone with a remote control. A dreamy, light-headed feeling had come across me and I was struggling to care any more about anything. All of it had hurt so much, it was as if my sense of feeling, my inner pain threshold, had been knocked off-kilter and now couldn't function.

I found Lord Ashton in the main hall, talking to two men, both tall enough to rival his own notable height. Before I could focus on their faces, I heard Lord Ashton say, 'I'm very much obliged to you, Mr Quinn.' For a second, I felt a jolt of panic, mistaking the surname for that of the recently deceased tutor. Then I recognised the men properly, and it only took me a moment to place them. The slightly older of the two was a gentleman named Bartholomew Quinn; he'd visited the house a couple of times before. As I walked further down the stairs to face them, I realised that the younger man was Michael Allerton. It was strange to see him here again, just a matter of weeks after his last visit, under such different circumstances. He didn't smile as I came into view, just looked at me intently for a few seconds, then switched his attention back to Lord Ashton.

'Of course, it's best if Clive is spared some of the finer details of what's occurred,' Lord Ashton was saying. 'Perhaps you could have a discreet conversation with him later today and make that clear to him. He just needs to be forewarned that his son may talk about it at some point and we need to be certain we've got a solution to every eventuality.'

Both men nodded, then Michael Allerton said, 'I'm sure we can find ways to manage the boy. Clive had already asked me to try and smooth things over with his school. He's keen for him to get back into ordinary life, so I'm certain we can make sure the family as a whole is, well, on the right page.'

'Good,' Lord Ashton said, then he turned round to me as if he'd always known I was there behind him. 'I'll meet you in the kitchen, Mrs Medlock.'

I took this as a sign he didn't want me listening in any further and walked off towards the back of the house. I was desperately hungry: a feeling that only kicked in properly when I saw the bread on the kitchen worktop, awakening a need for food I must have subconsciously repressed for hours. I cut myself a large slice and collapsed into one of the chairs at the table, cramming the food into my mouth, marvelling at how I could find joy and comfort in something so plain, so trivial, when the world around me was in such disarray. One slice wasn't enough. I went back for more – a thicker slice, layers of butter and cheese and cold meats, more desperate, delicious feasting, tearing the crusts with my teeth, the feeling of satisfaction tremendous.

'I don't want to interrupt your meal,' Lord Ashton said at the doorway when he entered. 'But as you can imagine, there are things we need to discuss immediately.'

'I know,' I said, setting down my crumb-strewn plate, looking up at him. It was a strange sight, seeing him in the servants' quarters. It was as if a very rare, endangered creature had just wandered into a shop and tried to buy a newspaper. This feeling was heightened further when he pulled up a chair and came to sit facing me, laying his large, strong hands on the heavily grooved and scratched tabletop in front of him. 'I also know what you're about to tell me,' I added, meeting his eyes.

'You do?' He frowned.

I nodded. 'He hasn't made it, has he? Mr Oakwood?'

Silence for a few moments. Then Lord Ashton said quietly, 'No, he hasn't survived. Mr Oakwood died of his injuries a little while ago.'

I nodded again. He waited a moment, as though expecting me to have some dramatic breakdown, to start smashing things up, turning over the table, wailing on the floor. I did none of these things. The inclination for anything of that sort had long since left me.

'Well ... I realise none of this is easy, but there are some other things.'

'Please continue,' I replied.

He took a breath. 'As I'm sure you've seen, the house has been thoroughly ... sorted out.'

'I'm glad,' I said.

'The fact that neither Mr Oakwood nor Bessie had any family makes things ... simpler.'

'I agree,' I said, trying to stop the very worst memories – the very worst images – taking over my thoughts.

'I just wanted to check if you or anyone else phoned the police at any point.'

'The phone lines had already been cut when the attempt was made. They were fixed temporarily, but I think Mr Quint damaged them again. So no, I don't think the police were called.'

He looked satisfied by this, and moved on. 'The children are going to be a complication for a long time to come. I've made it clear to Rupert how important it is we treat the situation quite delicately. I suggested his mother's health and mental well-being would suffer if she ever found out what happened here. I think he will keep his word, but we'll have to watch him closely.'

If I had more energy, I might have mentioned some concerns I had about this arrangement, but I chose the easy route and just nodded.

'The doctors have said that Mary should make a full recovery. Her injuries are not serious. She is going to be sent to America.'

My eyes widened. He noticed.

'I know, a bit of a change, I realise that, but I think a new start away from this is best. There's a family in South Carolina who ... Let's just say they owe me a favour or two. They will take her in. I'll keep tabs on her, but she's going to get a new identity. Mr Quinn and Mr Allerton will sort that.'

Again I did my best to push away the ethical and moral concerns I had about this. The lies that would be told to the girl, the emotional blackmail, perhaps, the manipulation of her trauma and memories of her early years. The whole thing made me tremble.

'Are you able to give me a summary of who knows ... details that could be difficult? And if so, how much do they know? As you can imagine, Mary's letter worried me.'

I waited a few seconds before I answered. Then I said, in as dispassionate, businesslike a tone as I could manage: 'Mary, Rupert and Ernest all know about the bones. They knew Mr Quint suspected the bones came from a ... a baby. Mr Oakwood and I told them they were actually from a dog.'

Lord Ashton appeared to ponder this for a moment, then asked, 'What about Honoria?'

A tear made its way slowly down my cheek. I didn't brush it away. 'I told Bessie. Not everything, though. And I'm certain she never told a soul. She couldn't. She didn't have time before . . . '

He put out a hand. He kept it on mine. I allowed it to be there.

'Everyone has a breaking point. I understand why you needed to speak of it. But we're going to put it behind us now. For ever. You understand me?'

I tilted my head forward to show I understood, unable to look up from the table as more tears blurred my vision. 'For ever.'

Chapter 54

Recollections

Natalie

'But ... I still don't understand,' I say, trying to remain patient, given everything this poor woman has told me. 'What really happened to the first Lady Ashton? And the graves in the garden, the ... '

'The babies?' Mrs Medlock says in a faint, faraway voice. She gets up and walks over to a large box in the corner of the room, removing some folded blankets and magazines that are piled on top of it. The contents seem to be an untidy mess of papers, but she navigates them easily enough, and picks out some notebooks – cheap looking, scuffed and old. 'There are still some things I can't talk about,' she says. 'But after everything I've told you today, I think you deserve to know the full story. The story of my ... my children. How I was a mother for the briefest of minutes. And how the woman I did it all for died that same night.' She hands me the notebooks, and I take them, noticing the years on each one.

'They're your diaries?' I say, looking up at her. 'They're all still here?'

She nods.

I'm desperate to start reading them, but there's one more thing I feel I need to say. 'I'm so sorry to hear that Mr Oakwood didn't survive the ordeal. That must have been very difficult for you, on top of everything else. To lose someone so close.' I say this as gently as I can, realising it may cause her great upset.

She doesn't break down in sobs, but I see a small tear form in the corner of her left eye. A moment later, though, it has gone and she's composed herself again. 'Our relationship wasn't a typical romance. It didn't follow a classic love-story trajectory. He was a man I held close to me once, when we were both young and caught in that sudden first spark of love, across a dazzling summer many, many years ago. And then we found that connection again, briefly, during that difficult time twenty years later. Perhaps, had he survived, our bond would have solidified. The foundations were there. We just didn't have the time. Or maybe we did, we just squandered it. But so many things in life only become obvious to you when it's too late. Regret is a bitter but familiar companion as the years go by, I find.'

It's my turn to cry now. I move a hand up to my face to brush away the tears. Mrs Medlock notices. 'Oh goodness, I'm so sorry. I've upset you with all my rabbiting on about the past.' She gets up from the table. 'It's time for you to meet Master Rupert. You can get to know him and even have a preliminary lesson today, if that would suit? I know some tutors like to start things off with an assessment in order to work out the direction to go forward.'

It's almost too much for me. I swallow back the tears, the memories, the buried pain of it all and try to speak as calmly as I can. 'Mrs Medlock ... we're not at Marwood Manor.'

She appears only mildly confused at first, frowning at me as if I've tried to make a joke that she doesn't quite get. 'What ... sorry, what do you mean?'

'We're not at Marwood Manor. You haven't lived there for years. This isn't the kitchen, or the servants' quarters. We're in your flat in Henley.'

She looks properly puzzled now. 'I'm sorry, I don't know what you're talking about ... Henley? Why would I be in Henley?'

'Because this is where you live,' I say, standing up myself now and walking round to her. 'I'm not a tutor for Master Rupert. Because Rupert doesn't need a tutor any more, does he? He's nearly fifty.'

She's staring at me as if I've just told her the earth is flat. 'Nearly fifty? What nonsense. He's just a boy ... just ... he's up in his bedroom right now ... ' She raises her eyes to the ceiling, as if there might be some visible evidence up there to prove she is right.

'Mrs Medlock,' I say, laying a hand on her arm, 'everything you told me about happened a long, long time ago. I'm grateful to you for talking to me. Some of it I remember, some of it has been gaps in my mind for so long. Gaps that have haunted me. And now, thanks to you, I'm starting to piece it together.'

She's shaking her head, looking at me sadly, as if she suspects I'm insane and doesn't know what to tell me. 'I'm sorry, my dear, I really don't know ... '

'I introduced myself as Natalie, Mrs Medlock. But that's not the name I was born with. That's the name I was given when I was adopted when I was a child. My birth name was Mary.'

Chapter 55

Mrs Medlock's Diary

October 1959

2 October 1959

As soon as I held the little bundle, I knew it was too late. I'd felt him leave me. Just like his sister. But the other baby was still crying. The last and smallest of the three. I picked him up, trying to soothe him.

At first I didn't know if it was Honoria screaming or me, but when I looked up, I saw it was her. She had collapsed over the little bodies, her arms wrapped around them, leaning against the end of the bed.

'It's OK,' I told her. 'We still have this one. This little boy.'

'Give him to me,' she said, looking up, her eyes wild.

'Not yet,' I said. 'Let me hold him. In case he goes too.'

She tried to take him off me, but I told her again I wanted a moment with him. I worried he wouldn't survive much longer, that he would soon leave us like his brother and sister had. Even though I'd tried to reassure her, I feared we were on borrowed time.

She wouldn't listen. She reached towards me and snatched the baby with desperate arms. 'He's not yours!' she cried. 'He's mine! My son!'

This wasn't true, and I told her as much.

'Give me back my little boy, please,' I begged her, hauling myself off the bed, trying to ignore the pain. She backed away from me, out of the room onto the landing, shrieking and shouting as she went. I could barely make out what she was saying. I think she was unravelling in that moment, all the hopes and pressure and build-up over the months finally breaking her. Although it was my body that had gone through the trauma of birth, her mind had still suffered deep ruptures.

'Get away from me,' she shouted, trying to get a grip on the baby in her arms. That was when I realised she was still holding the letter opener she'd used to cut the umbilical cords. I didn't know if she was brandishing it as a weapon to make me keep back or if she'd forgotten she was holding it altogether. All I could hear was the baby's sobs worsening, and a protective rush built within me like nothing I had ever felt.

I didn't wait. With an energy I would previously have thought impossible, I stepped towards her, determined to lift the infant from her arms. I was just in time. She had lost her hold on the blankets and he was about to tumble to the floor. My arms closed around him, lifting him up, and I tried to walk away from where Honoria stood.

That was my mistake. She came at me like a wild thing, a creature spooked, some beautiful, terrible angel sent down to punish me. My whole body was in pain, but I moved back as her hand jabbed forward, nearly catching me with the blade. We were pressed up against the railings of the gallery landing, her weight now against me as she tried to take what I had, fingers too harsh, too rough for the fragile creature in my arms. I worried that at any moment I would hear something break, his little body injured in the fray; or that the knife in her hand might find me, sink into me and render me incapable of protecting the piece of my soul clutched in my embrace.

I pushed her. It was the only thing I could do. I pushed her so hard and thoroughly, I saw what was about to happen just before it did. And I heard the fall echo through the house, as if every room knew a calamity had occurred. As if its walls would never be free from the taint of it.

Honoria's screams stopped when her feet left the floor. The baby's cries stopped seconds later, his little body limp in my arms, just like his two siblings. And then I was alone.

Mr Oakwood found me, huddled on the landing outside Honoria's bedroom. I was holding the little bundle, rocking it gently, even though the child was no longer present to be comforted. It was to comfort me. 'Promise me you'll get Lord Ashton,' I said, gripping hold of his sodden shirt, rainwater dripping onto me. 'Him and only him. Nobody else.'

It was Mr Oakwood who tried the phones throughout the night as the storm raged on around us. He who got through to Lord Ashton at last and had him drive back from London in the early hours. I will never forget this night. It will become a part of me. For ever.

3 October 1959

Lord Ashton visited my room at eleven o'clock last night. It was a short meeting. 'My wife's boat has been found,' he said, his voice neutral. I didn't know what he meant at first. 'What?' I said, confused. He went on to explain: 'Don't you remember, Mrs Medlock? My wife decided she was going to spend this week with a friend in Cornwall. She was advised not to go sailing since the weather was going to be rough, although of course it would have been very irresponsible in her condition whatever the weather. It seems she didn't heed this advice and went out alone. Her friend said she was adamant she would be fine. You know how headstrong Honoria could be. It seems she got into difficulty. The boat has been found. Her body has not. I dare say it never will.'

    I lay awake nearly all night, both horrified and impressed with how calmly he had told me all this. Could such a story really work? Would people be satisfied with it? Would her mysterious disappearance go on to become a curiosity in the press for years to come? Part of me feels incapable of dealing with such a weight of doubt in my life. In the end, I gave up on sleep and came to write this. The sun is rising at last. It's the first we've seen of it for three days now. A new dawn over Marwood. I daresay I'll find a way of coping. I've always been one for soldiering on, as my father used to say when I was a child. Better that than get lost amid the reeds. But if the reeds have secrets, snagged within their whispering stems, surely it's impossible not to get dragged back into the past. I suppose I'll have to wait and see.

Chapter 56

Where It All Began

Natalie

During the night, I dream I am back at Marwood. The house is on fire and I am chained to the floor in the main hallway, facing upwards, with views of the many gallery landings above. They go on for miles and miles, stretching into space, defying any sense of time or place or reality.

I wake with a start, pulling myself out of the covers, almost expecting to see flames around me. It takes me a second or two to realise where I am, why I am here in England. Confronting my past. Confronting ghosts that have found no peace.

The car arrives for me outside the hotel at 11 a.m., as promised. I sit in the back as the driver takes me out of the main city centre of Oxford and into the countryside. Soon the car slows and we turn off along a gravel road. A driveway.

The house comes into view like a speck on the landscape, getting nearer and nearer. An enormous, hulking beast. An animal waiting to pounce.

A man opens the front door and walks down the steps. My

memory of Rupert is indistinct. At times I feel I can see his face clearly. There were moments amid Mrs Medlock's recollections when I felt as if he was almost there beside me. Then the image blurred, and I wondered if I was just inventing my impressions of a troubled little boy, neglected by his parents, uncertain of his place in the world. But I know this is Rupert.

I'm struck by how remarkably well he's aged. His brown hair is flecked with grey but has held its colour well. His frame looks firm and surprisingly athletic. He's dressed in beige chinos and a grey and dark blue patterned sweater. If I had to imagine what a British aristocrat would wear around his country estate, this would be it.

As I climb out of the car, I'm unsure whether to stare up at Rupert or the house. Both are competing for my attention, but the house wins. Its presence has featured so heavily in my mind – both conscious and unconscious – for so many years now that standing in front of it, seeing the cracks in its walls, the sheer size of it, is nothing short of astonishing.

'Do you need a moment?' Rupert asks, clearly realising I'm struggling not to become overwhelmed. I nod in response, and he stands next to me and turns to face the house he's just walked out of, taking in the same view as me. 'I can't imagine what this must be like for you.' I nod again, feeling bad that the response is inadequate, but it's all I can manage. After a while he says, 'Do you feel able to come inside?'

I take a deep breath. 'Yes. I think so.'

Whenever people describe memories 'flooding back', I'm always jealous. My memories of my childhood are like a patchwork quilt, with most of the squares greyed out and only a few rendered in murky colour. Even while listening to Mrs Medlock, things were still difficult to define. But coming back to Marwood, walking through these doors into the hallway, looking up at the main staircase, seeing the gallery landings above ... the floodgates really do open. It feels as if they're now open for good.

Rupert is patient with me as I stand in the middle of the hallway, taking everything in. And for a moment, I feel as if I'm back there, frightened and confused, on a cold December night forty years ago, trying to comprehend my parents' deaths, trying to make sense of my new surroundings.

As soon as I feel able, he leads me into the library. He isn't to know what happened in here. I strongly suspect nobody has ever told him. He will soon, though. And when he does, he may not be able to stride so confidently into the room ever again.

I take a seat on a sofa. Rupert sits in one of the single-seaters. He offers me something to drink, which I decline. 'It's rather extraordinary to see you again,' he says. 'Should I call you Natalie? Or Mary?'

'Natalie, please,' I say firmly, then give him a quick smile to dilute the bluntness. 'I can barely remember being called Mary. It doesn't feel like my name.'

'I understand,' he says, nodding slowly. 'Although there is a lot I *don't* understand. I know you've said some of this in your emails, but you ... well, you've left a lot out. Gaps in your memory, as you say. Am I right in thinking that your visit to Mrs Medlock yesterday was helpful in filling in those gaps?'

I look at my hands. 'Some of them. She certainly confirmed a lot I thought I knew. And told me some things I didn't. Her recollection is quite remarkable.'

He raises his eyebrows. 'Is it? I've barely seen her since she left Marwood. I understand she's starting to develop dementia.'

I nod. 'She thought she was still here. Still working here. It was quite disturbing in a way. But the details she could recall ... I never expected ... never dared hope ... '

I twist my fingers together, as if trying to scrub them clean – a habit I have when I'm stressed. 'Do you live here alone?' I ask, looking up at him. I see his eyes widen slightly at the change of subject.

'No, I live with my partner, Charles, and his adopted son, although they're both out at the moment.'

I smile again and nod, although this wasn't quite what I wanted to know. I decide to come straight out with it. 'Your parents ... they're not ... ?'

'As I said in my email, they don't really live here any more – not permanently.'

I'm tense. I cast my eye around the room, looking for something to distract me, but the rows of books on the shelves offer me no solace. 'I'm surprised you can be here, like this ... so calm and happy. After everything we went through.'

Rupert raises an eyebrow. 'Everything? Well ... I remember you used to visit me,' he says, 'when I was up in my bedroom. And Ernest Kellman was staying here at the time with his tutor, who invited his friends around, which I remember irked Mrs Medlock somewhat. I think that might have been what pushed her over the edge. She didn't handle changes in routine very well.' He looked up and to the left as though he was trying to bring forward faded memories, things he had forgotten. 'It was around that time that she had a bit of a meltdown, made us go to the gardener's cabin one night. I think I was quite frightened. Is that what you're referring to?'

Although I had suspected as much, it feels strangely sad having my presumptions confirmed: that Rupert too has buried a lot of his memories of the past. Both of us have unconsciously chosen to suppress and forget. Or perhaps dismiss and minimise.

I nod my head. 'Yes. Yes, that is what I'm referring to.'

My eyes fall on the fireplace. It doesn't look as if it has been lit in a long time. To its left is another sofa, not dissimilar to the one where Mr Oakwood lay after he'd been carried in by Mrs Medlock and Lord Ashton. I half expect to see blood on the upholstery, an indentation of his body as he fought for his life. But of course, it is pristine.

'Is there something particular about this room that upsets you?' Rupert asks, trying to follow my gaze, turning in his chair to look around.

'This room is important, yes,' I say, keeping my voice slow and measured.

'Important ...' He repeats the word, almost to himself, his brow creasing. 'Would you find it easier if we go somewhere else?'

I nod. He gets up and tells me to follow him. I'm led through the house and out of a back door. We walk round the house, the autumnal sunlight bathing the grass and trees in a golden-orange glow. Then a sight takes me by surprise. A swimming pool comes into view, surrounded by sunloungers and a number of little cabins. 'Oh wow,' I say, pausing to take it all in. 'This is ... this is very different.'

'Oh yes, I suppose it is,' Rupert says, brushing the leaves off a pair of wooden chairs situated to the left of the pool and indicating that I should sit down. 'This was installed in the summer of '79.'

I take a seat and look at the pool, watch the leaves on the water's surface glide in the gentle breeze.

'There's an indoor pool too,' he continues. 'Although that was put in a bit later.'

Silence falls between us for almost a full minute. Then he says, 'So, shall we begin?'

I look at him fully now and find it impossible to keep the intense sadness from my face. Sadness for what's passed. Sadness for the anguish to come.

'You'll have to read Mrs Medlock's diaries to understand the full truth. It's going to take time to unravel it all. There are many pieces to this story. Secrets she has kept all these years. But I think we're going to have to start where this began for me.' I raise a hand and point across the lawn, past the little cabins, towards the cluster of trees swaying gently in the afternoon breeze. 'For me, everything started there. Down in the garden, behind the stone wall.'

Acknowledgements

Each book is a unique journey, and this one has had a winding road to publication. I started it in 2019 and wrote a large portion of it during the pandemic lockdowns of 2020 and 2021. It was a dream to write, offering an escape during a time of uncertainty. Of course, some time has passed since then, and I'd like to thank my agent Joanna Swainson for her unwavering encouragement and enthusiasm for this book in the intervening years.

Thank you so much to Cal Kenny for having such a wonderful vision for *Medlock*. Every step of the editorial process for this book has been a joy. Thanks to Nithya Rae for such a keen eye for detail during the copyedit, to Ben Prior for an amazing cover design, and to everyone at Sphere and Little, Brown for bringing this book out into the world.

Special thanks to my family: my partner Leno for being so wonderful (and for baking delicious treats featuring Biscoff and Nutella), my parents, sisters Molly and Amy, and my granny and uncle. Thank you to Rebecca and Tom and all my close friends. And last but not least, thanks to Meg Wallace, to whom this book is dedicated, who has helped shape and encourage my love of gothic novels, atmospheric classics and horror fiction through our many chats and shared cinema experiences within these genres.

Author's Note

This book is, in some ways, a love letter to a number of classic novels, drawing inspiration from and paying homage to Frances Hodgson Burnett's *The Secret Garden*, Daphne du Maurier's *Rebecca*, Henry James's *The Turn of the Screw* and Thomas Hardy's *Far from the Madding Crowd*, along with many others. I'd also like to give a special nod to Alejandro Amenábar's 2001 film *The Others*, which had a huge impact on me when I saw it as a teenager. If you haven't yet had the joy of discovering any of these works, I thoroughly recommend picking them up as this novel couldn't have existed without them. I'd also like to mention Agatha Christie's *The Pale Horse*, specifically the 1964 Fontana paperback edition featuring a cover illustration by Tom Adams, details of which are referenced within this book.